SWORD OF THE BLACK ROSE

LEGEND OF THE BLACK ROSE 2

A.W. HART

WOLFPACK
PUBLISHING
— EST 2013 —

WOLFPACK PUBLISHING
— EST 2013 —

Paperback Edition
Copyright © 2020 A.W. Hart

Special thanks to Richard Prosch for his contribution to this novel.

Published in the United States by Wolfpack Publishing, Las Vegas

Wolfpack Publishing
6032 Wheat Penny Avenue
Las Vegas, NV 89122

wolfpackpublishing.com

Paperback ISBN: 978-1-64734-072-8
eBook ISBN: 978-1-64734-071-1

SWORD OF THE BLACK ROSE

There is story the Sisters of Sorrow tell about a pair of brothers — one of them heir to a fortune, the other cast out of the family for a perceived slight. The first man ruled a kingdom from high in a castle built upon a hill of tradition and looked to the past for glorification. Fortified by the souls of his ancestors, his every whim was accounted for by scavenger birds and jackals. The other man was made unfairly destitute and forced to work in dire conditions for every scrap of bread he received. He looked to the future for a just reward, and the vultures paid him no mind. Over the years, the first man's castle decayed, his fortune drained away into the coffers of others, and he suffered great misery. How different from the second man, who rose up through individual effort and achieved his own great happiness. In this way, the sisters teach the most unhappy are not the souls whose life is taken from them by force, for justice is their handmaid. Rather, the most unhappy are the men and women who give away their life for adulation, for their handmaid is envy.

FROM THE SECRET DIARY OF THE CONVENT SISTERS OF SEÑORA MARIA, MISSION OF SANTO TOMAS SISTER ADELINE O'MALLEY, ANNALIST.

CHAPTER ONE

During the course of her twenty years, Catalina Cristiana Rivera had consumed the finest lagers available to Rancho Rivera and the scions of Contessa D'Mores of Madrid. She wasn't about to drink the goat's piss Colonel Perry Sullivan offered her in his ramshackle roadhouse.

But she accepted the cloudy mug from the old man with a smile, as befitted her masquerade as a nun of Señora Maria, and she batted her lashes with mock gratitude.

"Drink up, sister, drink up and listen to the words of the Sainted Brothers of Monterrey."

Lina lifted the glass in mock salute, then put the beer down on the stained table top and ran her hands along the sleeves of her gray-blue habit.

In her memory, she relished the warm flavor of *Estella Dramm* hitting the back of her mouth before gliding smoothly down her throat. She remembered breathing in the aroma of pit-fired venison.

Those days were gone.

Here in the present, near the back door, Sullivan's Way smelled like a full latrine at the height of summer. And it was only May.

The Colonel pulled a copper token from his pocket and handed it to her.

"The memory of Monterrey be blessed," he said as she accepted the roughhewn coin.

Then the old Fenian raised his flagon and, with arms wide spread, called to the four and twenty louts of varied age gathered inside the cramped, stuffy parlor. "Harken ye to my words. Tis the true Lord's legacy we honor tonight, friends."

A framed portrait of a bearded man, not unlike Sullivan but twenty years younger, hung at an angle from a twist of baling wire, and the wall's peeling pink paper bowed to past glory.

Catalina rolled the token between her fingers and watched the Colonel squeeze through the horde of tables to the front of the room. He positioned himself behind a crude wood lectern and faced the crowd. She had sympathy for the man.

She understood about legacies.

At Rancho Rivera, Lina's mother had been protector and servant, warrior and nurse, matriarch, and keeper of the New World Spanish porciano. A 300 year-old land grant, gone in one blistering day of war landing Lina into the fold at the mission of Santo Tomas.

And into the exclusive Order of the Black Rose.

Sullivan cleared his throat. "Erin go Bragh," he said. *Ireland forever.*

"Ereen. G'brag," said a weary old graybeard, half-heartedly lifting his mug at the next table.

"Braa." A grunt from a pair of Mexicans near the front, a pair of copper tokens on the table in front of them.

"Hear, hear." A *gringo* drummer in a bowler hat with his sample case in his lap.

In Lina's palm, her token echoed the sentiments of the room. Erin go Bragh. The slogan traced the circumference of the copper. In its center a stamped angel posed as the pillar of a stringed harp, her outstretched wing forming the instrument's neck. And she was surrounded by specks of four-leafed shamrock.

Clasping the coin tight in her fist, Lina felt it dig into her flesh and she dropped the crude piece into a pocket of her habit.

"Who's for a touch of the old Nick?" said red-haired Mary Rosetta spinning in from the side kitchen, her hair piled in a flaming stack. Mary's linsey shirt was open at the collar, clinging to her breasts. She wore tight canvas pants like a man, but there was nothing male about her waistline. The men in the room weren't shy about salivating over her curvy shape.

Mary swept past the drummer and tipped an amber bottle toward Henry Hodges.

At his table, Hodges nodded and wiped his fat lips with the back of his hand.

"Aye, and bring y'r pillow lovelies o'r to old Henry."

Catalina watched with satisfaction as Mary poured a healthy dollop of cheap whisky into Hodges's tin cup, bending at the waist decidedly more than necessary, breathing soft peppermint breath across his cheek.

The railroad man was clearly entranced.

Just as Lina and Mary hoped.

A teamster with drooping yellow whiskers and a battered McClellan cap dropped his copper token on the table and raised his glass. Mary swiveled to oblige, pointing her backside at Hodges and shooting Catalina a wink.

"Here, gal, don't you tarry now," said white-haired Colonel Sullivan. "I'm calling this meeting of the Sainted Brothers to begin."

Rather than jump at the old man's brogue, Mary flouted him with a mocking expression meant for Henry alone. Hodges returned her sly smile and the trade was like a silent pact between them.

"Hear, hear," cheered the drummer.

With a deliberate sway of her hips, Mary crossed the room in front of the open front door, shooing a stray chicken back out into the front yard. As the last bands of crimson and pink showed behind a shadow of mesquite trees, Sullivan banged a heavy ladle on the podium.

"Let's come to order now," he said. "Order, order."

The Sainted Brothers murmured a final few words to each other, then offered the Colonel their full attention. All except Henry Hodges, whose lazy left eye swam around the room while his right orb stayed glued to Mary.

The redhead continued to ply the crowd with rotgut.

Sullivan cleared his throat and started into his speech.

"The Batallón de San Patricio, or St. Patrick's Battalion, was the culmination of..."

Lina wasn't paying attention to the history lesson. Like a cat watching a mouse, she focused her attention on Hodges. A husky northerner with a gut gone south, his oily hair dripped across the back collar of his yellow stained shirt. His face was a pan of dust and his left eye rolled in its crinkled socket like a marble.

She'd seen him come in to town on a rangy buckskin three weeks ago. He'd lost weight off his belly since then. Working for the Sioux City and Orient company to repair a long stretch of the Santo Tomas spur in summer's blazing heat drained the starch out of the toughest men. From what she'd learned, Hodges was a hard worker, he put in a day's work and didn't slack off. He was also an angry drunk.

Savannah Diaz and Emilia Martinique, cousins and novitiates of Senora Maria convent, had gone missing from Santo Tomas since he'd arrived. A third, fifteen year-old Lucia Hernandez, a ward of the mission, had also been attacked. Lucia had barely escaped Hodges's filthy grasp and foul intent. In sobbing remembrance she'd told Lina about Hodges's long blade, and she showed her a fresh cut on her shoulder. She told how Hodges played with her red hair, and Lina had gotten a chill.

Both of the missing girls had reddish hair, too.

Hodges liked to play with Bowie knives.

Lucia's ordeal had revealed the wolf hiding within the usually peaceful fold of Santo Tomas.

Lina clutched her dark rosary tight.

Attacking one of the Order of the Black Rose was Hodges's first mistake.

Tonight, the hunter became the prey.

Mary scurried toward the back of the room, not giving Catalina a second glance as she slipped to the edge of the door.

Over her shoulder, she gave a wink and blew Hodges a kiss, then vanished outside.

Sullivan's voice droned on, encouraged by an occasional smattering of applause from his followers. "With this sought-after boon soon in our grasp, we have reason to expect the Batallón de San Patricio to rise again for the first time since 1846..."

"Damn near seventy years ago," the graybeard told Lina. "Who gives a good god-damn?"

Catalina ignored the comment.

Hodges played with his copper token, spinning it idly on the table before looking over his shoulder at the back door. Eventually, he gently pushed back his chair, careful not the let the legs scrape too loudly on the floorboards.

Sullivan continued to preach. "These young martyrs, branded traitors by the so-called *United* States, were summarily executed for treason. But I say unto ye, if not for holy crusaders..."

Foxlike, Hodges squirmed through the tables, moving quickly away from the martial drumbeats, away from the two Mexicans and the yellow haired teamster.

Away from the drummer with his case and his bowler.

At the back of the room, it was clear he was thinking only about what waited for him on the other side of the rough batten and plank timber door.

But as he grasped the iron handle, he didn't notice Catalina rise up behind him.

His second mistake.

******

"Woo-hooo, li'l darlin'?" Hodges was careful to tread lightly in the dry chaff behind Sullivan's Way, watchful of the broken glass bottles and piles of rusted tin cans on the path to the privy.

Under half-rotted timbers and decades of neglect, the old frame outhouse sagged into the desert sand, a snarl of black grama grass and knobby mesquite trees bunching up at its base. The door creaked with a night's breeze and a bustling flutter of sparrows burst out, across the dusky indigo.

Hodges scratched his oily chin. Now where had the little vixen got off to?

"Pretty girl?" he said. "I was hoping to introduce myself to ye," he said, shoving a full load of charm into his raspy wet voice.

Silence.

"Pretty girly, pretty girly?" he sang under his breath. "Come out, come out, wherever you are…"

Behind him, the door to Sullivan's decrepit old shanty clicked shut.

Hodges spun around in surprise, but there was nobody there.

"Huh," he chuckled. "Hee-haw, haw." Hodges cocked his head, strained to hear anything above the night's breeze.

Inside, Colonel Sullivan was beating home his speech, emphasizing each pedantic point with a sounding of the gavel.

A hornet buzzed from the eaves of the house, its whipsaw drunken flight pushing Hodges back a step.

He waved his arms and took a step back.

"You lookin' for me, Henry?"

Hodges peered into the thickening darkness past the privy. The redhead was perched on the edge of a bosquecillo of brushy trees, her arms stretching above her head, her breasts half-uncovered, on co-quettish display.

Hot damn, it was just like he'd thought. The buxom tart had led him outside on purpose. Like the others, she couldn't resist ol' Henry's two-dollar haircut and splash of bay rum.

The redhead hooked a finger in his direction.

By God, Hodges wanted her more than all the others combined.

Since coming to Santo Tomas, he'd been stopping in at Sullivan's Way for a pint after work. He liked the old Colonel's sermons, and he liked collecting the lassies even more. He'd fallen into a stroke of Irish luck here.

And tonight he'd be kissing something better than the blarney stone.

Hodges tried to stroll casually forward. "What's your name, lass?" Hodges called, working to slow his advance.

"Mary," said the girl. Incredibly, she put a hand to her blouse and loosed another button.

This one sure enough was full of the old salt. He'd known she wanted him, but he was surprised at how much.

Truth be told, the gals didn't always go for Henry. They were scared of his wandering eye. Nothing he could do about it. He'd lived with the condition ever since a kid named Clay Buckhead shoved a pencil into it when he was seven.

He told everybody it had happened on San Juan Hill with Teddy.

"You're a mischievous one, Mary," he said.

"I canna' deny it, Henry me lad."

"I like 'em mischievous."

"Are ye from around here, Henry?"

"I'm here now. That's what matters."

Not ten feet in front of him, Mary stretched again, putting her arms behind her back. "I've been thinking about settling down here."

Hodges nodded and swiped a string of drool from his chin.

"With a gal like you around, I'd settle in hell itself," he said.

"I'm so glad to hear it," said Mary.

Hodges took two more steps, bringing him directly in front of the open outhouse door.

"Hold it right there," said a male voice from inside.

Hodges jerked around. The mestizo facing him wore a black shirt and a clay-colored charro jacket. His chin showed a day's growth of whiskers and a shock of black hair hung limp over his forehead. He gripped a tall hickory walking pole in his right hand, and on his lapel was pinned a tin star.

"Howdy, constable...Cassidy, isn't it?"

Cassidy tipped his hatless head. "We need to talk, Henry. Just you and me."

The way Hodges had heard it, the new lawman of Santo Tomas was an ex-drunk who dallied with the nuns of Santa Maria because he couldn't get a real gal for love nor money. Probably didn't like gals. Cassidy was probably one of those *abnormals* Hodges read about.

"You regularly do your talkin' at the outhouse, boy?"

"Don't *boy* me, Henry."

Hodges hitched up the waistband of his pants over his sagging gut. "I heard about you. The lawman who don't carry a gun." He spit at Cassidy's feet. "Guess I don't have to talk to you if I don't want to."

Cassidy nodded like the idiot half-breed he was. "I 'spect you do."

"*I 'spect ya do,*" said Hodges, mocking the constable's high-pitched voice. Then with a hard challenge, he said, "I guess I'm done talkin' boy. And since you rudely interrupted me in my evening's pleasure—" Hodges glanced toward the brush were his lovely Mary was waiting.

The redhead was gone.

Hodges turned back to Cassidy. The prissy breed lawman had done scared away his pretty girly. For no reason at all, he'd stuck his nose into Hodges's business.

Nobody messed around in Henry Hodges's business. Not his mama. Not his former wife. And especially not some pansy-assed lawman with a stick.

He sneered and made his voice hard as thunder. "You little bastard. Now I'm gonna have to ram your pole straight up your—"

A rustle of wings behind him, and a dark smear in his peripheral vision made Hodges turn in place once more and the twilight vision before him was impossible to comprehend.

The woman crouched in a landing position like she'd leapt from the top of the house or fallen from the sky, her endless black cloak suspended in the air, merging with the dark of night itself. When she stood, the crown of her raven-tressed head was higher than Hodges and her face was a nightmare of Apache scarlet and black warpaint.

"What the hell are you?"

Dressed in a black silk tunic with flared sleeves and laced leather gauntlets, trousers with nickel conchas and leather tassels, she advanced on him with remarkable speed, driving the heel of one of her knee-high boots into the side of his knee, putting him on the ground.

Through a haze of red misery, he reached for the small of his back and brought out his big knife.

Long and glistening in the first shine of the rising crescent moon, honed to hair-splitting perfection, the weapon had drunk its share of blood, mostly from nosy bitches like the one hovering over him.

Her voice rang in his ears. "What is it you were saying, *perro*?"

"I peg you for the Black Rose they talk about. Am I right?"

"I'm Savannah Diaz, I'm Emilia Martinique," said the Black Rose. "I'm Lucia Hernandez."

Hodges gripped the knife and shook the fog from his head. "Never heard of 'em."

"Lucia's blood is on your blade."

"Drop the knife, Henry," said Cassidy.

It couldn't end this way, thought Hodges. Brought down by a flowery boy and a circus freak? He wouldn't have it end this way. If they took him in, they'd toss him behind bars. Henry couldn't stand being behind bars, the walls closing in, the constable watching him eat and sleep and piss.

"You all picked on the wrong man, tonight," said Hodges, feeling the fear boil up inside him like a musical crescendo. Inside the house, Colonel Sullivan was at it again, yelling at the top of his lungs.

Hodges felt his own cry spilling over his lips. Fear turning to rage. He fought to keep it in as beads of sweat popped out across his forehead and his lungs spasmed for breath.

His legs were coiled springs, ready to lurch up and forward. His arm was a lever of oak, ready to send the long knife into an arc designed to fairly gut the circus wench in front of him.

And then the wheel of fortune turned and three men came around the side of the house.

Calvin, Carlson, and O'Rourke. Co-workers from the rail yard. Three *friends*.

"What the devil?" said Calvin.

"Get them," said Hodges.

CHAPTER TWO

Catalina had thought twice about wearing the garb of the Black Rose under her nun's habit. Henry Hodges was one man, and with Cassidy's fighting prowess, she'd doubted her presence would be needed. Mary, too, was formidable in battle, having been trained in the arts of savate and jousting by a French paramour.

In the end, she presented herself in cloak and warpaint out of a sense of honor. The legend of the Black Rose had spread all over southwest Texas and across the border to Chihuahua and beyond like a cloud of locusts, a bleak warning to those who would bring harm to Santo Tomas and its sacred springs.

Lina had a reputation to protect and cultivate.

Plus, Mother Mercy wanted her here. And Lina owed Mercy her life.

When the three brawny roughnecks rounded the corner of Sullivan's Way, she was glad she had dressed for the occasion.

Two of the men each out-weighed her and Cassidy

combined. Walking tombstones — scarred and built of thick white slabs in the moonlight. They wore only cotton shirts, trousers and boots. One of the devils wore a Colt .41 double-action gun in a holster at his hip. The other had only one good eye paired with a blank socket.

The third polecat was tall and slender, and his furry chaps clung to his legs like rangy overgrown otters. He wore a dirty slouch hat and loose bandana, and his rolling walk was right out of the moving pictures.

The lead man with the gun took in the scene — Hodges on his knees in a crouch, Cassidy behind him with his wooden pole. He said, "What the devil?"

"Get them," said Hodges, even as he exploded upwards, his blade held far out in front.

The Black Rose leapt backwards, landing with a light thump near a sandy patch of prickly pear and manzanita shrubs. Hodges gave her no time to rest, darting in fast with the knife, rolling away from her out-thrust boot, leaping in again to try and bury the knife between her breasts.

He almost succeeded.

Had she not spent most of her life in training with her brothers in the caverns of the holy springs, her young life would have been forfeit.

As it was, the Black Rose dodged at the last instant and followed up with a hard side-hand chop to Hodges's neck, a blow which would have staggered a mountain lion. The impact sent the bastard toward into the thorny bush, but his sweaty mitts hooked onto her forearm and together they tumbled down to the ground with a crash.

They rolled through the brambles like mad lovers, nails scratching and teeth gnashing. Hodges played dirty and cranked his knee hard between her legs, sending a wave of anguish rippling into her torso. The Black Rose clutched at the bushes, scraping Hodges's face and neck, but the man came out on top, screaming, his left hand clamped around her windpipe.

Like a feral horse, the Black Rose knocked him sideways, putting Hodges off balance as he brandished the knife with his right hand fist. She managed to draw her knee to her sternum and plunged the heel of her boot deep into Hodges's guts. She owed him that much at least.

Letting out a hard grunt, he toppled over, arms outstretched and flailing, retching up a stream of amber bile.

The Black Rose regained her feet and saw Cassidy at the outhouse squaring off with the gunny. Warily they circled each other, the constable taunting his opponent with his hickory pole. "C'mon Calvin, if you think you can take me." Calvin's arms were like iron girders, his chest twice as wide as Cassidy's.

"I've been itchin' for a good tussle," he said.

Behind them, Mary shouted with anger at the one-eyed man. The Black Rose recognized him as a drifter named Carlson.

"Try it again, you greasy possum." The redhead was deep in the bear grass at the bosquecillo and her bare arms were crossed in front of her. "Go on, try it."

The one-eyed man must've appreciated her challenge.

He tried it again, descending on her like a bleached adobe mudslide.

Balanced on the balls of her feet, Mary was instantly in the air. For a few brief seconds, gravity had no power over her, and the side of her foot crushed her opponent's nose with a spurt of blood and an audible pop.

Carlson screamed and cupped his face.

Reacting to the wail, Calvin took his attention off Cassidy for one fatal second. The constable's hickory pole was a bullet careening toward Calvin's jaw, smashing into bone and gristle. Whirling back around, Cassidy brought the stick down hard, a heavy club caving in the bull gunman's skull with a solid crack of wood on bone.

At the periphery of the skirmish, the movie cowboy held back, timid and indecisive.

The Black Rose turned back to Hodges as he made one last climb to his feet. She pounded sand from her trousers and flung her cloak around in a flourish. Like a bullfighter, she taunted him.

"Sure you don't remember the names of those girls? Savannah Diaz? Emilia Martinique?"

Hodges's eyes were china saucers, his face a riverbed of sweat and grime.

"They wanted me," he said. "Just as much as I wanted them. But I held back just like I was supposed to. I passed 'em on down the chain."

"Passed them on? To who? Where?"

"Don't you worry your pretty little head. They'll be tended to well enough."

The slimy son of bitch.

Until now she'd gone easy on him.

Stepping past Hodges's feeble reach to parry his knife hand away, the Black Rose drove the callused palm of her hand up under his jaw, knocking his teeth together with a clatter. Iron fingers clamped around his windpipe, she drove forward with her knees underneath of her like hydraulic pistons, lifting Hodges off the ground. His face turned the color of boiled beets and he pawed at her hand with a weakening frenzy. Chomping down into his own tongue, blood dribbled past his lips. When she could hold him no more, the Black Rose dropped him like a bag of rocks, and he hit the earth with a satisfying thud.

At the same time Cassidy's warning rushed to her ears.

"Gun," he said, and even as she turned, the Black Rose had her fingers at the glimmering steel whip-sword she wore wrapped around her waist.

The urumi was a twelve-foot blade of flexible edged steel, wielded by warriors on the ancient Indian sub-continent and brought to Argentina in the 17th century where secretive sects of gauchos trained with it in tandem with the boleadoras. Along with weapons like the man-catcher and the navaja blade, Catalina's brothers had presented her with the urumi at the appropriate time in her training, and she had mastered it with deadly efficiency, beyond anything her brothers had been able to accomplish.

The stringbean cowboy had both hands wrapped around a hunk of metal that looked like one of the compact European automatics her father had added to his collection years before. A Belgium model maybe. The muzzle bobbed up and down and Cassidy yelled again.

Her hand firm on the pomel, the urumi's expertly ground steel unwrapped itself from the Black Rose in a single smooth motion. Lightning swift, she hurled the blade out and away from her where it telescoped to its full length. Six feet, then eight, then twelve where the sharp edge bit deep into the flesh of the cowboy's throat and seared against bone. His shriek was muffled by a gurgle of blood, and the gun went off with booming percussion before tumbling harmless to the ground.

The night was quiet then except for the whimpering of Hodges and Mary's broken bully who sat propped up against a stump, cradling his nose and snuffling.

Cassidy rushed to the cowboy's twitching corpse and knelt beside him while the Black Rose kicked Hodges in the ribs. "Get up," she said.

"Kiss…my ass," he gasped, coiled into a fetal position, hands massaging his bruised neck.

"I should've broke your neck you rotten bastard," she said.

Cassidy's heavy tread came up behind her, his breath hot and fast, his fingers flung out behind him. "Damnit to hell, do you see what you did?"

Her eyelids were hoods against his wild emotion. "He's the one who tried to shoot me. I only defended myself," she said. "I have nothing to be ashamed of."

"You nearly took off O'Rourke's head."

"O'Rourke? You knew him?"

Cassidy shook his head. "By name only," he said. "El Chico estaba con la pandilla de Calvin." *The boy runs with Calvin's gang.*

"He aimed a gun at me. Yet you call him a boy."

Wild eyed with emotion, Cassidy confronted her. "What do you call him?"

"Muerto," said the Black Rose.

Dead.

"Y'all gonna argue all night?" said Mary clapping her hands together behind them. "Me? I think you oughta high-tail your spooky butt outta here, girl." She hooked a strand of long red hair around to the back of her neck. "I'll go in and sooth the Irish."

Even as she said it, the back door jerked open, and Sullivan appeared. "Was that a shot I heard?" he called.

"Sparrow hunters," said Mary, hustling him back inside. "Nothing to worry about."

"I thought I heard a shot…"

"The only shot you need to worry about is a glass of the old Nick. Now who's for a quick sip?" she said before closing the door behind her.

The Black Rose stood above Hodges, her urumi a coil in both hands. "For what he did to those girls, he ought to die too," she said.

"Don't you think one soul is enough for tonight?"

"We can't all afford to be as docile as you, Cassidy."

"Docile?" His jaw twitched and his teeth ground together. "I call it compassion."

"I call it meek. And one day, it will get you killed." She brushed past him toward the heavy dark bosquecillo, waving the mist away from her eyes.

Making sure to keep her voice steady, she added, "I don't want to be there when it happens."

CHAPTER THREE

Dressed in the pleated habit and veil of the Sisters of Señora Maria, Catalina walked with Mother Mercy, the convent's Mother Superior, along the adobe brick-lined path inside the west gate of the mission at Santo Tomas, noting the elder's blooming garden of violet desert willows and fiery red ocotillo.

But not at all admiring it.

The morning sun had burst over the tranquil walls and blazed hot and insufferable over the face of the church. At its crown, the four-eyed espadana — the bell gable — rose into the sky and showed a stifling blue through its four semi-circular arches. Each opening housed a single brass bell on its individual headstock with ropes falling down from wheels to a raised platform inside the mission.

If there was one sound Lina could live without ever hearing again, it was those bells. She'd lived with the nuns for several months, pretending to be a novice, but she would never be one of them. Every time the bells sounded, it reminded her of her status as an outsider.

"This is the day the Lord has made," said Mercy. "Let us rejoice and be glad in it."

Lina wasn't even sure she believed in God.

When she said as much to Mercy, the sister immediately stopped on the sun baked path and straightened the heavy white guimpe draped over her chest and shoulders. She looked up at Lina through horn-rimmed spectacles, a robust middle aged woman with a grim smile. Gently she patted Lina on the cheek.

"What matters," she said, "is He believes in you. We all do."

Lina looked away, glancing across the open plaza to where Raul Cassidy watered his cantankerous mule, from the mission well.

Following her gaze, Mercy replied to Lina's scowl. "The water of the sacred spring is too good for Diablo?"

"I said no such thing."

"It's what you were thinking."

Mercy shook her head, but said nothing. Then together they watched as a young man dressed in a black cassock strolled from the shadow of an arched walkway to join the constable. The priest laughed at something Cassidy said and slapped him on the back.

"Father Demetrius seems to be getting accustomed to the mission," said Mercy. "Those two have known one another barely two weeks. Already they're fast friends."

"Barroom buddies, is more like it."

"You're sour this morning, Lina."

"He who speaks truth tells what is right, but a false witness, deceit."

"Are you quoting holy scripture?"

"No. Aquiles Rivera. My father."

"We have work to do. May I assume you'll carry today's cheerful disposition into the meeting of the Order? If so, I'll ask Mary to bring a sidearm."

Lina ignored Mercy's jibe. Still fixated on Cassidy and Demetrius, she compared the two with lament. The new pastor was everything the constable wasn't. Tall and muscular with a heavy crop of dark hair. A firm jaw and shoulders as wide as the Texas plains. A good laugh, and a supreme sense of confidence.

All wasted on the white collar at his throat.

"Come along, child. The others will be waiting."

"I should like to get to know Father Demetrius better," said Lina. "Perhaps you could arrange a welcome supper to more properly introduce him to the Sisters."

"As it turns out, our meeting today concerns the young Father."

Lina's heart skipped a beat. "Does it?"

"And a supper isn't a bad idea."

"For the Sisters of Santa Maria only," said Lina. Her fingers brushed the octillo blossoms. They were quite lovely in the sunlight. "Nobody from the village."

Mercy nodded. "The constable isn't invited, if that's what you are hinting at."

"Good."

"But I'm afraid you won't be able to attend, either."

Lina spun on her heel, and the sun went behind a passing cloud. "No?"

"As I said, we have work to do. Your next assignment takes you to the New Mexico territory." Now it was Mercy's turn to lead the way across the plaza toward the secret entrance to the old limestone corridors.

"Surely there's work to do here," said Lina. "Something closer to…home." She couldn't help but glance over her shoulder at Demetrius.

"Catalina Cristiana Rivera," she said, "I do believe you're smitten."

"I don't believe it's any of your business," said Lina.

"She who speaks truth tells what is right, but a false witness, deceit." Mercy turned and offered Lina a mischievous smile before walking into a shadowed alcove. "Check your Bible. You'll find it in the book of Proverbs, dear. Twelve-seventeen."

******

More than two centuries before, when southwest Texas was still an undiscovered frontier, the Spanish conquistador Don Cicero Da Costa led an expedition to La Junta de los Rios, the junction of the Rio Grande and Rio Conchos, a place he believed had mystical powers. Lost in the wilderness, starving and sick with malaria, Da Costa's men were doomed, but a Franciscan traveling with them named Lopez, survived.

Attributing his recovery to the region's abundant springs, the priest founded a church near the bigger of the two rivers. And so Santo Tomas was born, named in honor of the old priest's benefactor, St. Thomas of Villanova.

Lina followed Mercy past the common room's portrait of Da Costa and through a narrow hallway where a wooden trap door led to the cellars under the mission. Mercy pulled back the hatch and slipped into the rock hewn corridor. Lina quickly followed, closing the ingress behind her. The cool air braced her cheeks, and the mineral-rich smell of the springs filled her lungs.

Mercy was deceptively agile for her age, picking her steps with ease, descending the heavy limestone stairway. She knew the corridors and vaulted chambers under the mission as well as Lina's family had known similar caves beneath their family hacienda.

After a maze of twists and turns they came to a locked steel door. Mercy withdrew a silver key from her habit, opened the door, and proceeded into a second hallway. Here, spring water trickled through the walls and the floor was a damp, heady red clay.

They emerged in an open meeting space, almost twenty feet square with low ceilings and an ancient bubbling pool in a far corner. The temperature of the water there was warmer than the initial chill of the place would indicate, but the room was eminently comfortable. Lina stripped off her veil and habit to reveal her black silk tunic, flared sleeves and laced leather gauntlets.

Here, Lina felt more comfortable.

Here, she was the Black Rose.

At a wide oak table surrounded by six mahogany

chairs, the other members of the Order nodded their greetings.

"Buenos dias, Madre" said an olive-skinned brunette, her hair dropping across her shoulders in two heavy braids. "It's good to see you, Catalina."

"And you, Sofia," said Lina, her mood improving with the reunion. "Hola, Caroline."

Seated beside Sofia, Caroline acknowledged the recognition with sparkling eyes and a nod. "Beivenidos," she said. *Welcome.*

Next to Caroline, the wide girth of Sister Adeline took up the remainder of the table's length and not only because she surpassed the sinew and bone of any three men, but because of her journals and maps took up more than her fair share of the table in front of her.

The only one of them still covered with coif and veil, Adeline was the convent's official secretary. It was her daily log and reports which Mercy sent to the Diocese in El Paso, but it was her second, secret ledger which recorded the legend of the Black Rose.

"Hola, Adeline. Como estas?"

Adeline's tone was hurried, her answer, breathless. "Hola, Lina. How am I? You mean besides all the shuffling to and fro like a worried hen over this business with St. Agnes?"

"St. Agnes?"

"All in good time," said Mercy, taking her place at the head of the table in a cushioned chair decorated with ornamental carvings. "Where's Mary?"

"Goddamn wasps." The familiar voice echoed through the cavern, and Adeline slammed down her pen.

The big nun's eyes were slits in a steel mask and Lina was sure she saw steam rise from under her veil as Adeline addressed the Mother Superior. "If you don't take little miss Mary in hand, I will. Sometimes a punch in the face helps one remember."

"Mind yourself, Adeline," said Mercy. "Like Catalina, Mary Rosetta has yet to take any vows."

"And I never will if y'all can't clean up the bugs down here," said Mary, tossing her veil onto a stone peg and breezing across the room. "Those damn wasps liked to gang up on me."

Adeline rose from her chair and met her halfway. "I'll not have you taking the Lord's name. Not in front of me. Especially not here on sacred ground."

"Better listen to her, Mary," said Sofia.

"One o' these days, them two gonna go to fist-icuffs," said Caroline, slipping into the southern African dialect used by the grandmother who raised her. "Missy Mary gonna be sor-ry."

Lina wasn't so sure. Before taking her vows, Adeline had been a rough and tumble girl true enough, rollicking through the West with the likes of Teddy Roosevelt and spending a fair amount of time in the ring. But Mary was hellfire personified.

Adeline would follow the rules of pugilism. Mary didn't acknowledge any rules but her own.

It would be an engrossing match.

"Ladies," said Mercy, interrupting the face-off. "If you'll please stop squabbling, and join us..."

On the table, each of the place settings was a compact paper envelope sealed with a pressed dollop of scarlet wax bearing the imprint of a rose blossom. As Mary and Adeline squared off on opposite sides of the table, Mercy continued to speak.

"As you all are aware, Monsignor Andronicus has taken on a young protégé. Father Michael Demetrius hails from the east coast, but comes to us by way of the College of St. Vincent Maccabees in the New Mexico territory."

"You don't need to remind me," said Adeline.

"I've heard of St. Vincent's," said Sofia. "Did Demetrius study there?"

"For several years — under Ellis Donovan."

"The famous historian," said Catalina.

"Demetrius sought out Donovan specifically because of the older man's archeological experience in the area of holy relics. While at St. Vincent's, he helped catalog Donovan's extensive collection."

Lina couldn't help but roll her eyes. "Let me guess. Slivers of the True Cross. The Holy Grail. The sacred veil of the Blue Nun."

"Donovan is no snake-oil huckster," said Mercy. "He's overseen three expeditions to the Holy Land and shepherds a faculty of seven in serious scholarship."

Adeline agreed. "He's published five reference works and earned numerous awards."

"No doubt he loves his dear, departed mother," said Mary, "but what's he got to do with us?"

"It's not Donovan directly," said Mercy, "but rather, what Demetrius found in his collection which hastens us to New Mexico."

"What exactly did he find?" said Lina.

"The Sword of St. Agnes."

Everyone was still, and Mercy's words seemed to echo through the chamber.

Sofia crossed herself. "Madre de Dios," she whispered.

"You're sending us to New Mexico to see this sword?" said Lina.

"No, my dear," said Mercy. "I'm sending you there to steal it."

CHAPTER FOUR

The young chairman of the History and Humanities department at the College of St. Vincent of Maccabees waved his sheaf of official papers in the air. "Who the hell would want to steal a thousand year-old sword?" he said.

Ellis Donovan loosened his collar and steered the young man to a neatly arranged sideboard of brandies and liqueur. "Fix yourself a drink." He scratched at his full, graying beard and examined a curved wall lined with hundreds of hardbound books and ancient texts with a certain degree of satisfaction.

Five of his own thick tomes, bound in leather, rubbing shoulders with the likes of Herodotus and Josephus, Clausewitz and Schopenhauer.

And underneath, on a shelf all its own and lit red, green, and gold by the afternoon sun through the room's floor-to-ceiling ocular rose window, a two-edged Roman gladius lay on a velvet lined walnut rest. The sword's bleached bone capulus marked it as the once proud property of an ancient officer. Its pristine blade stretched nearly two feet long.

"The Sword of St. Agnes is a good bit older, Mick. In fact, it's at least six-hundred and some odd years older."

The room smelled of leather and ancient papyrus. Cigar smoke and oak barrel aged scotch whiskey. While Mick Shanahan raged like a randy goat, Donovan rounded the desk in front of the stained glass, and sank into the comfort of his over-stuffed chair.

Shanahan wagged his blonde head. "It doesn't matter how old the blasted thing is," he said, tossing the funding request down on Donovan's acreage of a desk. "And no, I won't have a drink in the middle of a weekday, thank you very much. I've got a class on the Punic Wars to teach in less than an hour. If your damned cantankerous mechanical elevator doesn't stall."

Adjacent to the sword, the balance of his collection was on permanent display, lining the walls of the room floor to ceiling.

Mycenaean funeral masks and decanters of ashes from Pompeii, two fingers from the lost Statue of Zeus at Olympia and fragments of the Temple of Artemis. Donvan's life work was here, in the campus' most prominent structure with its belvedere room and dormers, gables and three story corner tower. He'd worked hard, and maybe bent a few rules in order to reach this little corner of paradise.

He thought about Shanahan's comment about the elevator. If ever there was a juxtaposition of the ancient world and the industrial age, it was Old Central.

The building, his office, and everything in it deserved to be protected.

"I can name any number of groups or individuals who covet the sword, and not all of them would be so obviously nefarious," he said. "You'll have to trust me on this."

Shanahan stormed to the sideboard and poured a drink after all. "But only one," he said, holding up a glass tumbler.

"Suit yourself," said Donovan, putting a finger to his head and tapping. "Your temper's showing."

The veins at Shanahan's temple pulsed in time with the twitch in his clean shaven lantern jaw. "The point is, your request for additional dollars to be spent on security — for your personal collection — isn't just out of line, it borders on...on insubordination."

The man should've been in the theater.

"Insubordination is a hyperbolic word, Mick, and curiously militant."

"We live in militant times," said Shanahan. "In case you hadn't noticed, the administration cut three positions last month. They're slashing the faculty to ribbons. I won't have your indulgence become a handy excuse for those fossils in the admin building to cut my position." He tossed back the remainder of his drink. When he spoke, his voice was full of the old country, and his tone was reverent. "I've worked a long time to get here, Donny."

"I should think your position with the school is more than secure than you think," said Donovan.

"The heart of the matter is you simply haven't justified the exorbitant sum of money you've requested. Armed guards for Old Central, plus uniforms and automatic sidearms? I'm not saying your curious assemblage of artifacts isn't important or somewhat…alluring."

Donovan's brow furrowed at the slight. "You're questioning the monetary value," he said.

"They already gave you your damned elevator," said Shanahan. "Despite the fact we had to tear out a perfectly good set of classrooms to do it."

"This is the second time you've framed this as a personal matter," said Donovan. "I thought you knew me and my situation better, Mick. And I thought I knew you. We've always made our archeological finds available to the entire College of St. Vincent's, not to mention the scholarly community worldwide. I've written more than—"

"Half a hundred papers on church history alone, I know," said Shanahan. "Though I suspect you kept your young priest Demetrius busy carrying a lot of the water for you."

"Demetrius wasn't overly interested in history. Social theory and charity were more along his line."

"I heard the church put him in some God-forsaken Texas armpit." Shanahan splashed a second helping of whiskey into his tumbler.

"A place called Santo Tomas," said Donovan. "But back to the matter at hand. I honestly don't see the problem in a new budget line for campus security."

"Funding is not what it was. There's trouble across the Mexican border. Rumblings in Europe. Old alliances being tested. New alliances being made."

Donovan opened a cedar box on his desk. "If I can't change your mind with my Scotch, I doubt I'll have better luck with Dutch Masters?"

Shanahan waved away the offer of a smoke.

"I'm sorry," he said. "If I take a financial request of this size to them, the regents would have my head."

Donovan clipped the butt of his cigar with a pearl-handled knife and rolled the opposite end in a lit match. He breathed in deep and gazed at the sword. Then he blew out a thick cloud of smoke.

A true scholar.

He always felt like a true scholar when he drank whiskey and smoked a cigar.

"That's how *she* got it, you know," he said.

"What the hell are you talking about? That's how who got what?"

"St. Agnes of Rome. Born into a prominent Roman family in A.D. 291, she committed herself to Christ at the tender age of ten. When she was to be married at 13, she refused, and her faith was revealed. For such an offense, the Romans took off her head with the very sword you're refusing to protect." Donovan rolled the cigar between his lips. "The irony is delicious."

"Look, if it were up to me—"

Donovan wearied of the conversation. "Funding is at the discretion the Chair of the Humanities department, which is what the brass plaque on your office door reports you to be. The sword alone has doubled the value of this collection. If not financially, then culturally, and dare I add — spiritually."

"Next you'll be telling me we have to accommodate the pilgrims who want to come to pray in front of the blasted thing."

"It is rumored to possess occult powers beyond our ken."

"Naturally."

Shanahan's tone was dry and sarcastic, but he glanced at the sword with a nervous tick.

"If it's a question of authenticity…," said Donovan.

"No, no. The paperwork you showed me is proof enough. The provenance all checks out. I'm as convinced as you are the sword is real."

Donovan sat forward. "Then get me the funding, Mick. You, of all people, can make it stick. Nothing must happen to the Sword of St. Agnes. In many ways it's priceless."

Shanahan made one last feeble protest. "You've yet to explain my very first question — who you're protecting it from."

Donovan pressed his fingers together in a steeple and leaned back in his chair. How far could he trust his fiery young colleague?

Donovan remained circumspect. "We wrestle not against flesh and blood, but against principalities, against powers, against the rulers of the darkness."

Shanahan ran a hand across his blonde pate. "Have it your way." His voice was filled with resignation as he pulled a gold pocket watch from the pocket of his suit coat. "I've got to be on my way. If I'm not on time, some of my students become quite the classroom clowns. All it takes is one, and before too long they're all following along like a bunch of mindless nincompoops."

"I have no doubt," said Donovan. "Young men can be easily led."

The two men held each other's gaze. Shanahan was the first to blink.

"I'll make the request for you, Donny. But if the funds aren't turned loose, I don't want you blaming me."

"Understood."

Shanahan helped himself to two cigars. "You owe me," he said.

Donovan watched the younger man walk to the hall and shut the door behind him. He listened for the clatter of the elevator doors, the chuffing growl as the engine engaged. The squeal of the cables. Micky Shanahan complained about the elevator, but the novelty kept him from using the tower's creaky old stairs.

Alone in his office, Donovan marveled at Shanahan's performance.

It was how the game was played, after all.

The college board knew the value of the sword — worth a dozen new students next semester. Maybe more.

But at first, it was always good form to posture and harangue.

Donovan had no worries. The money was as good as delivered.

Slowly, Donovan pulled himself up from his chair to stare out a side window over the oval grassy plaza where students lingered in groups of two and three. From his tower office in Old Central, the unruffled campus of the College of St. Vincent of Maccabees had a sedative effect.

On the right, soporific brick classroom buildings and cozy white-washed faculty homes baked in the New Mexico sun. To Donovan's left, the senile old administration building sunk another fraction of an inch into the sandy loam, probably under the weight of bureaucracy.

It certainly wasn't under the weight of the student body — a thinning herd who came with less frequency each semester. When the village lost its bid on the railroad spur to a rival town, more than one resident predicated Candelaria's demise.

With the fortunes of the town, went the college. Unless they could lure in the students — make the College of St. Vincent's of Maccabees an exclusive retreat, and to blazes with the town around it.

But right now, lack of students meant lack of revenue. Lack of revenue meant more money went to keep administrators in their luxury jobs and there was less funding for special projects.

Donavon knew he was the exception. He was an academic wonder, and if he had to single-handedly pull students to campus on an ox-cart, he'd do it.

Everybody would know Ellis Donavon saved them. Some might hate him for it, but most would bask in the light of his presence.

He put his cigar on the edge of his desk and something on the hardwood floor, just off his Persian rug, caught his eye.

It must've fallen out of Shanahan's pocket when

he pulled out his watch.

Donovan bent over and picked it up.

The copper piece was unfamiliar to him, some sort of coin or token.

On the polished face, an angel acted as pillar for a stringed harp and she was surrounded by clover. Around the edge, three words had been stamped.

Erin go Bragh.

Ireland Forever.

CHAPTER FIVE

"The amount of work I'm doing here is astounding," said Mary, propping her right arm against the flank of the adobe brown Andalusian mare, its coal black tail swishing at the stable flies. Brushed and well fed, outfitted with an Apache skirt and Spanish saddle, the horse stepped forward and back, eager for the road. "I mean, compared to Adeline. Holy Jesus. Did you know she, —"

Wearing her full habit and veil, Mary tugged the billet and saddle bags one last time before swiping her face with the back of her hand before continuing. "She had the nerve to stand there and scold me for…"

Catalina ignored her friend's tirade and finished cinching the tack on her own horse, a rare cremello with pale blue eyes, 16 hands high at the withers with a brilliant mane.

The gelding was called D'oro. *Golden.*

Her father had raised Andalusians with pure bloodlines running back to the 16th century Iberian

Peninsula. Most of the remuda Lina and her brothers trained had been lost in the attack on Rancho Rivera many months before, but a few, like this fine fellow, had survived. Rounded up and kept behind the mission by her young cousin Paco, the animals brought a sense of peace to Lina she couldn't find anywhere else.

Especially when tempers flared and tension was on the rise. As was usually the case between Mary and Adeline.

"…and then she called me nothing less than a tramp. Can you imagine? Me? I mean, really, she should look in a mirror. Do you know she used to work in logging camps before taking her vows? I've been around the block a time or two, and I know how things run in logging camps."

"You'd best curb your tongue, Mary," said Lina, indicating the facade of the square stucco building across the way. Under twin cottonwood trees, Mercy stepped outside the constable's office into a smattering of evening sunlight and shadow. Even if she was beyond earshot, her presence was a fair reason for the redhead to button her lip.

It didn't really matter to Mary, because she tended to say what she wanted when she wanted.

"I wonder what business she's got with Cassidy? You don't suppose she's got him going to New Mexico with us?"

Lina's stomach lurched at the prospect, and she hid her face behind the canvas satchel she hoisted into place behind D'oro's cantle. "To the devil with it," she said.

"It's not like we need a chaperone. I've been on my own plenty and done just fine.

"Cassidy needs to stay right where he is, safe and sound in his Santo Tomas office with his prisoner behind bars until the circuit judge arrives," said Lina. "Besides, I think the job of a prison guard suits him better than sheriff."

"You think Henry Hodges will try to make a break from jail?"

"He attacked a nun. I'd put nothing past the cur."

They worked on the horses for another few minutes. Then Mary said, "The missing girls still bother you, don't they?"

"Yes."

Lina continued to arrange her travel gear.

Mary put her hands on her hips. "That's all you're gonna say? 'Yes.'?"

"What more do you want me to add?" said Lina.

"You could say how, with all this business about the Sword of St. Agnes, everybody but you and me seems to have forgotten about Savannah Diaz and Emilia Martinique. Doesn't Mercy want to know what happened to them?"

"Mercy seems confident Hodges will relate what he knows to the judge when the time comes."

"Meanwhile, those girls could be in trouble."

"I know," Lina whispered.

"Well, it irritates me," said Mary. She continued to watch Mercy and the Constable. "They sure are chummy."

"I assume Mercy is just being neighborly," said Lina.

"Hells bells, you oughta know you can't assume nothin' around here."

The declaration was answered by a robust voice. "There's wisdom in your words, Mary Rosetta."

Lina turned to see Sofia Lee padding across the dust of the open stable toward them. The olive-skinned woman was slim with an innate athleticism visible even when hidden behind her long pleated habit. She approached them without a veil, and her hair was the color of night, but shorter than Catalina's, cropped close to the scalp. At her waist swung the same black crucifix and series of beads worn by all the sisters Mercy chose to become a part of her special Order.

If the other Sisters of Señora Maria questioned the exclusivity of the unique rosary, Lina had never heard of it. If the Monsignor ever noticed — but no, thought Lina, the Monsignor never noticed much of anything outside himself. Still, she asked a question:

"Does Andronicus know of our mission?"

Sofia's answer was gentle, but direct. Her voice devoid of emotion. "Andronicus believes us to be on a pilgrimage to liaison with the Daughters of the Holy Cross, a convent giving aid and comfort to the Indians."

"What about Demetrius? Does he know we're going to his old school?"

Mercy clasped hands with Constable Cassidy and, smiling, walked across the inlaid brick street toward the stable. Glancing in her direction, Sofia offered a slight shake of her head. "I don't know."

Another mystery, thought Lina, but she didn't mind overly much. She enjoyed puzzles and games of deduction. It would give her something to think about on the ride.

"Tell me more about how wise I am," Mary said to Sofia.

Growing up, Catalina had always been the problem solver in her family, at least as far as brain-teasers went. She wasn't as good at geometry as her brother, Carlos, and among the Order of the Black Rose, Mary was better at word games and ciphers.

But Lina generally welcomed the conundrums of daily life.

And reveled in solving deadly enigmas as the Black Rose.

Mary too, enjoyed the adventure, but Sofia herself was a mystery. Older than Lina, but younger than the Mother Superior, she shared less of her past life's story than any of the other sisters, and showed even fewer emotions.

Maybe Lina would get to know her better on the New Mexico trail.

For now, the mystery of the Sword of St. Agnes was tantamount to everything else.

Savannah Diaz? Emilia Martinique?

Catalina tried to push the names out of her mind for the time being. Maybe Hodges would tell Cassidy what happened to the girls so they could be rescued.

If they were still alive.

Mercy stayed near the street, motioning for Catalina to join her at the fence. Leaving D'oro beside Sofia, she almost asked about Cassidy but something between Mercy's fingers stayed her tongue.

"Have you ever seen one of these?" said Mercy, handing the copper coin to Catalina.

"Yes, of course," said Lina, instantly recognizing the angel and the harp, the shamrocks and the Fenian mantra around the edge. "It's the token Colonel Sullivan gave out at his meeting of the Sainted Brothers of Monterrey." She shrugged with indifference. "I suppose you got it from Cassidy? Did he take it off Hodges?"

Mercy's expression was as smug as it was easy to read. "As a matter of fact, he did not."

Rather than be annoyed at Mercy's rejoinder, Lina's interest was piqued. An old campesino with a swaybacked mule clomped along the street, and she waited for him to pass before saying, "Where did it come from?"

"This was given to me this morning by Father Demetrius."

Lina pictured the young priest's robust Mediterranean complexion. "Demetrius isn't exactly an Irish name. And he doesn't seem the type to join secret societies," she said.

"He's not. But apparently some of the faculty at the College of St. Vincent's are quite easily persuaded to join. What do you know about Colonel Sullivan and the Sainted Brothers of Monterrey?"

"Next to nothing at all. I didn't pay much attention to Sullivan's rantings. We were at the house to entrap Hodges."

"Anything you may remember might help."

"Why not put Hodges on the rack to help jog his

memory?"

Mercy glanced over her shoulder. "Cassidy will find out what he can before the judge arrives in town."

Lina's spirits jumped at the words. For more than one reason.

"Then he's not going with us? To the College?"

Mercy assured her he wasn't. "I hardly think a former deputy U.S. Marshal would approve of a heist from a prestigious institute. Besides, you've proven yourself capable of handling problems on your own."

"I have indeed," said Catalina.

"All but the problem of humility," said Mercy. "But we're working on this, aren't we?"

Lina ignored the comment.

She especially ignored Mercy's use of *we*, since Lina wasn't working on humility at all.

"It's my hope Hodges will reveal what happened to the missing girls. The situation gives me a bad feeling."

"I've said as much to the constable," said Mercy.

There was nothing more to be said on the topic, so Lina asked about the heist. "Does Father Demetrius know the true nature of our mission?"

"It was his idea to begin with." Mercy seemed to be holding something back.

"To steal a prize item from the collection from the famous Ellis Donovan?"

"They had…shall we say, a falling out."

"Must be some kind falling out to make a priest break the commandments. Surely the Church wouldn't approve? The Bishop—"

"The Bishop lives in a convenient haze of deniability," said Mercy. "Much like our own Monsignor Andronicus."

"Tell me more about the Brothers of Monterrey. What is Demetrius afraid of?"

"From what Father tells me, there's a great deal to fear from the Brotherhood." For the first time during their conversation, Mercy's features darkened. "Their leaders are the descendants of the original Saint Patrick's Battalion, called the Batallón de San Patricio in Mexico."

"These men fought in the Mexican American war against the United States?" said Lina.

Mercy nodded. "Most of the battalion were deserters from the American Army. The Brotherhood practically worships the San Patricio's leader, John Riley, as a deity."

Lina recalled Colonel Sullivan's addled rant. "Old men reliving old glory to make themselves feel important. He sounds like so much hot air. I don't understand how such nonsense can pose a serious threat to anything."

"I didn't use the word deity in jest. There are those who believe John Riley will rise from the dead and lead a spiritual battle against this earthly realm."

"Surely you don't believe this?"

"Of course not. Only one man ever rose from the dead." Mercy made the sign of the cross as she spoke.

Lina resisted the urge to follow suit. "But you're still worried."

"Such fanaticism is always a breeding ground for trouble and strife."

"We'll be careful," said Lina.

"The school is a day and two nights' ride. If you leave now, you will be there in time for Sunday morning mass. Then, according to plan, you should be home with our bounty by Tuesday evening." Mercy offered Lina a gentle smile. "Don't forget to send a wire once you have the sword."

"I doubt Sofia will let us forget."

"I do wish Demetrius had told me about the Brotherhood sooner," said Mercy, rolling the token between her fingers.

"Is he afraid they'll try to stop us from taking the sword?" said Lina.

"He's afraid they've already taken it for themselves," said Mercy.

CHAPTER SIX

Lina's coif chafed her forehead and beneath the heavy veil, sweat trickled like a fresh-water spring down her neck. Wearing split habits, she and her companions rode their sturdy mounts over a recently graded roadbed, smoothed of rocks and soft from the late afternoon showers. The moon was bright, lighting their way, the stars above—serene. Even so the summer temperature was high, and the humidity from the rain made the air thick.

"They always told me West Texas nights would be cold," said Mary.

"I have shuddered through January's frost in the middle of August," said Sofia. "Whoever they were who told you this, speaks true."

"It sure ain't true tonight," said Mary.

The three travelers had left the mission at Santo Tomas shortly before sunset, picking up Arros Creek and following it to the Pecos. Their plan was to follow the river north and cross into New Mexico on a highland less than 20 miles from the college.

"El mattoral es pasado," said Sofia, commenting on the thick underbrush and Lina's horse high stepped around squat dry juniper and pinyon trees. Ahead, the undulating terrain was a dusty silver quilt spackled with rusty green black scrub and the blue black smear of Mesa Peligro where outlaw Mescaleros hid in the old poblado and ghosts raised the grito against the Conquistadors — the ancient call to Revolution.

Lina was content to let Mary ride the point position and D'oro paced himself alongside Sofia's splashed white pinto. "How long have you been with the Sisters of Señora Maria?" said Lina.

"Ten years," said Sofia, without offering any more.

"You're proficient with the navaja folding blade, and the French falchion," said Lina.

"Yes."

"You must be eager to see the St. Agnes sword."

"Not particularly." Sofia wasn't much of a conversationalist.

Lina chewed her lips, eyeing the long, leather boot mounted on the right hand side of Sofia's saddle. Long and wide, it was too cumbersome to hold anything less than a Sharps .50-caliber rifle. "I guess we're not hunting buffalo," said Lina, tilting her head at the leather case.

Prying out Sofia's words, tooth by tooth, was exhausting.

Finally, Sofia relented. "It's not a gun," she said.

The reticent nun didn't say any more, so they rode in silence.

With Mary still in the lead, they wound their way through the isolated peaks of the Limpia Mountains, over rolling hills of rock and chaff which would have strained lesser mounts. Just past midnight, Lina spied an open meadow of low grass and they made a cold camp around sandwiches of lard and molasses and a canteen of bitter cold coffee.

Mary made a game out of counting jackrabbits and white-tailed deer and she surpassed a score of each before they stopped again.

At dawn they found a depression cupped from the side of a rock strewn mesa in a thicket of montane grass. After tending their horses, they slept through the heat of the day, taking to the trail again in early evening as cityscapes of towering clouds hovered overhead, their wide gray bottoms casting long shadows across the creosote flats near the border.

In the night, they crossed into New Mexico riding three abreast and followed a painted blue board with white letters announcing their destination awaited them in less than five miles.

"Candelaria and the College of St. Vincent of Maccabees," read Sofia.

"Quite a lot of information to fit on one sign," said Lina.

"Got a question for you, sisters," said Mary. "Because since we're almost here, I've started to get mixed feelings about this whole business."

"Better to share now, than to keep it inside," said Lina.

"And you're the one who needs to know, Sofia," said Mary. "I mean, unlike me and Lina, you've taken your vows. You're a bona-fide bride of Christ."

"What is it you think I should know?"

"Whether or not what we're doing is right," said Mary. "I was never any kind of church-goer, but I seem to recollect a commandment about theft."

"It's the eighth commandment," said Sofia, "and it doesn't apply to our mission at the college. Mercy explained all of it during our initial briefing."

"I guess I don't think so good. Does the sword belong to us? No. Are we swiping the sword and taking it home with us? Yes. To me it still adds up to stealing." Mary patted her satchel. "I've got Mercy's map of the college and floorplan of the Old Central building right here."

"The Sword of St. Agnes belongs to the Church in Rome," said Sofia. "We are the Church's good right arm in this part of the country. We're simply taking back what is truly ours to begin with. We are righting a great wrong."

"Before we left, Mercy told me it was Demetrius' idea," said Lina. "Apparently he had some kind of row with Ellis Donovan over the sword. Anyway, Donovan won't know we have any connection to Demetrius or Santo Tomas."

"But he knows we're arriving today," said Sofia.

"Mercy has a gift for misdirection. She sent word of our arrival to Donovan through one of her friends in El Paso. He thinks we're coming in from one of the missions there."

Mary tried to recall Mercy's words from the cavern meeting. "Our convent in El Paso is called the Sisters of…who?"

"The Daughters of the Holy Sepulcher," said Lina.

"And who are they?" said Mary.

"They don't exist except in Mercy's imagination," said Sofia. "And as far as anybody here knows, we're here on a pilgrimage to pray over the sword."

"It's a cover story," said Lina, "and not a very good one, to be honest. The coffee in my canteen is stronger."

"It is true. I will be praying over the sword the entire time. You need to learn to trust Mother Mercy."

"I do well trusting myself," said Lina. "Perhaps it's you who needs to learn, Sofia."

"Good thing we're not going to be here long," said Mary.

Lina agreed. "From what I've read about him, Ellis Donovan is no fool. He most likely has plenty of friends and colleagues in El Paso and his had more than enough time to wire back and forth and inquire about us."

"There's no point in speculating," said Sofia.

Weary of the conversation, she spurred her mare to the top of a clay mound and reined her back around to face them even as the first streaks of dawn lit the horizon. "I can see the tower of Old Central on the campus mesa," she said, pointing the way. "The main street of Candelaria is quiet enough. I suggest we make haste." Her long saddle boot burned a bright rusty ochre.

"You ever find out what the contraption is she's got in her saddle boot?" said Mary in a tone so low, Sofia wouldn't hear.

"It's called a Man-Catcher," said Lina.

"Hell, you don't need it as long as you've got me along," Mary joked.

Lina thought about the scene behind Sullivan's Way with Henry Hodges. "I do believe you're both designed to catch the same vulgar sort of fellow."

Mary's response was full of alacrity. "I just knew you were going to say something like that."

Lina couldn't help but smile as she rode ahead to meet Sofia and the morning lifted over the mesa.

******

Dismounting at the edge of town, the three travelers walked their horses along the main street with lowered faces in accordance with the humble tradition of the convent. From here on in, every word and deed must conform to the teachings of the Holy Father and the eternal Church.

From beneath her veil, Lina got a quick glimpse of each building. The white-washed corner hotel with its tattered American flag nailed to an anemic Alamo cottonwood. A barber's shop with a weathered candy-cane pole. The long rough-planked saloon. A corner mercantile covered in advertising tins with a small livery tucked behind.

Situated in the flood plain of the Rio Grande, Candelaria was colonized in the early 1600s by the Spanish. According to Mercy's quick history lesson during the briefing and was part of the First Mexican Empire, then claimed by the Republic of Texas until the end of the Mexican-American War in 1848 when the Treaty of Guadalupe Hidalgo.

Aside from a broken down automobile parked halfway down the street, there was no sign of humanity. As they passed the Ford, two shabby donkeys peered over the edge of a sagging barbed wire fence, and one of them wagged his fat head.

A passel of chickens scattered out of Lina's way when she turned right, toward the college, setting a course for the hilltop campus.

Approaching a row of dilapidated one-room shanties, they heard a woman's whiskey-torn voice from the house nearest the road. "Eres un hombre muerto!"

Immediately came the reply, "Come on then, bitch. Come on and try."

"I'll split your skull open, Josiah Woolard."

"C'mon, Estrella…c'mon."

Lina picked out the combatants, a doughy man with a moon-sized gut and a shrunken middle-aged woman dressed in a man's red long-underwear, even as the iron head of an axe whistled past her chin to land half-buried at her feet with a thunk.

Estrella was almost as startled at Lina, standing on the lower step of a dilapidated shack, a naked axe handle still raised above her head. Her black hair was stick straight and her teeth, crooked.

"You rum-soaked idiot," said Lina, doffing her veil and unruffling her coif as she strode toward the site of the ruckus.

Josiah Woolard, maned like a lion and brandishing a shovel, ignored Lina's charge and squared off with his opponent. The man could be neighbor, father, or lover. It didn't matter. If Lina didn't stop him, within seconds he'd be a killer.

"You want a set-to, Estrella, then God-help-you, I'll give you a blasted set-to!"

Gripping tight to the shovel's handle, Woolard swung the square steel blade in an overhead arc. It would have crushed Estrella's skull if Lina hadn't shoved the drunken woman out of the way.

"Who the devil?" said Woolard.

Balancing on the balls of her feet, Lina swung around and hit the bearded man at the base of his neck with the edge of her hand. Woolard staggered and dropped the shovel, but stayed upright.

His face was a stew of emotion. "A nun?" he said.

Behind her, Lina heard the hammer click of a revolver.

"Leave this to me, sister," said Estrella. With a hiss, she dropped into a crouch, pointing her pistol at Woolard. "I should've sent this dog to hell long ago."

Lina barely had time to utter a single syllable, "Dios!" and lurch out of the way before the lead flew.

Leaping past Catalina, Estrella jerked the trigger twice, and the booming muzzle of her old Colt spat fire, missing Woolard both times.

Seething with rage, but sober as a hangman, Woolard went for the small of his back and came out with a silver, single-shot pistol. The old man had sand.

Lina was caught in the crossfire.

In the nick of time, Mary soared in, scooping up the shovel, spinning the long wooden handle like an August dust-devil. She caught Woolard under his chin with the smooth knobby end, then reversed the spin to pancake the flat steel business end across his raging scowl.

Suddenly, from out of nowhere, a third man appeared, blustering into the fracas from inside Estrella's house. He too was dressed in long underwear, with sloppy big mud-covered boots, and he carried a rifle. "I will take care of this."

Casually he threw the gun to his shoulder. "Die, you son-of-a-goat," he said, and bearing down on Woolard, worked the carbine's lever action.

Three rapid shots tore through the street as Lina crouched low, pulling Mary down with her. There was no place to go as the barrel of the rifle swayed back and forth like a cobra, spitting out a volley of death.

Suffering a row of bloody thunder, Woolard waved his little gun above his head, popping off his final load, as he fell dead in the street. But the rifleman's percussion continued, and he laughed like a maniac as shells plundered the ragged grass and dirt in front of the shack. "Nobody's so big as Miguel is now," he screamed.

"Nobody will tell Miguel where to plant his trees," said Estrella. She spit on the ground.

Lina caught Mary's eye. "Trees?" she mouthed.

The deadly fandango was an argument over trees?

Lina gripped the urumi at her waist, but there wasn't time to uncoil the weapon as the carbine's iron eyes landed in her direction.

Lina rolled away from the fire as the muzzle spat and geysers of dirt and rock flew up from the earth.

Estrella's expression was full of horror as the nuns' uniform registered with her. "Miguel, debes parar," she said. *You must stop.*

Miguel wasn't paying attention. He was entirely caught up in a drunken frenzy of destruction. As long as the rifle held rounds, he'd shout and shout again, without discretion, killing anyone who happened to cross his path.

Lina stepped in beside Estrella and hammered the drunk woman's wrist. The Colt toppled sideways to the ground like a rock even as Miguel's rifle sounded off once more.

Again he yanked for the trigger. "All motherless goats must die—"

And his words were cut off with the thud of impact and a soggy wet rasp.

Lina focused her eyes on Miguel, and Mary stepped up beside her.

The gunman's desperate hands clawed at an iron ring and steel pole clamped around his throat.

At the other end of the pole, Sofia secured her stance, then jerked Miguel off-balance, yanking him down by the throat. Once the gunman was prostate on the ground, Sofia put all her weight into pinning him there without air.

"The man-catcher?" said Mary as Miguel's face turned purple and his hands grew more feeble. With one last, desperate effort he pawed at the spring-loaded iron collar pressing into his throat, kicked twice and then lay still.

Sofia released the catch and withdrew the weapon, allowing Estrella to kneel at Miguel's side.

"What do you think of the man-catcher now,

Mary?" said Lina.

The redhead cocked her head at the bloated blue face with its bulging frozen eyes, like hailstones embedded in a rotten eggplant.

Before Mary could reply, a new voice from behind answered for her.

"I think if your weapon is called a man-catcher, then you sure enough caught one."

Lina folded her hands and watched a lanky, raw-boned hombre saunter toward them. "But I'd say you in some trouble at the same time."

The man wore tan pants and a short-sleeved linsey shirt. His hair curled up over his collar in back, and his Stetson rode at an angle just opposite his laconic smile. "My name's Jeff Rayburn. I'm the law in these parts."

"Ain't we in the soup now for sure," said Mary.

Rayburn's cheeks puffed up with a smile. "You ladies do me a favor, and don't move one damned muscle."

CHAPTER SEVEN

After Sunday mass at the College of St. Vincent of Maccabees, Ellis Donovan and Honey Shaw led Catalina, Mary, and Sofia down a clean swept concrete walk toward Old Central.

Decorated with ostentatious dormers, steeply pitched gables, and iron crestings rimming the perimeter of its roof, the palace of higher learning presided over an egg shaped acreage of lawn. The building's centerpiece was a round tower, four stories tall with an immaculate stained glass rose window embedded under a steeply pitched gable.

Lina had never seen so many useless architectural ornaments glued to a single structure.

"It's lovely," she said, forcing sincerity into her voice.

"My humble abode," said Donovan with cheerful alacrity. He squeezed Honey's hand. "Or should I say, *our* abode, my sweet?"

Honey was Donovan's fiancé.

"The great street o' the city was gold, as pure as transparent glass," said Honey. "It says so in the Good Book."

"It's not quite the New Jerusalem described in scripture, but Old Central is as close as we're likely to get."

"Aye, and it's the way with all flesh," said Honey.

Mary stood in the shadow of Old Central, head tipped back, her languid expression taking in the tower window.

Donovan approved. "You admire St. Catherine's window, Sister Mary?"

Glinting red, green, and gold, the tower window was divided by four diagonal spokes and ornate lines of decorative tracery. Like the single, all-seeing eye of some great owl, thought Lina. Unblinking, making eternal judgement of all within its domain.

"I do," said Mary. "Why St. Catherine's?"

"I would've expected even a young novitiate to remember St. Catherine of Alexandria, condemned to execution on a breaking wheel in 305." Donovan waved away a horsefly. "Such windows are often named in reference to Catherine's mode of death."

"Young female martyrs appear to be a specialty of yours, Mr. Donovan," said Mary.

"I should say the same for your profession, Sister."

Donovan motioned with his head toward the heavy electric cable drooping from a high cornice of the tower to a tall pole nearby. "We were the first building on campus to be wired for electricity."

"It's quite magnificent," said Mary.

Lina resisted the urge to flinch as Donavan put his free hand on her shoulder. "Again, I'm so sorry about the trouble you encountered in town. You'll find Sheriff Rayburn is a fair and honorable man."

Considering the lawman's laconic reaction to Mary's account of Miguel's attack, Lina couldn't disagree. Rayburn releasing the three of them into Donovan's custody until a formal inquiry could be called the next morning spoke to the integrity of both men.

Later today she would don cloak and cowl and steal the Sword of St. Agnes before fleeing into the night — betraying them both.

What did this say about the Black Rose?

Donovan cleared his throat. "I shouldn't worry about the inquest tomorrow. We've had trouble with those folks before, especially young Miguel. In fact, when he worked for the groundskeeper, tending the lemon orchard here at the college, he was quite a caution."

"How so?" said Lina.

"He had to be dismissed." Donovan making a thumbs-up gesture with his fist, then raised it to his lips as if it were a bottle. "He drank and didn't know his limits."

"Aye and it's the way of all flesh," chimed in Honey.

"Miguel was plenty soused this morning," said Mary. "His girlfriend and neighbor, too. All of them were plenty loaded."

"The woman, Estrella Gomez, is everybody's girlfriend," said Donovan. "If you'll understand my meaning."

"You mean she's a whore," said Mary.

"Er...I mean...yes." Donovan blushed and abruptly turned to Sofia. "Sister, I understand you controlled the situation with an ancient weapon. A Sasumata according to Sheriff Rayburn's description? I'd enjoy seeing it before you leave."

"The Sasumata is a forked tool of Oriental origin. It's not quite the same as my Man-Catcher. What I wielded today is a more esoteric polearm of medieval European design." Her lips pressed tightly together. "The Sasumata is only meant to entrap and detain."

"And your weapon?"

"The Man-Catcher is designed to kill."

Honey crossed herself as Donovan's heavy eyebrows jumped to his forehead.

"I'd still like to see it," he said.

"Of course," said Sofia, bowing her head. "It is currently safe at the campus stable with our horses."

Lina watched an athletic young man saunter around the corner of the building toward them. Wearing a light spring jacket, slacks and a tie of the latest European fashion, he exuded an arrogant confidence even Ellis Donovan lacked. When he spoke, he delivered his words with a New England accent, an affectation almost good enough to be real.

Almost.

"You must introduce me to your guests, Donny," said the slim man. He nodded at Donvan's fiancé. "How are you, Miss Shaw?"

Honey offered him a demure bow.

Donavan took two steps back. "Ladies, my I introduce my colleague, Mick Shanahan, doctor of philosophy."

"I must say the pleasure is mine," said Shanahan, thrusting his hand out with the hint of a lecherous smirk. His handshake was cold and damp, and Lina resisted the urge to wipe her palm on the folds of her habit.

"These are Catalina, Mary, and Sofia of the Daughters of the Holy Sepulcher from El Paso. They're here to see the Sword."

Shanahan's visage was cheerful and inviting. "I hope you're making them feel at home, Donny."

"Dr. Shanahan is the chair of our History and Humanities department."

"Such a tremendous responsibility," said Mary.

"We do our best," said Shanahan. He addressed Donovan and Honey as one. "I certainly hope we're still on for dinner this coming week?"

"It's on my calendar," said Honey.

"I'll look forward to it," said Shanahan. "Is there any chance the Sisters might join us?"

"I believe the sisters are only staying for the one night," said Donovan.

"We're traveling on to the Indian Reservation," said Sofia. "But thank you for your generous offer."

"Thank you, dear ladies, for gracing us with your presence."

Shanahan touched each of their hands once more before excusing himself.

Lina watched him stroll across the campus egg, a man without a care.

"Before we see your collection, Mr. Donovan, we should tend to our horses," said Sofia.

"Your horses — of course! Forgive me, ladies. Forgive me." In the shadow of Old Central, Donovan clapped his hands. "In my eagerness to welcome you to campus and show you my tower menagerie, I neglected to allow you to freshen up after your long journey. To say nothing of your arduous morning."

"Your hospitality is appreciated, Mr. Donovan," said Lina.

"But reckless and overly enthusiastic," he said. "You've had a long ride from El Paso. I'm sure the Daughters of the Holy Sepulcher would like to freshen up." Just over Donovan's shoulder, a burly guard stood watch at Old Central's front door. He wore navy blue with brass buttons and a polished belt and holster.

Donovan followed Lina's attention to the guard without comment.

Instead, with a peek at his pocket watch, he made a pronouncement. "Let's meet back here in two hours. Honey will help retrieve your belongings and get you situated for your overnight in one of the dormitories. Once you're rested, we'll have all afternoon to show you the sword."

"Your plan sounds very good indeed," said Catalina.

At least Donovan still had the thing. Demetrius could rest easy.

Donovan took both of her hands in his and again Lina fought not to resist.

"Until one o'clock then," said Donovan.

For an instant, the look on his face told Lina he intended to kiss her hand. When he refrained, it was from an obvious act of will and he waddled quickly away.

"I can tell his for sure sweet on ya," said Honey. She crouched low and motioned for Lina, Mary, and

Sofia to huddle close to her. "I have to keep my eye on him," she said, meaning Donovan. "He's a good egg, but he's one for the ladies, if you know what I mean."

"Aye, and it's the way—" said Mary.

"Of all flesh," finished Honey. "You've are so right, dear."

******

The white room was heavy with the scent of lilac, and the plaster walls had been hand-scrubbed, its wood floors swept and waxed. Three beds with iron headboards were dressed in stark pressed sheets, and a small wooden wash basin with a ceramic pitcher of fresh water waited on a low-slung chest of drawers.

As soon as Honey Shaw left the travelers from with their bags, Catalina let out a long sigh of relief. It was like she'd been holding her breath for the past hour without realizing it.

Mary's reaction was more animated as she pulled off her veil, tossed it into a corner and fell back on the bed closest to the door. "Hot damn, I think we pulled it off," she said.

Stoic as ever, Sofia stood by the wash basin with folded arms and eyed the rumpled clothing. "I begin to understand Sister Adeline's opinion of you."

Mary sat up on the bed. "Me? *You're* talking about *me?*"

She climbed to her feet on the mattress. "What I wielded today is a more esoteric polearm of medieval European origin," she said, in a deep mocking voice.

She jumped down beside Catalina with a loud thump. "Am I the only one who sees the irony in our masquerade being nearly betrayed by the only one of us who actually is a certified nun?"

"Go easy," said Lina.

Mary ran her fingers through her hair with vigor, then glued her knuckles to her hips. Again, she lowered her voice. "The man-catcher is designed to kill." She shook her head with disbelief. "What the hell, Sofia?"

In her corner, the nun's lip curled into a sneer while her eyes remained cold and level. "Your theatrics are wasted on me," she said.

"Your theatrics are wasted on me," repeated Mary in the same mocking tone.

"I couldn't help but notice the way you eyed Professor Shanahan. Take your act back to the bordello you came from."

"Lady, if you want a piece of me, you can—"

"Enough," said Catalina, striding between the two women, her voice holding each of them at bay. "Are we children to bicker over such meaningless things? We have a job to do."

"If Cassidy were here, there'd be no end to *your* bickering," said Mary.

Lina felt her face flush with heat.

"She is right, Lina," said Sofia.

Lina moved her head, looking from one woman to the other and back again.

"I said, enough."

She waited while Sofia moved to a chair beside the window and sat down, facing the grassy campus.

Mary fell back on the bed to stare at the ceiling.

For several heartbeats, the room was silent except for the sound of a songbird perched on the brickwork outside the St. Vincent's dormitory.

"Pout all you want," said Lina, "but Mercy trusts the three of us to work together." She slid aside the wash basin, picked up her satchel and plopped it onto the table. "And we must work together if we are to follow the plan."

"The plan didn't include killing the first people we met," said Mary.

"You would rather it be one of us measured for a coffin?" said Sofia.

"What about poor Sheriff Rayburn? What's he going to say when we don't show up for the inquest tomorrow?"

Lina shrugged. "He won't say anything — not to *us* anyway. Tonight the Daughters of the Sepulcher will vanish into the dark and cease to exist."

Eventually Mary exhaled long and loud. "Okay, I'm sorry. I *apologize*." She sat up and directed her words at Sofia. "Are you satisfied now?"

Sofia lifted her chin. "I suppose it will have to do."

Catalina spread the floorplan for Old Central across one of the beds.

"We don't have a lot of time before Honey comes back to collect us," she said. "So let's review." Recalling their initial meeting in the caverns below the mission at Santo Tomas, Lina covered the general aspects of the plan with broad strokes.

"What about the guards?" said Mary. "Did you see

the slab of blue marble standing out front? I wonder how many more fellows like him are around?"

"Mercy never mentioned armed guards," said Sofia. "And he carries an automatic. If reclaiming the sword was Demetrius' idea, it's funny he didn't say something to warn us."

"It's entirely possible he doesn't know about them," said Lina. "The guards might be a new addition since Demetrius left here." She studied the floorplan with a furrowed brow. "If I were trying to protect the contents of the tower, I'd station guards here." She put her finger on the floor plan. "Here, and here," she said, pointing.

"This spot is awful close to Donovan's door? What if the guard sees you?"

Lina smirked. "Let's just hope for his sake he doesn't."

"Each of us will be acting alone," said Sofia. "If we're discovered, and depending on the number of men employed, Donovan's squad might overwhelm us."

"Then we'll just have to be careful so we're not discovered," said Lina. "Or if we are, we need to make sure the guards are in no position to share the news with one another."

With that, Honey's voice beckoned from the hallway. "Sister Catalina? Are you ready to proceed to Old Central?"

According to plan, Sofia called out. "One moment, please, Honey."

Lina swept the plans away, threw back the sheets, and crawled into the bed.

Mary reclaimed her veil and straightened her habit.

Both women nodded in readiness.

Sofia opened the door. "I'm afraid Sister Catalina's taken ill. Sister Mary and I will be making the final pilgrimage alone."

There was no turning back.

CHAPTER EIGHT

After Mary and Sofia left, Catalina slid out from under the sheets and dropped lightly to her feet. At the footboard, she dropped her coif, wimple, and veil and stripped away the blue broadcloth of Mother Mercy's order. Beneath, she was dressed in the silk black tunic of the Black Rose with short flared sleeves and laced leather gauntlets. Her long legs were covered in ebony pants with nickel conchas and leather tassels running down the outer seams to where they met knee-high, lace-up boots.

Around her waist, the razor-edged steel urumi was wrapped like a belt.

From her saddle bag, Lina pulled a compact rectangular tin with a snap lid. Opening it revealed a tray with two compartments. One was filled with a greasy black tallow, the other's contents were blood red.

Pushing her fingers into the black side, she scooped up an ebony wad and drew the sign of the cross on her face, from forehead to chin and then across the bridge of her nose. She followed with a slash of red to each side of the black line her forehead.

The Apache war paint felt cool on her skin and the smell of its animal fat and herbal foundation energized the Black Rose. Catching sight of herself in the mirror, she realized there was one more thing to be done. With one deft motion she swept her long raven locks up into a twist.

Mercy's plan put the Black Rose in close proximity to moving cables and pullies. For the same reason she wasn't wearing her long cloak and cowl, she pinned her hair behind her head and out of the way.

Before pushing up the window sash, she took one last inventory of the room. Out of necessity, her nun's habit and shoes would be left behind, as would Sofia and Mary's mostly empty satchels. They had carried a change of clothes and other provisions in the warbag still with D'oro in the stable.

Besides the urumi at her middle, she carried a coil of knotted hemp and a cylindrical steel tube vital to the success of the mission. Inside the hollow black rod were four dry-cell batteries and a carbon-filament bulb.

Beyond the rope and electric torch, she would need to rely on wits alone.

And Mary Rosetta's skill as a pick-pocket.

The Black Rose opened the window and vaulted over the sill, landing with stealth in a rock garden of creeping yellow ivy.

On a lazy summer Sunday afternoon, with most of the students on sabbatical, the temperature was nearing three digits and a shimmering haze of dry heat permeated the egg-shaped plaza. Within the ring of seven brick buildings, two men were visible, conversing in the shadow of a young ingénue's lacy green parasol and these three were far across the emerald lawn. Every window on campus was flung wide with hopes of securing the faintest breeze, but nary a conversation nor snippet of music could be heard. It was the most lackadaisical of days and the Black Rose would have preferred more noise.

With a cacophony, she might blend in. With a certain activity and bustle, she might slip to the street behind the chapel unnoticed.

As it was, all it would take was one snoopy-drawers with time on his hands.

"Hello, gorgeous. Mind showing me what you're wearing?" said the young rummy hanging out the dormitory window above her. "Going for a swim are you?"

It couldn't be helped.

Damning her luck, The Black Rose ignored the lone undergrad's volley of ignoble questions and darted for the chapel, a blonde brick box of a place with a row of leaded glass windows, pleasantly locked down. She rounded the backside of the place without incident and, just off Wyckoff Street — exactly where it was supposed to be — she spied a hinged iron lid on a round stone foundation.

Without thought or worry of catching her breath, she gripped the cistern's iron ring in hand, lifted the cover, crawled inside, and pulled the hatch closed behind her.

******

It took a few minutes to adjust to the dark of tunnel, but hearing and other senses rapidly filled the gap left by her dimmed sight. Somewhere on the street above, the clip-clop of a horse advanced with the ongoing crunch of wagon wheels rolling over the brick lined street, and ahead in the distance, she heard the slow steady drip of water into a pool.

Like the tunnels beneath Santo Tomas, the College corridors were native to the region, ancient limestone carved by fresh water springs. At the dawn of the new century, industrialization had finished what nature began. Conduits for indoor plumbing and discreet coal delivery were like blood vessels for the school and the Black Rose thought about the electric line she'd seen earlier. Old Central certainly benefited from its network of veins and arteries, but just like with men, blood vessels left it vulnerable to attack.

An uneven roar and trundle of wheels passed over the surface above her head, a gasoline powered truck.

Crouching on a patch of bare granite, the Black Rose slid the switch on her electric torch and a beam of luminescence shot forward to light her way.

Ahead of her, the floor was a powdery white dust, marred here and there with brown mud basins for trickles of spring water and condensation. The air carried a light tang of death and with her first step, she splintered the stale carcass of a deer-mouse.

Pressing forward, willing herself to breathe easy, she recalled the drawings Father Demetrius had given them.

As she'd studied this labyrinth, she realized as long as she kept to the widest path, there was no way for her to get lost. With no major forks between the site of her ingress and the cellar under Old Central, she'd make good time. Maybe even arrive at the elevator shaft before Honey, Mary, and Sofia.

She certainly didn't expect to meet one of Donovan's guards down here.

And lucky for her she had never been afraid of the dark.

Following the subterranean path, picturing Mary and Sofia strolling along with Honey to keep their appointment with Donovan and view the St. Agnes Sword, the Black Rose reflected on all she knew about the treasure.

Agnes of Rome was a Christian martyr from a wealthy Roman family. One of seven women commemorated by name in the Canon of the Mass, Agnes is the patron saint of girls and chastity. Devoted to purity, she refused to marry because of her faith and so was condemned by Roman authorities.

Mercy had shared a handful of fanciful legends about Agnes. After her arrest, she was taken into Roman custody. Dragged through the street without clothes, her hair grew miraculously to cover her nakedness. She was lashed to a stake in the public square, and the men who attempted to violate her were struck blind. She was condemned to be burned alive, but the pile of wood where she stood would not ignite.

Finally, a Roman centurion drew his sword and beheaded her.

Not for an instant did the Black Rose believe the sword in Donovan's office was the actual blade which took Agnes's life. But she couldn't help wondering how far Donovan or his friend Shanahan bought into the story.

It didn't really matter one way or the other. What mattered was the Church and Mercy believed it.

And the Sainted Brothers of Monterrey, apparently they believed it too. By the time Demetrius had arrived in Santo Tomas, he feared the Brothers might already possess it.

The Black Rose wondered the same thing.

A choice line popped into her mind, filtered out of the past from her evening at Sullivan's Way. The old Colonel pounding on his pulpit, the fervor in his voice reaching a crescendo.

What exactly had he said?

"With this sought-after boon soon in our grasp, we have reason to expect the Batallón de San Patricio to rise again."

This sought-after boon? Yes, those were Sullivan's words.

But had he been talking about the sword?

If the Brothers of Monterrey gained possession of the thing, they could ransom it back to the church at a high cost. The church, of course, would pay, and the gold could go to the Brothers' war chest.

It made sense to Lina's way of thinking.

Or maybe they planned to sell it back to Ellis Donovan. That would work too.

Like Demetrius, maybe Donovan suspected something was afoot. It would certainly explain the new cadre of guards stationed in and around Old Central.

Either way, the Black Rose was determined to get the sword before anyone else. She owed Mercy her life and she was committed to her secret identity and her mission.

Another mouse, this one very much alive with a twitching pink nose and opal black eyes stood on its hind legs as the flashlight beam hit. The animal skittered along the edge of the tunnel, and following its progress, the Black Rose noticed a heavy heel-print in a spot of dust.

Somebody had been down here before her.

Quite recently from the looks of the print.

She swung the light back and forth, perusing the dark passageway, probing for more signs of life. Here and there were partial footprints. Along the wall, a muddy handprint.

A hard right hand corner forced the Black Rose to squat low to pass under a steel lintel beam. She crossed from the street into a stone lined dungeon under Old Central, and her fingers touched a lock of hair caught up on the edge of a rock.

Who had been down here?

She held the hair up into the light. It was blonde and smelled of lye soap.

Honey?

Another turn led her down three steps into a wider rock cavern supported by wood beams and steel stantions. Here she could almost stand upright, and a wood ladder was fixed to the wall.

The sub-basement to the elevator shaft.

According to Mercy, Donovan had convinced the college to install the Otis Elevator in Old Central two years ago. In her mind's eyes, Lina recalled the drawing and the building's network of ironworks. The electric motor and pullies were mounted high in the tower ceiling, and the car hung in an open shaft on steel cables. Behind the car, a tall, square duct ran the height of the tower.

The service chute was included in the construction, but was unnecessary to the design of the elevator they had installed.

The Black Rose was betting it had been forgotten.

She climbed up into the chute through a scaffolding of hardwood and steel, catching a web of jumping spiders on her chin.

She brushed the sticky web from her face. It wasn't enough to stop her.

Only one thing would stop her from achieving her objective of returning home to Mother Mercy with the Sword of St. Agnes…and it wasn't spider webs.

What if Donovan chose not to show off his Otis electric elevator and lead Mary and Sofia up Old Central's side stairway instead?

For the plan to work, it was vital to take the nuns for a ride up into the tower.

Trusting in the hubris of puffed up men like Ellis Donovan had never let her down.

She didn't think this time would be any different.

CHAPTER NINE

Clinging to the back of the cold steel Otis electric elevator car, the Black Rose waited for what seemed like hours. In reality, it wasn't more than a few minutes.

It had always been her intention to reach the shaft ahead of Mary and Sofia and hold on to the rungs at the back of the car, it was the only way their plan would work. While her friends rode up to Donovan's office museum inside the car, she would ride on the back, soaring up the extraneous service chute.

Then, as Donovan showed off his collection, the Black Rose planned to position herself on the electric motor scaffolding just within reach of the fourth story's outer doors. When the car dropped back to ground level, she would remain up high and steal into the abandoned building.

She was so distracted reviewing the plan in her mind, she almost missed the start of it.

Donovan's voice was muffled but intelligible and the sound of the car's inner accordion gate folding open echoed through the shaft.

"I'll welcome your opinion on the arrangement," he said. "I dare say the collection has grown so fast, I've hardly kept it as orderly as it should be, but it's a monumental challenge and quite humbling for me. To know pilgrims might find it worthy of a special journey is always gratifying."

Mary's tone was reverent and well-rehearsed. "Simply to be in the presence of the sword is humbling indeed, Mr. Donovan. I hope we're not taking up too much of your time."

"Most assuredly, you're not."

Then came Honey's voice. "Sugarplum welcomes any opportunity to share his work."

"I don't think I've ever been so excited," said Mary. Lina imagined the redhead batting her eyelashes.

"It's to be expected," said Donovan. Then: "First time in an elevator, dear?"

Sofia assented. "Yes. I'm not sure what to expect."

"Don't you fret even for a second, dear," said Honey.

"This is the finest model on the market," said Donovan. "I'm honored to share your, er…first time."

The Black Rose sighed to herself.

Men.

Still, in her estimation, the most important benchmark was crossed. They were inside.

Always count on hubris for the win.

They occupants of the car were silent. Finally, Donovan said, "Just a few more minutes."

The words were unexpected, as was the car's stationary status.

Sweat broke out on her palms, and the Black Rose tightened her grip on the iron rungs.

Why weren't they moving?

A pounding of footfalls, and a hollow bump and sway to the car, let the Black Rose know an additional passenger had joined the party.

"Ah, here we are," said Donovan.

The inner door of the elevator folded open again and then shut. In her mind, the Black Rose imagined Donovan, Honey, Mary, and Sofia.

Who was the new man?

As if in answer to the unspoken question, Donovan said, "Sisters, allow me to introduce you. This is Mr. Nolan, my chief of security."

He was broad shouldered, dark haired and good looking. Lina could hear it clearly in the way Mary said, "Hello there."

If Nolan acknowledged the greeting, it was with a silent expression.

The next voice from inside the car belonged to Honey. "Sugarplum had a devil of a time getting the college to accept his demands for security. Didn't you, dear?"

"Yes, indeed," said Donovan, emphasizing his agreement with a forced laugh from deep in his chest. "These Philistines simply have no ken as to the true value of my collection."

"Especially Dr. Shanahan," said Honey. Then to her guests, "Oh, don't get me wrong, he's not a bad sort. It's simply, with him, everything comes down to the almighty dollar. He has no sense of adventure."

"I see," said Sofia.

"The fool has no sense of history or the power the sword brings us."

"Power?" said Sofia.

"To bring in new students, of course," said Donovan. "And, of course, the value to pilgrim such as yourselves."

And still they weren't moving.

Something was wrong.

"It's a shame your Sister Catalina couldn't join us," said Donovan. "Odd her coming down ill so suddenly."

"I'm sure it's a result of this morning's debacle," said Sofia. "Sister Catalina has always had a diminutive constitution."

"Weak as a kitten, she is," said Mary.

"Spends most of her days at the convent in bed," added Sofia. "We tried to talk her out of even coming with us on the journey, but she wouldn't hear of it."

"I shouldn't be at all surprised if the poor dear expires at a young age," said Mary.

"We'll keep her in our prayers," said Honey.

"She'll be glad to hear it," said Mary.

The Black Rose scowled. She wanted to hear one thing and one thing only — the sound of Donovan tossing the wall-mounted rheostat lever forward and the engaging growl of the elevator engine.

Why was Donovan stalling?

"I do have one request before we visit the sword," he said.

Here it came.

"It's my utmost desire to have the three of you

stay through next Wednesday when we'll unveil the sword and celebrate the feast of St. Agnes."

Silence.

The Black Rose held tight to the elevator.

Donovan was testing them, damn him!

"With due respect, Mr. Donovan, the feast of St. Agnes is January 21. This is the month of May," said Sofia.

Donovan's expulsion of mirth was clean and robust. "That's a fact, my lovely. It certainly is a fact." He let his laughter go with a series of throaty chuckles. "Of course you would know when the feast day is — if you are, in fact, who you say you are."

Sofia's words were bitter. "I've taken the vows of my order, sir. Should I feel insulted?"

"Oh, don't let it weigh on you, dear," said Honey. "He's forever the paranoid."

"Just making sure," said Donovan. "Let's be on our way than, shall we?"

There was a hard, piercing buzz — like a thousand bees had been loosed in the steel shaft — followed by a snarling whirr from the big Otis engine and the clack, clack, clack, of the central pully mechanism hauling up its freight.

The car wobbled and started to rise.

The Black Rose held tight, but progress was slow.

They moved toward the fourth floor at a snail's pace and conversation inside the car continued, jumbled and hidden behind the noise of their assent. Truly it would have been faster to use the stairs.

When they arrived, the stop was sudden, the car freely falling an inch into its steel levered braking notch. Inside, the inner door came back and the outer doors were opened, allowing a haze of light from the sunlit hallway to penetrate the dark elevator shaft.

"Welcome, welcome all," said Donovan as the occupants made their exit.

Somebody closed the outer door, and darkness once again surrounded the car.

Immediately, she hoisted herself to the top of the shaft and felt with blind fingers for the series of well-spaced girders so prominently outlined in the building's construction plan.

They weren't there.

The Black Rose carried her electric torch in a deep pocket at her hip, but she didn't dare turn it on, lest the light give her away.

Wary, feeling her way along the front edge of the car with her arms held high and above her head, she tried to be quick, tried to stretch her fingers and feel for something to grasp.

She craned her face to the tower rafters and strained her senses. There was nothing, only empty space, and it took all her training to stay poised in the vacuum.

All her strength of will to keep from falling.

She imagined her cramped fingers, slipping and sliding as they groped desperately for the cables, her strained arms and bunched shoulders flailing against the steel slick sides of the shaft. She imagined falling, careening into the hardwood platform four stories below, her spine snapping like the frail bones of the mummied mouse she crushed under her boot.

Annoyed by the picture, the Black Rose shoved it out of her mind.

Pin lights of sun poked through here and there, and her eyes started picking up heavy, lumbering forms. The impressions had a familiar construction, a predicable regularity.

She found the main crossbeam, identified the engine mounts, recognized the massive assemblage of pullies. The structure supporting the electric Otis motor was, in fact, in reverse of the drawings Mercy provided.

The Black Rose made her roost at the rear of the shaft, above the service chute instead of near the doors.

It was a minor setback. Heart racing, she pulled herself into place and uncoiled the knotted rope hanging near her waist from the same loop securing her razor-edged urumi.

She wrapped several lengths of rope around the beam she sat on, then secured it one-handed with a tight bowline knot as Carlos had shown her. Her brother had taught her how to tie and untie all manner of knots when she was a child. Lessons she never forgot.

Before long, she heard snatches of conversation from Donovan's party in the hallway outside his office. Bits and pieces of pleasant small talk grew louder and more comprehensible as the group came near.

"Not at all."

"…you're always welcome."

"Next year, we plan…"

When the outer door opened, a slash of light cut into the shaft just under the Black Rose's station. She held her breath as one by one, the elevator filled.

The outer door swung shut, the inner cage clanged into place and the rheostat was engaged.

Gritting her teeth against the deafening squeal of the elevator car's plodding descent to earth, the Black Rose gripped her rope and waited.

The car dropped away into the darkness.

When the shaft was again quiet, the Black Rose let the rope uncoil into darkness, its full length stretching down into the gap, parallel with the iron cables.

From her high perch, she slid along the length of hemp, hands alighting on knots tied earlier in preparation for the task at hand, using momentum to swing over to the lip of the outer elevator door.

At the last second, she let go of the rope, snatched the door latch with her right hand, twisted it open and rolled through with the force of her short leap into the hallway of Old Central's top floor.

She came up on her feet nose to nose with Mr. Nolan, chief of security.

CHAPTER TEN

Nolan was the same uniformed fireplug she'd seen installed outside Old Central's main entrance earlier in the day and his name was embroidered in white thread on his uniform. With a thick hairbrush mustache and lantern jaw, he stood an inch lower than the Black Rose, but was twice as wide at the collar. His arms were lampposts welded to a chassis of v-shaped steel culminated in a hydraulic lift of a waist and legs like cannon barrels.

She levered a side hand chop into the cleft between his earlobe and shoulder. The same explosive blow had caused Josiah Woolard to stumble, but Nolan didn't seem to notice.

Instead of reeling from the attack, he advanced. Right hand like a steel-pronged trap, his quick iron fingers snapped around the Black Rose's slender neck, and his left hand clutched her tunic. Thrusting up and to the side, he lifted her off the floor and slammed her into the wall's oak chair rail.

Losing wind, the Black Rose slumped forward to let Nolan toss her like a rag doll down the hallway. She came to a stop on her back at the threshold of Donovan's office.

The deep polished door's frosted glass front picked up glints of color from the immense rose window in the room beyond and gold leaf spelled out the history professor's name and rank in blurred letters.

Doctor of History and Metaphysics.

Under the knob, in the faceplate, a long key with a crescent handle protruded from the keyhole.

Mary had apparently been successful in picking Donovan's pocket and leaving the key according to plan.

With renewed optimism, the Black Rose rolled to her right, away from the office as Nolan stomped forward, addressing her with prejudice. "You some kind of Injun girl with a painted up puss?" He licked his lips. "You must be deranged taking a swipe at me."

She rolled up onto the balls of her feet and slowly circled around him, stepping back, staying out of his mechanical grip until her head cleared.

"That's it, isn't it? You're some kind of lunatic." Nolan was massive, bison strong, and he knew it. "Come on to daddy and I'll make quick work of this scuffle."

If he grabbed the Black Rose again, he wouldn't let go until she was broken and gone. She couldn't let it happen.

But she wasn't about to run.

Nolan clasped his hands together and his knuckles cracked like gunfire. "I'm gonna enjoy taking you down, Injun girl."

The short hallway spanned the diameter of the round tower and was cool with filtered daylight coming through a single double paned window. Opposite the window and near the elevator, a closed door led to the stairway.

The Black Rose expected Nolan's comrades to burst through the door at any time and she kept one ear on the elevator shaft.

Nolan came in slow and confident. Too confident.

Planting herself like an oak tree in his path, she felt his hot breath and twisted to the side at the last instant, cranking her elbow around fast and hard, driving it into his puffy, open maw, tearing at his lips, snapping off his bottom front teeth.

Abrupt dental damage will slow even the toughest man.

In Nolan's case, he absorbed the concussion faster than most. But as blood poured down his chin and onto his dapper uniform, the Black Rose knew she'd stung more than his pride.

"Hope that…ain't all…you got?"

"Oh pooh," said the Black Rose. "It hurt like hell, and you know it."

His next grab was sloppy, a wide open, half-assed arc she easily ducked under, pivoting in behind to launch the heel of her boot into his spine.

Nolan spat blood and phlegm with a frothy grunt, pinwheeling into a long wooden waiting bench opposite Donvan's door.

He hit with a crash, but bounced back around with a loosely formed fist, clipping the Black Rose on the shoulder. The shock sent her reeling into the wall. Had Nolan's full weight been behind the strike, her arm would be useless for days.

Then there wasn't time to think, only react.

He came at her with fists like pistons, welling through the air, pounding in front of him, always just a fraction away from connecting. She whirled through the hall in defiance of gravity, launching kick after battering kick, punishing Nolan's mouth and chin. Hit a man hard in the same place twenty times, the frustration becomes as agonizing as the pain.

Now Nolan's attention was split between the Black Rose and the fount of blood welling up over his lower lip. He was still dangerous, but also distracted.

The Black Rose meant to capitalize on it. She beckoned him to her with wagging fingers.

"You promised to enjoy taking me down," she said. "I'm waiting?"

Giving in to her taunts, Nolan did just what she hope he would do. Giving in to anger and frustration, he charged forward with head, neck and shoulders in the lead, his elbows bent and thrust out with the makings of a bear hug.

The Black Rose wasn't about to let him cinch the embrace.

Instead she tossed off another kick, a blow to the knee, and she followed up with a hammer blow to his bruised face.

This time, Nolan expected it and caught her wrist in his vicelike grip. For his size, he was unbelievably quick. Before she could think, he snatched up her other arm. Nolan had the advantage now, heaving himself on top of her, bending her backwards down to the hard polished wood floor, crushing her beneath his mass.

His putrid breath smelled of bile and pipe tobacco. His uniform reeked of sweat.

Nolan's teeth were stained with blood and his crimson smile came straight from hell.

He was dead weight, like a steam engine chuffing its last, tipping forward…

The Black Rose held her pain within, refusing to cry out as her spine threatened to rupture, her rib cage to collapse like child's paper mache under Nolan's mass. Spasms of agony shot through her body and her feet tried to find purchase on the slippery floor.

Her legs begged for leverage.

Dark gray and fuzzy scarlet blobs spread through her brain.

"This is me…taking you down…," said Nolan, the air whistling through his missing teeth.

On the brink of oblivion, the Black Rose slammed her forehead into Nolan's bloody tender gash, folding back his top incisor with a crack. It wasn't enough to make him let go, but he lost his own precarious balance and they tumbled together to the floor.

The Black Rose grappled hard with fingers like deadly talons raking skin and seeking to gouge Nolan's eyes. For his part, Nolan was slowing down, drawing wind as he did his best to heave himself to the top.

He wasn't used to this kind of exertion. He didn't expect anyone to fight back.

They rolled across the floor, coming up in front of the elevator where the fight began.

"You're not going to let a girl beat you?" said the Black Rose.

"I'm…not…beat, yet."

The knotted hemp from before lay on the floor at his feet, one end still tied to a beam in the elevator shaft.

A garden snake relaxing in the sun.

When she was five years old, Catalina Cristiana Rivera wandered down a narrow trail bursting with purple flowered copperleaf shrubbery into the desert. Away from her sky-ranch hacienda in the rocky hills, she met a coiled rattler on the path. Not knowing to be afraid, she reached for the snake with predictable results.

But the fangs didn't touch her. Through luck and a natural grace, Lina swerved away from the lancing attack, curving back around to catch the snake under the jaw and toss it away.

She had no more fear of snakes than she did of the dark.

As swift as she had been one memorable day so long ago, today the Black Rose had honed her coordination and polished her accuracy. As Nolan barged ahead one last time, she whisked out of his way, seized the loose end of the rope, and wrapped it around his neck.

Caught off guard and panting, he put his paws to his throat.

The Black Rose showed her teeth and lowered her shoulder. "What's the difference between a cowboy and a horse thief?"

Legs churning ahead, she hit Nolan with everything she had, pushing him through the outer elevator doors into empty space. For a single tick, he realized his defeat.

"It's all in the way he swings a rope," said the Black Rose.

Then Nolan was gone and the rope snapped tight, quivering violently before it broke under the heavy man's weight.

A dull, wet thunk sounded far below and the Black Rose walked to Donovan's office door.

"Bless you, Mary Rosetta," she whispered, grasping the cold iron key. She twisted it counter-clockwise and felt the bolt slide.

Finally alone, Lina ignored the loud click echoing through the hallway. Mercy's plan had been based on complete stealth, but Nolan's disruption left little room for subtlety.

The Black Rose was behind schedule, and now since her rope was lost, she tried to imagine a new route of escape.

One thing at a time. Solve one problem at a time.

Still listening for the rush of additional guards, she turned the knob and opened the door.

Donovan's office opened to her like a sun painted Christmas morning.

Awash in shards of colored light from the ocular window, the room towered high above her head. Glass cases and cedar wood shelves lined with pulpy cloth-bound books pointed skyward, and jars of liquid and glittering pieces of gold and silver invited her touch.

According to what Demetrius had told Mercy, Donovan kept the Sword of St. Agnes on a velvet lined rest directly in front of his desk.

A prominent place.

Conspicuously empty.

The Black Rose swiveled her head to the left and right, frantically searching for a treasure that wasn't there.

The Sword of St. Agnes was gone.

Then the stairwell door opened with a crash and a new band of guards rushed to fill the hallway.

CHAPTER ELEVEN

"What now, you chickenshit bastard?" said Henry Hodges from behind a locked jail door. "You expect me to get down on my knees and pray?" Dressed in the same soiled clothes he'd been sleeping in for the past several nights, he stood with both fists gripping the bars, his unshaven face thrust into Cassidy's office.

In Santo Tomas, the morning breeze was hot and dry as ever, but the sunlight sky was filled with song. Under the direction of Sisters Adeline and Sara, the mission children's choir sang *Bring Flowers of the Rarest* on this fifth Sunday of Easter.

The constable laid the heavy leather bound book on his desk. "It's Sunday, Hodges. It'd do you well to clean up your language in the lady's presence." Leaning on his hickory walking stick, he glanced back at the door and spoke with soft assurance. "Go ahead and take a seat, Mercy. Don't pay any attention to the windbag in the corner."

Mother Mercy pushed the office door shut and picked up a wood folding chair from where it leaned against the wall beside the door. "I'm praying for you, Mr. Hodges. Whether you like it or not. We'll be lighting a candle each night in the convent until Judge Meredith comes."

Her compassion fell on deaf ears. "Where the hell's my lunch, Cassidy? Or are you planning to feed me bread and wine?"

Stick in hand, Cassidy walked past the front of his desk and poured from a tin carafe into two ceramic cups. "You take sugar in your coffee, Mercy?"

Hodges didn't cotton to being ignored. "What's all the racket coming from the square?" He forced a laugh. "Sounds like somebody chasing the chickens again."

Outside, the Marian hymn entered into its refrain.

"Hey, constable — I'm talking to you turds-for-brains," said Hodges.

Cassidy whirled around and the hickory slammed into Hodges' knuckles with a loud thwack. The prisoner wailed and fell back against his iron bunk before sticking the bent red fingers of his right hand into his mouth.

"I'll take sugar, yes. Thank you," said Mercy.

Smoothing her habit, she sat on the hard backed chair and received her coffee with a nod.

Cassidy hooked a thumb over his shoulder at Hodges. "Me and him are still working on our relationship."

Mercy sipped from her cup and offered both men a bemused smile. "How's it working out so far?"

Cassidy carried his mug to the other side of his desk and propped his stick beside a tall oak filing cabinet. After settling down in his chair, he shrugged. "He lips off, I smack him one. He calls me a name, I poke him in the eye."

"The lesson of the carrot and the stick."

"Mostly stick."

"Not a lot of carrots around these days?"

Cassidy shook his head. "There surely aren't."

Mercy's eyes sparkled. She was a fine looking woman behind those spectacles.

For her age.

Cassidy figured she was somewhere north of forty. Not old enough to be his mama, but nearly so. Looking at the series of beads and jet black wooden crucifix at her thigh, he couldn't help but think of Catalina. She carried a rosary equally dark.

"Something you'd like to say, Constable?"

"I was just looking at your…at your, er…forgive me."

"Yes?"

"I noticed your rosary. It looks like it was burned at some point."

"I suspect it was."

"Lina—that is, the rosary Sister Catalina carries is the same."

"Sister Catalina's rosary has been through hell itself."

"As has she," said Cassidy, recalling the night he rode with the Black Rose and a Mexican revolutionary named Garcia to liberate Santo Tomas from an oppressor's army.

"As has she," agreed Mercy.

"But not all of the nuns wear black rosaries," said Cassidy.

"No," said Mercy, the same benign smile plastered on her face. "Not all of the sisters do."

Cassidy realized he was pushing for more information than Mercy was willing to give. At least in mixed company.

He was privy to some of Catalina's secrets, but not all of them.

He had hoped that would change with time. Then came the evening at Sullivan's Way.

Now he wondered if they had any future together at all.

Cassidy leaned forward and pulled the book across the desk, then opened it to a page marked in the middle with a long satin ribbon.

Hodges' voice from the cell was less belligerent than before. He was curious. "Never pegged you for a bible reading man, constable."

"This ain't a Bible," said Cassidy. He bent back the first half of the tome and read the title aloud, "*Saints at War: 1846-1848. Being the History of One Man and the Right Glorious Batallón de San Patricio.*" He cleared his throat. "I guess you'd know all about it."

"I don't know spit."

"You were at Colonel Sullivan's meeting."

"I wasn't there for schoolin'."

"No, you were there to prey on the women Sullivan hired to host his meetings."

"Not my fault if a lassie likes the smell of bay rum."

"Lucia Hernandez didn't like it," said Mercy.

Hodges answered with an exaggerated stroke of the chin. "Can't rightly recall the name."

"Good thing you keep your stick behind the desk," said Mercy.

Cassidy nodded. "You get a hankerin' to swat him, you let me know and I'll hand it over to you."

"What became of the other two girls, Hodges? You might as well tell us now. It might be worth a good word to the judge."

"I've got no idea what girls you're talking about."

"Save us a lot of time if you told us about them," said Cassidy. "Same with what you know about Sullivan's social club."

"I told you, I just go out there to drink."

"Ever hear Sullivan mention the Sword of St. Agnes?"

"Knew a gal named Agnes once back in Houston. Except when it came to Agnes and me, I was the one with the long sword." Hodges bucked his hips back and forth. "You know what I mean, Sister?"

"The Sword belongs to the Catholic Church," said Cassidy, "and I think Sullivan wants it."

"Free country," said Hodges. "What's it got to do with me?"

Cassidy flipped a few pages away from the center of the big book on his desk. "And so in remembrance of the mighty battery who staved off the Imperialist American horde on 21, September 1846, we call ourselves after the city in question, beloved Monterrey, passion of our heart and soul."

"Too flowery for my blood," said Hodges. "Who wrote it?"

"This was penned by Colonel Sullivan's great grandfather," said Cassidy. "Arthur Q. Sullivan. He was one of the original members of the St. Patrick's Battalion. One of the few who wasn't executed for desertion by the American army."

"Where'd you find the book?"

"Our Father Demetrius brought it with him from New Mexico," said Mercy. "Father has grave reservations about a resurgence of the Battalion."

Hodges cackled at her tone, waving away her concern. "Bunch of harmless old coots, the lot of them and Sullivan's the king of coots. *Loco en la cabeza.*"

"I've heard that a lot, lately," said Mercy.

"What's the big, hairy problem, anyway?" said Hodges. "So what if a bunch of creaky oldsters want to trade their grandpas' war stories?"

"The St. Patrick's Battalion were traitors," said Cassidy. "Irish immigrants and expatriates who turned on the United States and fought against us in the Mexican War. They've got American blood on their hands. They should be reviled, not commemorated."

"Reviled they were," said Hodges, a new note of tension creeping into his voice. "Hated, despised and hanged for it in the end."

"You said Sullivan's grandfather was one of the few not executed?" said Mercy.

Cassidy flipped to a page at the end of the book. "In 1847, fifty men were hanged in three separate locations. They were accused of joining forces with Mexico after the declaration of war."

Outside the jail, in the town square, the children took up a new hymn: *Hail Queen of Heaven, the Ocean Star.* It wasn't exactly a toe-tapper, but

Cassidy drummed his fingers on the desk in time.

"The ones who were hanged had it easy," said Hodges. "Does your book, with all its fancy words, talk about the others? Does it talk about John Riley, the man who founded the San Patricios, but left the American service *before* the declaration of war? What about him and the others like him?"

"What about them?"

"Shackled, whipped," Hodges held a shaking fist up to his cheek, "branded on the face with a 'D' for deserter. Forced to wear iron collars." Hodges jerked his head toward the tiny square window in his cell. "Can't those bloody kids shut-up with the singing for a while?"

"You know a lot for somebody who claims to know nothing, Mr. Hodges," said Mercy.

"I got ears, ain't I?"

"And you hear things," said Cassidy. "Which is what I've been saying." He closed the book and came around the desk to stand in front of the jail bars. "I want to know about those missing girls. And I want to know about the Brotherhood's interest in the Sword of St. Agnes."

Hodges curled back his lip to expose yellow chipped teeth. "You'll have to ask Sullivan…if you ever manage to catch up with him."

But the answer was in Hodge's eyes. He couldn't hide it.

He knew what Cassidy wanted to know, but it was masked with raw defiance. The prisoner could feign indifference to old Colonel Sullivan's cause all he wanted, but his fussing and fuming proved he was part of it.

"Now that you mention it, I think I will take a ride out to Mr. Sullivan's place. I reckon a God-fearing man like him would be home on a Sunday afternoon."

"What about my lunch?"

"What's the verse about man not living by bread alone, Mercy?"

"Mathew four, verse four."

"I believe you are correct," said Cassidy. "You need to get right with God, too." The constable turned and, putting on his slouch hat and picking up his walking stick, put an arm around Mercy and led her to the door. She stepped out onto the boardwalk in front of him and Cassidy looked back at Hodges.

"I'll have one of the men from the livery check on you 'fore too long. Meantime, Mercy will have the choir sing you a few more numbers."

"You just try," said Hodges. "You might come back and find me gone."

"Oh, I don't think you want to try to get away," said Cassidy. "Unlike me, those boys from the livery carry some mean old hoglegs on their hip, and they'd welcome any excuse to use 'em for a little target practice. You know, something to break the monotony."

"One day I'm gonna wring your chickenshit neck," said Hodges.

"One day I'm gonna let you try," said Cassidy and he closed the door.

CHAPTER TWELVE

The Black Rose stared at the empty space across from Donovan's desk.

There was no doubt. The Sword of St. Agnes was gone.

Martial shouts of anger and fear followed the crash of the stairwell door and a rumble of footsteps sounded along the hallway.

Damnation! She was trapped inside Donovan's office.

"Here, Captain! Look here at the elevator." "My God, Danny-boy." "He can't have gone far, the bastard." "We'll get 'im, sir."

There were at least three of them. Maybe four.

Big men from the sound of their voices, brawny and uniformed. Carrying guns.

And unlike Nolan, these men probably had the weapons already in hand.

The Black Rose wheeled around Donovan's desk and caught his heavy, upholstered chair in both hands. She shoved it into place behind the closed office door, hoping the security team's own noise would cover the sound of her action.

It didn't.

"What's that, then?" said one of the men.

"Donvan's office," said another.

Boots made a clamor through the hall. Within seconds, they'd be on her.

Grabbing the piece of furniture nearest to the door, she pulled herself up and dropped back, tipping the glass front cabinet over the chair, showering the way with scattered shards and broken pottery.

It wouldn't hold them for long, but maybe enough to buy her some time.

She looked up, past the top of the immense bookshelves to a ceiling of ornamental tin tiles. Off center, high above the desk, an iron hook protruded from its anchor, presumably a rafter behind the decorative tin. Designed to hold a light of some kind, maybe a chandelier, never installed.

In one bound, the Black Rose surged to the surface of the desk even as she uncoiled the steel whip-sword from her waist.

The office door shuddered and the chair slid ahead. "Who's there? Hold on, now. We've got firearms on you."

As if his words needed backing up, a thundering boom echoed through the hall and a jar on Donvan's shelf exploded with a spray of yellow liquid. The choking smell of formaldehyde clouded the atmosphere. The Black Rose tried not to think about what might've been inside the jar.

Instead, she held her breath and measured the distance between the hook and the door. If only she had her rope, she could swing above their heads.

And be cut to ribbons in a deluge of lead.

A second shot pealed in, scuffing the edge of the desk at her feet.

The men at the door increased their shouting and the Black Rose took a frantic inventory of Donovan's collection for anything she could use to help her.

The lucent glow from the tremendous round window colored everything with a luminous rich spectrum. Mounted on wood and brick the diameter of the glass was more than eight feet and the assemblage lined with traceries of soft lead. From outside, the color had appeared dull and cloudy, but in Donovan's office, the installation earned its miraculous relation to Catherine with a heavenly brilliance.

In memory, a tidy square patio trimmed with an iron trellis squatted just outside.

Another shot and this time the combined clout of the assembled guards shoved the door partially ajar.

There was only one avenue of escape.

With a smooth pirouette, the Black Rose flung out the urumi, sending it on an unerring path straight for the center of the bright circle. The tip of the flat razored steel telescoped out four feet, eight feet, twelve, and struck the window with the force and speed of a rifle bullet even as the Black Rose propelled herself up in its wake.

The guards burst into the room, pitching slugs left and right in a hot barrage.

She hit the window in a symphony of lead and shattered glass. Shards rained down and over her as she tucked into a ball, tumbling through open air to a cacophony of destruction.

In a hail of colored shards, she landed hard against an iron wail. It screeched away from its moorings and gave way, leaving the Black Rose to roll over the side of the patio as the window collapsed above her and an abyss of death beckoned below.

There was no purchase, nothing to hold onto.

Two of the security men were already at the edge of the splintered round window pane, guns wavering, a string of oaths spilling from each of them. "Son of a bitch," said the older one. "What next?"

Next, the Black Rose needed to stay alive.

The collision with the heavy stained glass had left her dazed. Head ringing, vertigo telling her sideways was up and up was down, she hovered over the entrance to Old Central like a specter in midair while her urumi coiled into a spiral spinning earthward.

A slow ripping sound lifted her from her cloudy haze and focused her all of her attention.

At her beltline, a corner of her loose-fitting silk tunic had snagged a single spear-shaped pineal on the broken wrought iron rail, a thin strap of fabric between her and eternity.

It was the only thing holding her in place.

Under her weight, the shirt tore again.

The Black Rose had mere seconds before the fragile material gave way and she plunged more than forty feet to the poured cement sidewalk below. A breeze whipped through her hair, and she heard one of the guards shout, "She's there! By God, it's a woman."

Glass crunched under foot and a ruddy face popped over the precipice.

"She's here—"

Before he could say another word, the Black Rose clutched his leg with her right hand and, using the man as an anchor, pulled herself up to the edge of the patio. The guard kicked free, but stumbled backwards, slipped on the glass, and landed hard on his backside.

The Black Rose slipped, held on with one hand while the urumi fell from her other, twirling down, clashing with the pavement.

Her fingers let go.

But salvation was right in front of her nose.

Affixed to the curved stone walls was a braided metal cable traveling down the tower from an ornate lightning rod at its peak. Held in place every couple feet by a lead clamp, the cable ran straight to the ground. The Black Rose fell into the side of the tower and wrapped both hands around the cable.

"Shoot her," said a voice from above, followed by a round of percussion. Brass careened through the air as the automatics blew hot sparks and lead hit the wall, sending up splinters of stone. A bullet nicked the Black Rose on the cheek, and another tugged at her trousers.

Holding firm to the cable, she was a simple target. If the men hadn't been flustered as they were, she would already be dead.

She only had seconds to act.

From the pocket below her belt she slid out a compact geometric shape with a spring loaded switch in the center. She pressed the button with her thumb and three-blades shot out, their points projecting around the center at different angles.

"Bless you, Caroline," she said, hurling the ancient throwing knife with unerring accuracy. The weapon buried itself under the short ribs of the guard closest to the edge of the patio, rocking him backwards with a cry of anguish. Still firing his .45, the shots went wild and he caught the second man in the shoulder before toppling over the ledge.

Taking fast advantage of the brief respite, the Black Rose scurried down the electrical grounding cable, hand over hand.

Once her feet touched cement, every muscle screamed out and she willed herself not to collapse. More guards were coming at a gallop across the egg-shaped open lawn and she still needed to retrieve her urumi.

Shots sizzled past and crashed into the sidewalk, plowing up turf, and smacking the sides of Old Central.

Her whip-sword was lost.

All the Black Rose could do was flee for her life.

CHAPTER THIRTEEN

Catalina Rivera had always been a fast sprinter. First off the blocks, she had dominated her brothers and cousins in games. Even twelve year-old Paco was no match for her in a short run.

But in the marathons her endurance was lacking. Her athletic prowess, like her personality, was explosive. She was highly flammable, but burned out too fast.

Having expended her energy fighting Nolan in the hallway in front of Donovan's office, the Black Rose barely had enough energy to save herself and slide down the side of Old Central.

Now she was in a footrace across grass and pavement, rock and clay. Her throat was dry and felt as if it were laced with strands of barbed wire and inside her head a spiked steel ball rolled around and around and around…

She felt dizzy and each beat of her heart was a rail spike between the ribs.

Nolan had hurt her. The broken window had left her arms and face bruised and sliced open.

She tasted blood and salt and the sickly air around smelled of lemon tree blossoms.

Bam, bam, bam, her boots hit the ground, one after another, each footfall an electric jolt to her aching back, a strap across her screaming shoulders and neck.

The afternoon sun was the white hot flame of a forge and she was running a gauntlet the length of a hell of itself. Her body and brains were melting into a sluggish pile of mercurial nothingness.

Behind her, the shouts wouldn't let up and soon they were followed with the rushing clomping of hooves.

On horseback, Donovan's army was sure to catch her.

Through bleary, sweat saturated eyes she saw St. Vincent of Maccabees' brick chapel come into view. Behind was the cistern she'd crawled into, a lifetime ago, less than two hours before. The hoofbeats came closer, the shouts more garbled and confused.

Somebody called her name — Black Rose — but who knew her by that name here?

And then they were upon her and she felt a strong arm swoop down under her breasts, tighten around her ribs, pick her up, and carry her to the side of a racing horse. They reined in behind a stand of fir trees and she dropped to the ground in a wobbly fighting stance, shaky fists on point in front of her face.

"Come on then, you sons of bitches," she said, "and you'll know you've been in a fight."

"Catalina, it's us," said Sofia from high on her ivory pinto. "It's me."

"Sofia?" The Black Rose lowered her elbows a fraction.

"Mary's got D'oro. Your horse is behind you." They both turned as Mary flew into the grove. "Mount up," said Sofia. "Now, while we have time."

"They're coming," said Mary.

D'oro cantered around and the Black Rose took the reins and hoisted herself into the saddle. She breathed deep and focused on the warm smell of the horse, the supple muscles rippling beneath her.

She had her second wind, and she addressed her friends. "How many men are there?"

"Six or seven at least," said Sofia. "At first they were on foot, but then they were met by men on horses. One of them looked like Sheriff Rayburn."

"How is he so quickly involved?"

"Who cares. What I want to know is where's the sword?" said Mary.

"I don't have it."

"What do you mean, you don't have it? I left Donovan's key in the lock just like Mercy said."

"I got into the office without trouble."

"You didn't lose the sword?" said Sofia.

"I never had it. There is no sword."

"There is," said Mary. "We saw it. Donovan showed it to us in his office."

The Black Rose was unsure.

"It was there when we left," said Sofia. "On display directly in front of his desk."

"Something happened to it. Somebody got to it before us. Because when I opened the door, there was nothing there."

A ruckus closed in around the curve in the road. "They're coming," said Sofia.

"Where can we hide?"

"Nowhere," said the Black Rose.

"They will know the town better than we do," agreed Sofia. "Our only hope is to outrun them."

"Go," said the Black Rose, "we head out of town and try to lose them on the open range. We have good animals, better than what they're riding. We have a chance."

She spurred D'oro into the street and Mary and Sofia came swiftly behind.

The news about the sword was disconcerting. How had Sofia and Mary seen it in his office mere minutes before she got there? It was a mystery, a case of "now you see it, now you don't." Where was the sword? Who had it?

As D'oro swung around the green, three men on horseback bounded toward her. One of them held his automatic out in front with both hands, steering his horse with his uniformed thighs. The Black Rose instinctively reached for her urumi.

"Dammit," she said.

It was going to take time to get used to the weapon being lost.

Crouching low in the saddle, she urged the Andalusian into a mad charge at the man with the gun. Not holding the reins, his control of his mount would be indelicate at best.

His aim looked to be off by a mile.

D'oro slammed a shoulder into the stallion, screaming a challenge, nipping at the smaller animal's neck and withers. The smaller horse shied away, then careened onto the grass. His rider fell sideways, pulling the trigger of his gun two, three, four times before sliding from the saddle into a rolling heap.

When the second and third riders saw their comrade fall, they pulled back and came around behind Mary and Sofia. But they were on the heels of the Black Rose, who was already several lengths ahead, pushing D'oro through her paces, leaving the street, crossing over rough ground and over a series of newly cut trails on the edge of the college grounds.

A few stray shots sounded through the hot afternoon air, but they seemed less than serious.

The Black Rose and her friends continued to ride, out across the open desert, circumnavigating Candelaria, then retreating back the way they came.

They tore past the shanty houses where Woolard and Miguel had warred over lemon trees, and, kicking up a cyclone of dust, made a hard left back toward the clay ridge where Sofia had first described the dawn's early skyline and the blue five-mile sign had pointed the way.

They were barely a stone's throw from main street when the Black Rose came around a sharp curve and saw a string of three wagons parked in the road ahead of them. One of them had lost a wheel and was listing to port, propped up by a teetering pile of lopped-off railroad ties.

A blob of a woman, dressed in gunny-sack material, waddled out from behind the broken wagon and turned her face in the three riders' direction. She waved her fleshy arm.

Bounding along beside the Black Rose, Sofia nodded at the wagons.

Keep going...or stop?

The rocky outcroppings on either side of the road were high and left little space to creep past the brightly painted vans. To pass without stopping meant turning around to backtrack a quarter mile.

Slowing the Andalusians to a walk would afford them passage, though they would undeniably be caught up in conversation.

The Black Rose looked over her shoulder. To go back would be suicide.

"Be quick," she whispered, as much to D'oro and herself as her companions. They stretched out singled file, the Black Rose, Mary and Sofia, aiming for the open crook between the ailing wagon and the hard sandstone of the shoulder.

Wind whipped up a dust devil to herald their way and when they got close, the fat lady walked in front of D'oro to greet them. If the woman was curious about the Apache war paint or the various injuries the Black Rose displayed, she didn't let on.

"S'prised to see you all out here," said the lady. "Most folks these parts know to ride at night."

"We're not from here."

"Guess, I kinda figured as much. My name's Martha Grell. You can call me Ma."

The Black Rose nodded. "We'll just be on our way."

When she urged D'oro on, Ma didn't move.

"I wonder if we could impose on your good will," said Ma. "Only for a moment."

"Not today."

"What is it you need?" said Sofia.

The Black Rose felt her face flush with anger.

"If you could be so kind," said Ma, stepping backwards and bringing her arm down into a welcome motion.

The Black Rose began to speak, "We must—"

But Sofia was already on the ground and Mary dismounted behind her. The redhead showed her index finger to the Black Rose and shrugged.

Wait one minute.

Ma explained their predicament. "We need help lifting up the back end of this wagon. We got the wheel fixed and ready to go back, but it's got to be raised up some and…," Ma smiled. "With my hernias and all…"

"You said 'we.' Who else is here?"

"Me and the girls," said Ma. She clapped her mitts together and when she blew air through her teeth it sounded like a cat calling her kittens.

Two of them strolled from behind the second wagon. One was blonde, the other of Native descent. Both were buxom with ample tops and narrow waists, dressed in lavish dresses more suited to the center of an opera stage than the middle of a windy desert gulch. Their faces were thick with warpaint of a different kind, flowery pink rouge and blue-green mascara, and their feet were covered with silken Chinese slippers.

The Black Rose couldn't deny they were quite lovely. For men.

Because despite the frippery and ornamentation, they both needed to shave the whiskers off their chins.

"Lookie here, girls — we got us some help." Ma introduced them with enthusiasm.

"Hello," said the blonde, the one Ma called Frank. "My sister's Dixie."

"Of course she is," said Lina.

Mary turned to the Black Rose. "Are you gonna come down here and help?"

"No."

"Ain't you the snoot," said Ma. "But I guess it'll be fine, enough. If Red here would just help Frank lift the wagon."

"We don't have a lot of time," said Sofia.

"Yeah, yeah," said Ma, "I heard you." She shoved between Frank and Dixie and shouted to one more member of her odd tribe. "Hey, girl! Get that wheel out here, already."

"Coming, coming," said a feminine voice. "Christ almighty, can't you let up with the nagging?"

"These holy ladies need to be on their way," said Ma.

"Holy ladies?" A woman came from behind the third wagon rolling an iron-shod wheel before her.

The Black Rose drew D'oro back as the newcomer joined them.

Mary and Sofia each took one step toward their mounts.

"What holy ladies?" The voice was as familiar as the face

The newcomer froze and the wheel fell over flat in the dust with a loud bang. She jerked a big Army revolver from her waistband and hoisted it into position with both arms straight out in front of her.

"Get down off the horse, Señorita. Get down slow and easy."

The Black Rose had seen the gun, and the woman, before.

It was Estrella Gomez.

CHAPTER FOURTEEN

"Sullivan's Way was deserted," said Cassidy. "Empty as the tomb on Easter Morning."

Hodges sat with his back pressed into the corner of his jail cell, facing the barred window on rumpled sheets. The last rays of evening marked him with long skinny shadows, stripes against his sunburnt skin. When he snarled, his white teeth belonged to a caged tiger.

"Easter?" Hodges spit on the bare stone floor and poked a stub of a finger in Cassidy's direction. "I knew you'd get to preachin' sooner or later. Said as much this morning when you came in with the old mother hen. A man holes up with a bunch of holier than thou virgins too long—"

The constable hit the bars of the prison door with his stick. "Shut up, Hodges."

"Step on a nerve, did I?" Hodges ran his tongue around the inside of his mouth and grinned. "Well, a man's got a lot of nerves to step on down there in—"

"I said, shut up." Cassidy walked to the wall and, unfolding a wood chair, set it in front of the jail doors, just outside Hodge's reach. He sat down and laid the stick across his lap. "You and me need to have a talk about Sullivan." He leaned forward, and his voice was a rough whisper. "Mano y mano."

"Let's just do it. What do you want to hear, constable?" Hodges spread his palms in mock surrender. "I've got time on my hands and nothing better to do."

"I want to know where Sullivan is. You and I both know he lived in that side kitchen. When I rode out there this afternoon, everything's cleared out. Clothes, belongings, saddle and tack — all gone."

"Could be he got fed up with the clientele around Santo Tomas. I sure couldn't blame him."

"Or maybe he went to see a man about a sword?"

Hodges shrugged, then spat on the floor, narrowly missing Cassidy's boots.

"You mean them dried up ol' nuns put the fear in you? They want something and so they got you running around for 'em like a pansy-assed errand boy?" Hodges stood up in his cell and stretched. Then he pulled up his belt and made it tight around his thick middle. "Or maybe I was right the first time? Maybe you got a little something going on the side with some of the veiled trim?"

Cassidy felt his throat constrict. Felt the muscles in his jaw tighten and flinch.

Careful not to show his anger, he leaned his walking stick against the wall.

"I'll tell you what, Hodges. How about you and

me make us a deal?"

"Yeah? What kind of deal?"

"How about we cut through all the bluster and lay our cards on the table? You want out of here, and I want to know about Sullivan."

"A trade?" Hodges buried his laugh in his hand, then pushed his fingers through his tangled mop of sweaty hair. "You're too much a stick in the mud for your own good, constable. You'd never go against the letter of the law."

"Try me."

"Okay, lawman. Okay, I'll call your bluff. I tell you where Sullivan is and what he's doing, you open this door and let me walk out a free man." Hodges put his hands through the bars. "I'll even tell you about them girls from the nunnery, Savannah and Emilia. Is it a deal?"

Cassidy shook his head. "Not quite. See, you're the one used the word *trade*, not me. The way I see it, this thing needs to be more like a contest."

"How so?"

The constable walked to the edge of his desk, opened the top drawer and removed the ring of keys waiting there. "Get away from the door. Back on your bunk, into the corner."

Hodges' teeth showed again in the dusky red sun. "Why not?" He backed up.

Cassidy put the key into the door, cranked it sideways and let the door swing out. He stepped inside and stood in the opening. "You get past me, boy... well, then I guess I can't stop you."

Hodges put his hand over his mouth and looked out over the street. When he turned his face back to Cassidy, there was the slightest hint of fear. "How does this get you information on Sullivan or the girls?"

"When I whale the spit outta you, you'll tell me what I want to know."

Hodges looked away, letting his lips curl back. He nodded. "I see," he said. "I win, I get to walk free. You win, I spill my guts."

"In more ways than one."

"You must think pretty highly of yourself, runt."

Cassidy's fingers clenched tight, but eyes didn't waver. "Take it or leave it."

"I'll take it," said Hodges, coming off the bunk like a wild boar.

Cassidy sidestepped like a matador, catching Hodges' loose shirt at the collar, using the prisoner's own momentum to slam him face first into the steel door latch. His nose popped with a spurt of blood.

Hodges rebounded up and backwards, floating his fists in front of him.

Cassidy parried the man's big paws away and pummeled his broken nose a second time. Cartilage cracked and Hodges blew a sticky pink foam from his nostrils as he landed hard on his tailbone. Tears brimming in his eyes, he scooted reverse until his back was up against the bunk.

The constable knelt down beside him. "Ready to talk?"

"You can kiss my—"

Cassidy stood up and buried the toe of his boot into Hodge's guts.

"I love these little talks we have. When you get done being sick, we'll have another chat."

It wasn't long before Cassidy had all the information he wanted.

******

"You're sure you can trust what he told you?" said Mercy.

Cassidy tossed the Mexican saddle across the mule's blanket and cinched it tight around his heavy barrel. "I'm not sure of nothin.' But what I got now is better than what I had before and it makes an odd kind of sense."

"Explain to me how trusting the words of a known scoundrel like Hodges makes any sense at all? It's bad enough I was supposed to have heard from Catalina's party, now you're chasing off to the Lord knows where."

"What's this about Catalina?" said Cassidy, pausing his work. Between him and the Mother Superior, the constable's mule, Diablo, fidgeted with cantankerous abandon. "Hold still, damn you."

"If all went according to plan, Catalina promised to send a wire from Candelaria this evening. I have yet to receive it."

On the twilight street, Cassidy tilted his head back toward the post office and its burning lamp light. "You told Mr. Carpenter to stay on in the office?"

Mercy admitted it. "No message has come in yet. They're well overdue."

Diablo held firm while his owner piled on a bag at the saddle's cantle. Then Cassidy picked up a lever action Winchester and secured it to the animal in a leather boot.

"The lawman who doesn't carry a gun?"

"This is for rattlesnakes," said Cassidy.

"You're not going to tell me where you're going?"

"I'm going after your missing children, Mother. I'm following Mr. Sullivan to Candelaria and the College of St. Vincent of Maccabees."

"Hodges told you where Sullivan went? Is he after the sword?"

"Sullivan doesn't care about the sword. Sullivan cares about the money his friends in the Brotherhood of Monterrey will have after they sell the sword to the highest bidder."

"Meaning who? Who will be the highest bidder?"

Cassidy didn't know. "The college? The Catholic church?" He grimaced. "Might want to loosen your purse strings, Mercy."

"If the sword is lost, it would be a tragedy. But I have to admit, right now I'm more concerned about Lina, Mary and Sofia. I'm more concerned about you, Raul."

At the use of his first name, the constable reached out and took the nun's hand.

"Raul Cassidy has been looking out for himself a real long time." He bent over and kissed Mercy on the cheek. "I'll bring your gals home," he said.

"Or maybe it will be the other way around?" said Mercy.

Cassidy gave her hand a squeeze. "Might be that way, too."

"What about Savannah and Emilia. What did Hodges tell you about them?"

He put his foot into a floppy stirrup and tossed a leg over Diablo. Once situated he answered. "Guess I'll be bringing them home too," he said. "Sullivan's got 'em with him."

Cassidy doffed his slouch hat to Mercy and spurred the mule toward the edge of town. The air smelled dry and free of inclement weather. And he carried multiple jugs of water.

He planned for a hard, fast ride for him and Diablo.

He knew the mule would never forgive him.

If he came back dead, he knew Mercy would feel the same way.

CHAPTER FIFTEEN

"I said get down off the horse, Senorita."

Estrella Gomez was a small woman with a big gun and the Black Rose felt like she had been pulled through the south end of a northbound mule. She had little choice but to obey.

Grimacing against the pain, she crawled from D'oro's saddle, stumbling in the washboard ruts of the road. A quick brown lizard spiraled away from her feet and blood flowed freely from cuts on her arms and legs. "A house lizard," she said. "We used to call them house lizards."

She fought against a dizzy nausea.

"But what do we call you, Indian Girl?" Estrella kept the gun level on the Black Rose and pulled a red bandanna from her tight fitting corduroy trousers. Poking the barrel of the gun forward, she came close and wiped the war paint away from Catalina's face.

Lina flinched at the touch and Estrella laughed.

"Maybe I call you Grandma Nellie, after the famous Apache?"

Beside Catalina's neck, the smaller woman cocked her head and inhaled slow, her eyes partially closed. "I know you, Grandma," said Estrella.

Abruptly, she pushed the gun back into her pants and turned to pick up the wheel. "Esta bien," she told Ma. "It's okay. These are the women I told you about from early this morning."

Ma's face was a mix of shock and good humor. "The ones killed ol' Miguel?"

"In defense of our own lives," said Sofia.

Ma laid a hand on her shoulder. "No need to pretty it up for me, darlin.' The little jackass had it comin' a long time. I'm just surprised you ain't still sittin' in Rayburn's jail."

"They never went to jail." Was there a hint of respect there? Or derision? Catalina couldn't decipher Estrella's tone. She recalled something Mercy once shared with her.

A woman of the night is a master of masking her emotions.

Having logged plenty of hours in the role before taking her vows, Mercy would know.

"These three have low friends in high places," said Estrella.

"As opposed to us, eh, girls?" said Ma, addressing the two men in female garb.

Frank and Dixie she had called them. The fellows were visibly amused. "We got the opposite, Ma — high friends in low places," said Frank. "Real low."

"For one, I'm glad for what you did to Miguel,"

said Dixie, bowing.

"Yes, gracias," said Estrella.

Addressing the woman, Sofia was confused. "But I thought you and he...I mean, you were *with him*... weren't you?"

Estrella rolled the reconstructed wheel over to the wagon and ran her bandanna around her neck. "Miguel was a filthy pig." She drew out the word, heaping it with derision. *Peeeeeg.*

For a few seconds, Estrella seemed to blur, as if a whirling dirt devil had come between her and Lina. Then the air cleared.

Ma reached out to pat her cheek. "My Estrella's a hard worker."

Hard worker.

Hard worker.

The words echoed against the wagon and came back to Catalina, rocking her skull sideways into her shoulder.

Now Lina saw two Estrellas, each lifting the wagon wheel.

"Let's get this old piece of junk fixed," said Ma. "If what you say is true, these may ladies have good reason to be on their way."

"Don't worry about el aguacil," said Frank. *The sheriff.*

"Rayburn es un bondadoso anciano," said Dixie. *A kind old man.*

"Dixie is in love with him," said Frank.

But Ma's voice was all work. "You two button it up. Either way, we gotta get this wheel fixed. Now, if you sisters get under there, we'll have Frank and Dixie lift from over here. You got the wheel, Estrella?"

Estrella...Estrella.

Lina pulled at her tunic closed and shivered against a cold breeze.

She couldn't remember ever feeling so cold.

"Lina?" said Mary.

Lina.

Lina.

"Are you—"

Mary said something else, but the rocky bleached road pivoted up on a fulcrum under Lina's boots and slammed into her side. The impact rattled her back teeth.

Funny, the earth wasn't supposed to do that. When everything else was in chaos, the earth at least was supposed to be stable.

Like the missing sword, it was another puzzle to solve. Lina decided she would think about it later, she told herself, when she was warmer.

She was so very cold.

A shroud fell from the sky. A hood of darkness enveloped her.

And for a long time, everything was quiet.

******

When Catalina woke up, she was tied and bound.

Awash in white light, and summoned by a loud, clanging bell, she wondered, if only for second, if she had slipped her mortal coil and landed in an unforeseen afterlife.

No, her head hurt too much for heaven. If she was dead, she'd definitely gone to hell.

Because, no matter what she believed, she knew paradise wouldn't include skull fractures or the ripe summer smell of horse apples.

Pressure on her arms held them to her sides, and her knees wouldn't bend. She struggled to sit up, but was constrained to a soft mattress of some kind.

A shadow slid between her and the sun and she gave in to a rough, rocking back and forth, the clang, clang, clang, keeping time with the motion.

Something soft, cool, and wet came to her forehead.

"Welcome back, sleepyhead."

Nobody but Mary could be so casual with Catalina and nobody's voice could have been more welcome.

Lina relaxed her arms, chest and legs and her breathing slowed by half.

"What...?" Her lips were two heavy to form the words. *What happened?*

"You left us for a while," said Mary. She replaced the cloth on Lina's head and with gentle fingers she massaged long her damp hairline. "Nearly two days."

Lina's thoughts were scattershot, her memories a crashing series of marbles spinning around at the bottom of a milk pail. "Where?"

"We're in Estrella's wagon," said Mary. "She's up front on the bench, driving."

"Candelaria?"

"We've left Candelaria behind, dear. We're out in the country now."

"Need to get back…"

"Shhh," said Mary, continuing to rub Lina's face, her cheeks. "You've lost a tankard of blood. For a while there, we weren't sure you'd stay with us. Let yourself rest."

Lina took in the words and swallowed hard. She understood injuries and fever, knew full well about facing death.

She'd done it before.

And she had no patience with death. Even less for recuperation.

Healing took too much time.

She forced herself to sit up. Constrained, she fell back.

At first she had thought she was tied down to the straw-filled day bed in the jostling van with its clanging pots and pans. The reality was more benign, but no less grim. Heavy bandages wrapped tight around her arms, midsection and thighs wouldn't let her sit up.

"Water?" she said.

Mary obliged with a cool, tin canteen. "Sip," she said. "Don't guzzle it."

That was one thing, at least, Lina could agree with. She had no desire to add stomach cramps to her banging head.

Finally able to put together an entire sentence, Lina said, "Please…quiet those goddamn tin pans?"

Mary held onto the swaying wall and removed the pans from their hooks in the van's enclosed ceiling joist. "You're lucky Adeline's not around to hear you curse."

"Or to see you dressed like a *puta*," said Lina.

"This old thing?" said Mary, with a wobbly sashay. "Ma says it's the latest from Paris."

The ruby red of the dress should have clashed with Mary's hair, but somehow it didn't. Even with a head injury, Lina could see the dress was made of soft, fine silk. The sleeveless bodice was low cut and fell in soft rumpled layers across Mary's breasts. The narrow cut skirt hugged her curves and resembled an upside down tulip blossom with one side draped over the other.

"Where's your habit and veil?"

"Sofia and I packed our old clothes away."

Lina rubbed her temples, trying to understand.

Mary continued to explain. "You were out for more than a day. We were supposed to be at the sheriff's office yesterday morning."

"He'll be looking for us," said Lina.

"He'll be looking for three nuns," said Mary. "Do I look like a nun?"

Lina had to admit, "Not like any I've ever seen."

Mary's hair was piled high atop her head and fell in soft curls at her neckline. A pair of teardrop ruby earrings dangled from her lobes and a matching necklace lay on her decotage with the teardrop pendant nestled in the crease of her cleavage.

Her lips and cheeks were rouged in a deep red and her eyes were lined with charcoal. She pursed her lips and blew a kiss in Lina's direction.

"Where's Sofia now?"

Mary nodded in the direction they were moving. "Riding with Ma on the lead wagon."

"There were three wagons."

"The girls, I mean — the boys — are driving the wagon ahead of us."

"We need to go back."

"You need time to rest."

"There may still be time to find the sword."

"The sword?" said Mary, crouching back down next to the thin daybed. With gentle hands, she pushed Lina back to her ruffled pillow and replaced the cloth on her head. "Our mission is over, Catalina. The sword is gone. You're lucky you escaped with your life."

"Luck?" Catalina winced at the sharp ache behind each temple. "I don't believe in luck, Mary."

"If you ask me, you don't believe in much of anything except showing off." She put her face close to Lina's. "Except maybe getting yourself killed."

"Tell me what happened in Donovan's office," said Lina. "When I was in the elevator shaft. You said you saw the sword?"

"We did," said Mary, pulling a sour face. "Maybe the ugliest thing I've ever seen: a hung of tin dross and yellowing bone."

"But Donovan had it on display directly in front of his desk?"

"Sure and he did. Had it mounted on a green velvet-lined rest with an electric lamp screwed into the shelf above to shine down on it."

"The sword was there when you left?"

Mary said it was.

"When you came back to the elevator, did Donovan close his office door behind you? Did he lock it?"

Mary closed her eyes for a moment as if to replay the events in her mind.

"Yes, I'm sure he did. Why? What are you thinking?"

"I think somebody must have been in the office between the time you left and when I broke in."

Mary chewed her lip and nodded. "But who? I mean, other than Honey."

"Honey?"

Mary brushed off the comment. "Oh, she forgot her purse or something, had to run back and fetch it."

Catalina pulled herself into a seated position. The ache in her head momentarily forgotten.

"Tell me about it."

"You know how Donovan is, all bluster and braggadocio. He made a big deal about showing us the sword, holding it up in the light, pointing out a variety of its features." Mary lifted her chin. "I made sure he knew I was properly impressed."

"But you weren't?"

"Like I said, it's just an old sword. Who cares about scrap of metal with fancy handle? Not too well made to my way of thinking."

"What did Sophia think?"

"She seemed less impressed than me, but she played along. She recited a long-winded prayer over the thing and, get this, went so far as to kneel down and kiss the hilt." Mary rolled her eyes. "Sort of disgusting if you ask me, but Donovan seemed satisfied enough."

"And afterwards, you left and came straight to the elevator?"

"We did, except, like I said about half-way down the hallway, Honey said she forgot her purse and ran back to get it."

"When she rejoined you, is it possible she had the sword under her clothes?"

Mary pondered Lina's words.

"I don't think so," she said. "She wasn't in the office too long by herself, and I didn't notice her acting strange or walking like she was hiding anything."

"Maybe she had a custom sheath concealed in her garment?"

"Maybe you need to do what I said and rest yourself," said Mary.

The wagon came to a slow halt.

Outside, Estrella climbed down from the wagon bench and stretched.

"We need to talk to Honey," said Lina. "Alone."

"Speak for yourself," said Mary. "This caravan is headed into the hills. We're traveling in the exact opposite direction of the College of St. Vincent's."

"Then I need to leave your company," said Lina, "and I won't bother to speak for myself. But I will speak for the Black Rose. I need to find Honey Shaw."

Estrella climbed into the wagon compartment. "Well, well, well. Look who's back with the living," she said to Catalina. Then she looked at Mary. "We're stopping to water the horses. What did you say about Honey?"

"Honey Shaw," said Lina. "Do you know her?"

"Yes, of course. She's a good niña. Taught her everything I know about the...ah, *bedroom art*," said Estrella.

"I don't understand," said Lina.

"Es no problema," said Estrella. "Before she went with the professor, Honey was…ah, how to say it — la puta numero uno de Ma."

Catalina understood only too well.

Ma's number one whore.

CHAPTER SIXTEEN

Ellis Donovan poured himself a stiff drink and tried not to look at the boarded-up shambles of his beautiful rose window as he rounded his desk. Most of the glass had been swept away, but he knew he would be finding splinters in the hardwood for years, not to mention his vast Persian rug.

Looking around at the devastation made him want to regurgitate. Instead, he jerked back his chair and let himself fall into it.

Sulking, he sipped his Scotch and let the woody oak flavors drift over his tongue and into his sinuses. He'd learned to appreciate the little things in the days since his sanctuary was so ruthlessly violated.

A good Scotch. His collection of books. The touch of a good woman.

He turned the framed cardboard framed photograph of Honey to face him.

At least he still had Honey.

Though he hadn't seen her since the previous

morning.

"Ah, time," he said to himself. "Time is the ruth-less enemy of us all. Too much of it spent together and familiarity breeds contempt. Too much apart and the green-eyed beast of jealousy springs to life."

Donovan wasn't sure who, exactly, he should be jealous of.

Honey was his forever love. Of that, he had no doubt.

A knock at the open office door was followed by a slow, easy voice. "Am I intruding, sir?"

At the sight of the sheriff, Donovan's eyebrows jumped and his cheeks puffed with joy. "Come in, Mr. Rayburn, come in."

"Hope I'm not bein' a bother."

"Nonsense," said Donovan, standing behind the desk. "Fix yourself a drink."

Rayburn cast a dirty eye at the wet bar and removed his hat. He was tall and lanky with a ruddy face and sun-wrinkled skin cast brown by the elements. Un-der his nose was a black and gray-streaked whisker hairbrush and his eyebrows were black and heavy. He wore horsehide gloves and smelled like a livery stable.

"Appreciate the offer, but this is an official call, sir."

Donovan couldn't help but respond to the sense of eagerness in the man's voice. "What is it, sheriff? What is it?"

"Think we might finally have a lead on them nuns."

"Do tell?"

"An old teamster named Sable thinks he saw a blue nun's habit and veil drying on a clothes line out about Stark Canyon."

The professor felt the air go out of his body. "There's a convent at Williamsburg," said Donovan. "Not many miles from the canyon in the other direction."

"Yes, sir, there is."

"It was likely one of the nuns from there. They often go on nature walks in the desert."

Rayburn wore a beige cotton shirt with the sleeves rolled up, jeans, and boots. In contrast, Donvan's jacket and heavy wool trousers hung heavy on him.

"Thing is, sir — this here habit and veil was blue. Like was worn by the women you described. The women over at Williamsburg, they look like penguins." Rayburn turned his hat between his fingers, hand over hand. "Anyway, I thought we ought to go see. I've got a right good posse of five, but if your men might accompany us, it would be right nice."

Donovan perked back up. He swallowed his drink and said, "How many do you need?"

"Four or five ought to do it. I don't mean to seem skeered, it don't do for a lawman to sound too damn skeered, but I've seen these three at work. They're cold-blooded killers and like I told you, the one had some fancy kind of pole weapon."

"The man-catcher," mused Donovan. "Yes, I never got to see it." Regret tinged his voice.

He put down his glass and bent across the arm of his chair to retrieve something from the floor beside him. Bringing up the wound bundle, he rose and carried it to his guest.

"Have you ever seen anything like this, Sheriff?"

Rayburn looked at the coil Donovan offered him

— a long, flat polished piece of steel rolled into a tight spiral and clipped together with a spring-loaded clasp. One end tapered to a sharp spear point. The other was hidden in the traditional hilt of a sword. "I believe I have," he admitted. "Around the waist of one of your nuns."

"Note it's not actually one blade, but several segmented pieces which telescope one into another."

Rayburn put a gloved finger to the edge. "Damn thing is sharp as a rattler's tooth."

"It's called a urumi," said Donovan. "A primitive whip-sword. Until the other day, I'd never seen one myself, though I've read about them enough in esoteric journals."

"I'll be jiggered."

"With one of these, a man with sufficient training could take on a regiment of armed horsemen."

"A man?" said Rayburn.

"Or woman," said Donovan.

"Your crazy nun, leave it here after her robbery attempt?"

"Apparently she did," said Donovan. "If it's the same thing you say you saw around her waist."

"That's it alright."

Donovan tossed the urumi to his desk where it landed with a thump.

"Got a question for you, sir," said Rayburn.

Donovan poured himself a fresh measure of whiskey and leaned against the front of his desk with his ankles crossed. "Go ahead."

"What kind of person are we dealing with here?

Your men said she wore some kind of paint on her face and was dressed in black pants with tassels on the side. Now you keep saying it was them nuns, and I guess I believe you, but…"

"But what kind of nun dresses in such a fashion and carries a weapon like this?" Donovan nodded toward the desk. "Traditionally, nuns don't wear pants, brandish weapons, and try to kill people."

"No, sir, they don't ."

"Then they aren't nuns," said Donovan. "At least, they aren't who they claimed to be when they arrived here. After this primitive attempt at larceny, I took the liberty of wiring my friends in El Paso. Apparently there is no such convent as the Daughters of the Holy Sepulcher. At least not in Texas."

Donovan walked to the bookshelf where his five books were prominently on display.

It was past time to share his suspicions with Rayburn. "One minute," he said.

"Sullivan…," he said, running his finger along the row of spines on the shelf beneath his manuscripts. "Arthur Q. Sullivan," he whispered. "Sull-i-van."

There was an empty space where the big book should be. "Hmmph," he said.

"Can't find what you're lookin' for?" said Rayburn.

"I wanted to show you a book. It's called *Saints at War: 1846-1848.*"

"Okay."

Donovan let his voice take on a powerful timber. *"Being the History of One Man and the Right Glorious Batallón de San Patricio."*

He scratched his chin. The book was gone. Then he realized — Demetrius.

He had allowed the young priest to borrow the book, and it had never been returned. If there was one thing he couldn't abide, it was a book thief.

He looked at the sheriff through lowered brows.

"I think these nuns are members of an unholy order, the St. Patrick's Battalion. Or, perhaps to be more clear, a resurrected para-military group who call themselves the Sainted Brotherhood of Monterrey."

"They said they came from El Paso."

"I have friends in El Paso, Sheriff. I've taken the liberty of sending a wire there. It seems there is no such order as the Daughters of the Holy Sepulcher. I have reason to believe they might be in league with certain faculty members here on campus."

"Oh, so?"

Donovan reached into his pocket and withdrew the token he'd found on his rug after the conversation with Shanahan the week before. He handed it to Rayburn.

"I've heard rumors about the Brothers of Monterrey." Rayburn studied the coin, turned it over in his hand. "Never seen one of these." Rayburn clutched the token in a tight grip. "Today you're showing me all sorts of things I've never seen before."

"You asked what kind of people we're dealing with. This is your answer. The demon who invaded my sanctuary here was no nun. *Demon* may, in fact, be closer to the truth."

Rayburn held up the token. "Mind if I keep this?"

"Be my guest."

The sheriff stood tall and proud. With his hat in his hand, he vowed, "We'll bring your demon in, sir."

"I'll have the men saddled and ready for you within the hour," said Donovan. "Reynolds Booth is my second-in-command on Old Central's new security team." The fellow was a big Filipino and Donovan prided himself on his lack of bigotry in hiring him.

Rayburn nodded. "I'll palaver with your man presently. I have no doubt we'll find these imposters. And God help them when we do."

God help all of us, thought Donovan.

He turned away as Rayburn left the room, feeling himself sink into a black pool of depression. He'd worked so long and at such great expense to possess the sword and now he risked losing it forever.

But seeing Honey's photo on his desk made him smile.

Her loyalty, at least, was one thing he could count on.

CHAPTER SEVENTEEN

Mick Shanahan sipped his beer and rolled the Irish copper token over his knuckles like a silver dollar. His old dad had taught him how to do that back in Nebraska, before the family moved south and west and he'd kept the habit all these years.

All these many years.

Hard years, too.

Watching the industrialists and the corporate barons rape the church, the family and a nation he'd been taught to doubt in the first place. All the time he'd spent climbing up the academic ladder until he became head of his own department — History and Humanities.

But at St. Vincent's, a once prestigious school in a piss-poor desert town.

Still and all — he was better off than any of the toothless old fools who drowned their sorrows at the tabled near the cantina doorway.

But not better off than the world-renowned Ellis Donovan.

Ah, but everything was about to change, wasn't it?

Shanahan loosened his tie and breathed in the smell of clean wood polish and furniture wax, sawdust from the wood floor and grilling steaks in the kitchen. The Snorty Horse was a cool respite on a hot week day afternoon. With classes over for the day and little to distract him, he could let his hair down and entertain guests.

The beanpole behind the bar (Max) and the girl servers (Edna and Louise) knew him here.

Shanahan rolled the token back and forth and watched Perry Sullivan finish his tall pint. Except for the grandfathers at the door, they were the only customers.

The Colonel was a bit of an embarrassment in his rumpled home-made uniform, a crude embroidered patch mimicking the design of the token adorning his shoulder. He wore oversized rubber boots on top of his shoes and each time moved a leg it was like he lifted a ten pound medicine ball.

Waving at Max, Shanahan told the Colonel to have another. "A healthy dose'll serve you in good stead after a ride like you've had."

Sullivan ran the sleeve of his old uniform over his upper lip bristle. "Aye, sir, you're right as can be. It ain't a bad hoof from Santo Tomas, but it ain't what I'd call pleasant, neither, not with them two fillies in tow."

Shanahan eyed the curvy blonde who carried a fresh mug of beer over to the table. Edna put it down in front of the Colonel and Shanahan nodded toward her backside. "We've plenty of pleasantries here in

Candelaria, sir. Plenty of fillies too. I'll wager we can make up for any discomfort you experienced."

Sullivan rested his elbow on the polished table top and dropped his whiskered chin into his palm with a whimsical expression. "I'm too old for such nonsense," he said. "Though there be times I wish it weren't the case."

"The two girls you brought along with you, Colonel. They're in your hotel room?"

"Ay-yuh, they are indeed."

"And what are their names?"

"Damned if I can remember," said Sullivan, sipping at the foam of his drink. "Emily and Sassafras, maybe. I didn't talk to 'em much. Didn't touch 'em, neither. Just like you told me not to. I just brought 'em along like a couple bags of seed grain."

"We'll deal with them later," said Shanahan.

He watched the two old men play cards, trying to identify the game. Not gin rummy. Not poker either. Sheephead by the looks of it.

The late afternoon sun cast long shadows through the cantina's proud windows. A breeze rolled along the boardwalk outside, kicking in a few stray leaves and a healthy modicum of peppery-smelling dust. Max scurried around from behind the bar with a short whisk-broom and pan.

"A ceiling fan would be nice."

"A what?" said Sullivan.

"Ceiling fan," said Shanahan. "Just thinking a fan would be a welcome relief in here. Something to stir up the hot air."

Sullivan drank some beer and paid no mind to the rafters. "I'm cool enough," he said.

"The problem of course is the cantina isn't wired for electricity," said Shanahan.

"No electric, huh?"

"Hard to believe, isn't it?"

"Not too hard," said Sullivan. "My place in Texas ain't wired."

"But that's Santo Tomas," said Shanahan. "My point is here, in Candelaria, less than a mile away from the College of St. Vincent of Maccabees, there's no power. We have telephone service, but none of the houses are wired for electricity. Power is provided on campus for only one man. It's absurd. Ellis Donovan wanted a working elevator for Jesus Christ's sake and he got it."

"You want to put an elevator in this place?"

"No, no. A ceiling fan."

"Seeing as it's only a two story building, I can't see as a cantina needs an elevator," said Sullivan with a condescending look from his watery blue eyes. He had some beer. "But to each his own."

"The point I'm making is what Ellis Donovan wants, Ellis Donovan gets. He wants electricity for his office, he gets it. He wants an elevator, the college installs one. His last request was for nearly $20,000 dollars. Twenty-thousand. Can you believe it?"

Sullivan was about to respond when he was interrupted by a catcall from the table by the door.

Shanahan watched Honey Shaw sashay across the threshold and stroll across the floor like it was her own personal hardwood. The slut had been too long on Ellis Donovan's arm.

Time to bend her over his knee.

The corners of his mouth pulled up at the image.

But first things first.

Honey bent at the waist and landed a casual peck on Shanahan's scalp. He was nothing special to her. Like an Indian, she was counting coup.

She was nothing special to him. But like his Irish ancestors, his blood ran hot.

They were hot together.

"Gimme a scotch whiskey, Max," said Honey without looking toward the bar. She tilted her face down to greet Colonel Sullivan even as she put a gentle hand on his shoulder. "It's an honor to meet you, sir. Mr. Shanahan's told me so much about you."

"Has he, now?" said Sullivan. He laid a wrinkled claw across her fingers and gave her a pat. "What a dandy. What'd you say your name was, dear?"

Honey told him and pulled out a chair next door, across the table from Mick.

"Has your boyfriend recovered from the loss of his beloved relic?" said Shanahan.

"Oh, Lord no," said Honey. Edna put a tumbler of amber fuel in front of her. "Thanks, love."

"I didn't speak with him today," Shanahan said. "But yesterday, he was damned near apoplectic." Shanahan raised his drink, inviting Honey to clink glasses. "Are we still searching for those rogue nuns?"

Honey finished the toast and downed her liquor before smacking the glass back down on the table.

"Oh, yes," she said. "Donovan has his band of merry men scouring every rock bluff and arroyo in the surrounding country. From what he tells me, Sheriff Rayburn has them all organized. Somebody said they might be traveling with Ma Grell's whorehouse on wheels. The posse's moving on into Stark Canyon tonight." Honey swallowed her drink. "Ma holes up there a lot. I'd say it's a good bet."

Listening between gulps, Sullivan was confused. "If you don't mind me asking, what's this all about?"

"The sword, Colonel," said Shanahan. "It's the reason you're here."

"Ah-ha," said Sullivan. "The talk of rogue nuns lost me, you see."

"Donovan believes a trio of thieves, disguised as nuns, stole the Sword of St. Agnes," said Shanahan.

"These same three are wanted here in Candelaria for the murder of a man," said Honey.

"And a dead college security guard named Nolan."

"Heinous blackguards," said Sullivan, shaking his head. "But surely murder had nothing to do with the business between you and me, I mean, you assured me…"

Shanahan motioned with his hands for Sullivan to speak low. "No, no — not to worry. Neither Honey nor I were involved in the least. Wherever these women are, they carry the guilt of their crimes with them."

"But do they carry the Sword of St. Agnes — that's the question, eh?" said Sullivan. "You told me…"

"We have the sword," said Shanahan. "Just as I told you. I, myself have held it."

Sullivan sat back in his chair and the years fell

away from his demeanor like the husk of a caterpillar's cocoon. When he spoke again, even his voice seemed ten years younger. "I can't tell you how good it makes me feel, son. How relieved I am."

"It's a relief to all of us."

"Where is it?"

"It's in a safe place."

"How did you get it?"

"Simple enough," said Honey. "Donovan opened his office to show off his collection to the nuns. As they departed, I pretended to forget my purse. I went back and took the sword from its resting place, hiding it within a special-made pouch in the folds of my dress."

"Isn't she glorious?" said Shanahan.

"But nobody suspects?" said Sullivan.

"Everybody *knows* it was the nuns," said Shanahan. "Everybody saw the stupid bitch crash through Donovan's window. No doubt they want the sword for their bloody church. Too bad for them, but it's not like they're completely innocent in the affair."

"I forgot to tell you," said Honey. "One of them, the ginger girl I think, lifted Donny's key and left it in the door. It was there waiting when I went back, so I just left it. It's how the one with the painted face got back into the office."

"Can we go see the sword?" said Sullivan, his eyes sparkling.

"Sure and we can. But after another drink?" said Shanahan. "To celebrate?"

"Why not?" said Sullivan.

While they waited for their drinks, Sullivan told Honey about his ride from Santo Tomas. "My old mare's a bit of a swayback. Just like me. Full of fleas, too, but we made it."

Shanahan laid the San Patricios token on the table, and Sullivan picked it up.

"Me old dad would be proud of what we're doing here," he said.

"I was just telling Colonel Sullivan about Mr. Donovan's latest request for funding," said Shanahan.

"Only $20,000," said Honey.

"Twenty thousand? Dollars? That's a lot, yeah. A whole helluva lot." Sullivan whistled. "Did he get it?"

"He did," said Shanahan, remembering how the request he'd carried to the board of directors sailed through the budget committee meeting with zero discussion.

Even with the additional thousands he had tacked on.

When his beer arrived, Sullivan sipped it and wiped his mouth. "What'd your friend do with all the money once he got it? What did he spend it on?"

Shanahan decided to be honest with the old man. Sullivan was a bit of a corker, but he had a direct line of ancestry to the San Patricios after all. He knew the history backwards and forwards.

He was vital to the plan.

Shanahan picked up the token and told the old man the truth.

"Donovan spent the money to outfit a campus security team," he said. "The fun part is since I'm the chairman of the department, I'm also the actual purchasing agent in charge."

"You are?"

"I am," said Shanahan. "Which means Donovan's men are loyal to me."

"This…uh, this campus security bunch is…"

"Is my personal army." Shanahan put his hand on Sullivan's shoulder. "Our personal army," he said. "The reborn Batallón de San Patricio."

The old man's eyes sparkled. "Begora, but it's got a sweet ring to it. I do believe John Riley himself is saluting us from the grave."

"We'll march across the desert and sweep through the plains," said Shanahan. "We'll take what's ours by God-given right."

Honey swallowed her third whiskey and giggled like a schoolgirl. "Manifest destiny," she said.

"Blood and iron," said Shanahan.

"Erin go Bragh," said Sullivan lifting his pint.

"With the sword forever in our possession," said Shanahan.

"Our possession?" said Sullivan. The old man put down his mug, confused once again. "I thought I was here to verify the authenticity of the sword before we sell it. Aren't we going to ransom it back to the church for gold?"

The old man wasn't confused, he was simply mistaken.

"Ransom it?" said Shanahan. "No, sir, not at all."

"What then?" said Sullivan.

"We have the Sword of St. Agnes, Colonel. With such power in our possession, we're going to take over the world. And we're going to start with the territory of New Mexico."

CHAPTER EIGHTEEN

Another day came and went in Stark Canyon and Catalina sat in the late evening breeze watching her black silk tunic and pants dry on a line of twine strung between two mesquite trees. She walked to a barrel of fresh water beside one of Ma's big-wheeled wagons and brought a full, cool dipper to her lips.

The camp was an open flat plain wrapped on three sides in the embrace of sloping horseshoe-shaped walls, a warm maternal comfort chock full of fat boulders and blooming wildflowers. Good luck for three travelers in need of rest.

The lazy evening sun dropped close to the western hill, painting the sky with a drybrush of warm lavender and rose.

Lina sat on a wood folding chair and watched her laundry dry.

Estrella came around the corner of the third wagon, wiping her hands on a towel. "The water is good, yes?"

Lina let the liquid trickle down her neck and down

the sheer white blouse she wore in rivulets. "It will do."

Estrella scoffed. "I apologize if it's not to your standards, your highness." She tossed her towel over the tall recently mended wagon wheel and leaned against it. "If our hospitality isn't good enough, maybe you and your friends should move on."

The pang Lina felt in her chest shook her from her reverie. She blinked and saw the pained look behind the defiance on Estrella's face.

Lina cursed herself. Her head wasn't in the here and now. It hadn't been since they arrived in Candelaria. The truth was ever since bringing in Henry Hodges, she'd done little more than chew on Cassidy's scolding words from the night at Sullivan's Way.

She'd let the constable crawl under her skin like nobody else. Not even Mercy could play such havoc with her emotions. Cassidy was a puzzle she couldn't solve. A Gordian knot she couldn't untie, but couldn't bear to cut.

She loved him.

Dammit.

And now she'd failed in her mission to secure the sword.

Had she been so wrapped up in affairs of heart and mind she'd missed something important? Some vital clue which could have led to success rather than failure?

And here she was busy second guessing herself, rebuffing Estrella's kindness.

"I'm sorry," said Lina. "It's been a long week."

"And it's not yet Friday." Estrella's expression was an invitation to start over.

Whatever tension had come between them, they reached a silent accord and they were both willing to let it drop.

Lina shoved her feelings for Cassidy into the back of her mind. He could wait.

"Stark Canyon is a beautiful place — calm, peaceful."

Estrella crouched down on her heels beside the chair. "We often camp here beside the stream." She pulled short measure of lightweight rope from her hip pocket. While she spoke, she practiced tying a series of complicated knots. "Few know about these springs, except the animals. They always return, looking for water. The rock walls are always fair shelter against the storm. Storms of all kinds — natural and man-made."

Lina admired Estrella's work — Dogshank. Monkey's fist. A figure-nine loop.

"Everybody needs a place like this," said Lina. "A retreat. Someplace to lick your wounds."

"Do you have such a place, Catalina?"

Lina pictured her plain, drab room at the convent, the cavern under the mission, her home in the sky country outside Santo Tomas — a residence burnt, pillaged and forever gone.

"No. No, I don't," said Lina. "Not anymore."

"Where do you go when the storm comes?"

Lina pondered the question. She knew what the other woman meant, but it didn't have the same meaning for her.

"I crave the storm, Estrella." She forced empathy into her voice. "When it comes over the horizon,

I turn to face it. Others run for shelter from the lightning and thunder. I run toward it."

Estrella's voice was quiet. "We run here to the canyon."

Catalina understood.

"I used to run toward men," said Estrella. "You? Do you have a man to run to?"

"I thought I did. I don't."

"But have you had…? I mean…."

"You're asking if I'm a virgin?"

"Forgive me," said Estrella, "I'm too bold." She continued to manipulate the length of rope.

"What do you call this knot?" said Lina, pointing out the latest. "It looks like a flower?"

"Ma taught me. It's called a Widow's Grip — tight and nearly impossible to untie."

"Show me?"

Estrella worked through the maneuver, tying several examples of the knot. Lina understood how the hitch worked, but didn't see why Estrella thought it so difficult to undo. Undoing the knot was an obvious process.

Out of a sense of being polite, she didn't say anything.

Estrella continued talking about Ma. "The old lady was born here. It's her home. My home too. When I was near the end of a very bad road, Ma pulled me back. She saved my life. Sometimes it feels like Ma truly is my mother. At least, she's like the mother I never had. Do you know what I mean?"

Lina thought about the day Rancho Rivera had been gutted and burned by an army of mercenaries, how she had escaped with her mother, only to see Theresa Rivera cut down before her eyes. She had literally crawled across the desert to the gates of the Santo Tomas mission where Mercy took her in. Sweet, impossible Mercy.

"I know exactly what you mean."

"I spoke with Mary while you were out. You two live with these…nuns?"

"We do."

Estrella sighed.

"It's not easy, living only with a family of women. This is something we both know."

The words forced a chuckle out of Lina's breast. "You're right." Then: "I think our Mother Superior would like your Ma Grell."

"Even if she did not approve of our livelihood."

Wouldn't Estrella be surprised, thought Lina, if she knew Mercy had also once, before taking her vows, engaged in the same occupation?

But it was not Catalina's secret to share.

"I think Mercy would be more forgiving than you imagine." She put her hand on Estrella's shoulder. "You've treated us like your own." She let her eyes play over the sloping inclines of the camp. "But you were right when you said we must be on our way."

"You need more time to rest."

"I am healed," said Lina. "As much as is necessary. More days here, locked away, as lovely as it is…" She shook her head. "It is time for us to go. We must turn to face our own storm."

She took in the hardpan blue of the late afternoon sky, the yellow orange soil. In the distance, a prairie dog hopped from scrub bush to bush before high-tailing it across the range.

Estrella was silent, and let her length of rope with its many tied knots fall to earth.

For a while they enjoyed the evening sound of a whip-poorwill. Finally Estrella said, "When will you go?"

"Tonight."

"Ma will want to prepare a meal." Estrella hooked a length of ebony hair around the back of her ear. "Frank brought in four rabbits this afternoon."

"I didn't hear any gunfire."

"He hunts with a sling," said Estrella.

"Not the normal way of doing things," said Lina, "but Frank isn't exactly a run-of-the-mill sort of person is he?"

"Don't judge him too harshly," said Estrella. "Or Dixie either. In our business, one learns there is hardly such a thing as *normal*."

"The brothers dress like women," said Lina.

"As you enjoy dressing as…whatever it is you are."

The accusation gave Lina pause. She stared at her billowing black cloak as the wind lifted it up on the line. "I am…"

What? Lina struggled with the puzzle. What role did she fill in Mother Mercy's order? With all her training and expertise with the urumi — a weapon no longer in her possession. What did she bring to the big table in the cavern under the mission at Santo Tomas? What now could she offer the job at hand?

Cassidy's words came crashing in again.

"Don't you think one soul is enough for tonight?"

Lina struggled with the puzzle. "I am…"

The realization was grim.

Death.

"Estrella, Lina!" Dressed in a cotton blouse and silk skirt, Frank clamored down the cliffside behind the three parked wagons and ran past the horses in their makeshift corral of stick and brush. "Alguien viene con pistolas."

Somebody comes with guns.

"Find Ma," Estrella told him. "I'll rouse the others."

Lina snatched her clothes off the line as Frank passed. She dressed in a hurry. "Get everyone out and away from the wagons," she said. "Into the hills."

Estrella ran along each wagon and hammering a fist against the makeshift apartment walls.

Dixie came out of the second wagon with three Springfield lever-action carbines

"Defensive positions," said Estrella, tossing one of the guns to Lina.

She caught it in mid-air, and turned to meet Mary and Sofia coming around the end wagon.

"We were mending our garments on the hillside. What's happening?"

"Men with guns," said Catalina. "One guess who they're looking for."

Frank ran around the front of the first wagon. In the center of the camp, he bent over and put both hands on his knees, working to catch his breath. Lina noticed the simple leather sling tucked into the waistband of his skirt.

He lifted his chin to speak. "Rayburn."

"How many?" said Lina.

Frank shook his head. "Doce. Más o menos."

Twelve.

And they were seven.

Better than two-to-one, thought Lina. She had been in worse straits.

And with warriors less equipped than Mary and Sofia.

Ma Grell stepped from behind the wagon next to Sofia. She carried a heavy old Texas-Paterson black powder revolver in a meaty fist. "You all get off your backends and into the them hills. Lina's right," she said. "Until we know what this is all about, we'll be discreet." She handed the gun to Mary. "I'll stay here and greet the sheriff."

"You should come with us, Ma," said Estrella.

"He's here for us," said Lina, "Mary, Sofia, and myself. This isn't your battle."

"We took you in when you needed it. We ain't gonna turn a blind eye now." Ma picked up the folding chair Lina had been sitting on. "Maybe I can convince him to go away."

Lina cut her eyes toward the makeshift corral and its population of Andalusians, including her D'oro.

"I don't think it will be so easy," she said. "The posse will know our horses."

"Vamose now," said Ma. "We don't have time to worry about the horses. You just get into the hills and cover me. We'll be okay, believe me. I know Rayburn. We've got a long history together."

Ma's eyes sparkled with amusement. "Unlike most of the men I know, he's not one to shoot first."

A scarf of dust appeared above the ridgeline of rocks leading into the canyon, and it trailed down the wide gravel road to the cactus lined clay bottom. Lina watched the men come on horseback in two columns There wasn't any more time to argue with Ma.

Frank had been wrong. There were more than twelve men.

Twice as many.

"They're coming," said Estrella.

Catalina bounded across an incline of boulders, holding the carbine high in her right hand, searching the wall of rock above her for a worthy place of concealment. Mary and Sofia were hampered by their skirts. As they jumped over the rocks, each held a gun in one hand, and a fistful of material in the other.

Lina found a clear platform of granite fronted by a row of cow-sized boulders and a towering stiff wall of red rock behind. The ledge offered a clear view of the camp below with its three wagons. "We can shoot from here."

Ma sat beside the water barrel, waiting.

"Where's Estrella?" said Sofia.

"Didn't see her," said Mary. "I think the boys are up there a ways." She tilted her head to the left. "Saw them scamper behind that row of brush."

Lina squinted into the shadow of the juniper and thorny dried-out weeds. A gaping black maw opened in the face of the canyon with a brow of sharp rock protruding over the top. There was no sign of Frank or Dixie, but if they were there, the cave would provide excellent cover. A faint trail was evident in the geography of the cliff, and Lina surmised it had served as a dwelling for untold centuries.

Down below, the men arrived in a torrent of dust.

The three wagons were parked front to back in a rough crescent moon and Ma sat at the end of van number three, the tin water dipper casually in her hand. The horses spread out into a broad semi-circle around her, two rows of muscular bays with polished black leather saddles and tack. Rows of navy-blue uniformed men sat on their backs. Men with brass buttons and big .45 automatic pistols on their hips.

Donovan's men.

One of them, apparently the leader, separated himself from the others and rode forward with Rayburn until they hovered only a few feet from Ma's chair. The soldier wore a white Stetson hat several inches taller than Rayburn's topper. The sheriff's chocolate brown steed cantered slightly left as if it didn't like the soldier's pony.

He greeted Ma and the wind carried his words up to them.

"Got some questions for you, Ma. Wondered if you knew anything about a break-in down at the college?"

It was the kind of casual inquiry you'd make of a neighbor or good friend. Familiar. Gentle. Maybe Ma had been right. Maybe the sheriff would simply move along.

Ma was busy shaking her head, and Lina couldn't make out her words — when the Stetson hat signaled one of his men from behind. Together the two soldiers stepped away from Rayburn toward the horse corral. Lina saw him point out the trio of Andalusian horses, heard him shout something to Rayburn.

The sheriff nodded and turned back to Ma. His tone was full of disappointment. "Are you sure you don't...hate it if you lied..."

"What is it they want?" said Mary.

"Isn't it obvious?" said Sofia. "They want us."

"Well, they oughta just say it, plain and simple."

Before Ma could answer him, Stetson was off his horse and marching forward toward the wagons.

"Here now, Mr. Booth," said Rayburn, but again his bay backed off, giving the man in the Stetson hat time to reach Ma's position. Booth reached down, grabbed the front of her dress with both fists and lugged her to her feet.

She spun around in his grip and Booth jerked his pistol from its holster. Before Rayburn could react, Booth jammed the muzzle of his gun into Ma's neck and called upwards in Lina's direction.

"Come on out, now. You three turn yourself in or the old bag gets a face full of lead!"

It couldn't get much more plain and simple.

Damn.

CHAPTER NINETEEN

Ragged waves of scarlet and pink scarred the violet of evening and a rope of gold stretched taught along the rim of the west canyon wall was the sun sinking away. Donovan's armed guards sat with nervous apprehension in Ma's camp, soldiers on a horde of identical bay mounts, shifting back and forth.

The coward holding Ma in the crook of his elbow was a big man with a swarthy complexion and a heavy waxed mustache. His tall white hat made him stand out from the crowd and his strident voice had a hint of a foreign accent.

When Booth bellowed out again, it was with an ultimatum.

"You filthy tramps got five seconds to turn yourself in."

Lina understood the directive was aimed at her and her cohorts.

The gutless swine started his countdown, "Five... four."

For a heartbeat nobody stirred.

With a gentle nudge, Lina brought the Spenser carbine to her shoulder.

Then she heard a whistle of air and a fist-sized rock struck Booth in the back of the head, toppling his Stetson off into the dust. He lurched forward into Ma and together they performed an awkward dance before pulling themselves upright.

Lina spun toward the source of the attack. Frank was perched high on a boulder in the distance, one bare leg bent up and balanced on a jagged ledge as he twirled his sling, preparing to loose another barrage.

Silly idiot. Another second and she would have pierced Booth's heart with a rifle shell. "Frank, no!" she cried, even as he sent the stone sizzling through the air.

The rock skipped through the air between Booth and Rayburn, cracking into a pan of granite and bouncing twice with a harmless clatter.

In the camp, Booth had his gun level with Ma's chest and pulled the trigger.

Inside the canyon walls, the explosion was overwhelming, its impact sending a shudder through every living body and dropping Ma to earth like a crumbled pillar of salt.

Then he swung his arm around in a steady arc and shot Frank through the head.

"What the devil?" said Rayburn, but the sheriff's next expulsion was cut short by crazed shouts of fury and earsplitting thunder from the lip of the open cave.

Hell bent on retaliation, Dixie plunged down the faint trail past his brother's twitching body, screaming his fool head off, working the lever action of his carbine like a pump handle. But Dixie wasn't the marksman Booth was. His shots smacked into the canyon floor around the sheriff and careened away in different directions.

Rayburn's horse reared up at the scattering clumps of earth and chaff, dumping him from the saddle into pile at Booth's feet.

Dixie kept pouring lead down through the rocks and prickly pear cactus. Over and over he cursed, "You dirty, weasel-spit sucking snakes," and a thousand more oaths Lina couldn't understand.

As one, the uniformed horsemen jerked their guns free and swung their steeds around to face him.

Booth stepped over Ma's inert figure and walked straight into the gun fire, smoothly working his automatic, sending a smoking surge of death up the hill.

The first shot took Dixie in the shoulder. The second blew out his throat.

Three horsemen followed Booth's lead, tearing the air with a volley of earsplitting booms, ripping Dixie to pieces like a marionette in a hailstorm.

What had begun as a neighborly inquiry had become a massacre.

On Booth's tunic, the third brass button down caught a last ray of sunlight peeking through an indigo cloud and Lina aimed for it.

This time she would have him. Gently she caressed the trigger…

At the last second, Rayburn wrapped both arms around Booth's legs and brought him down.

Lina's bullet passed harmlessly overhead.

"Blast it to hell," she exclaimed. Again she'd been robbed of a skirmish.

For his part, Rayburn reared up and pounded Booth with a right-fisted haymaker before staggering to his feet. It was clear he wasn't happy with the slaughter taking place but to Lina's way of thinking, he'd done precious little to forestall it.

And the truth was, he'd never been in charge of the expedition.

Lina knew for sure when, behind the sheriff, the gun-happy trio of guards who helped kill Dixie left their horses in a lurching stumble, leaping to Booth's defense. Each of them grabbed at Rayburn's tan shirt to pull him back. At the same time, another handful of men lifted their weapons and unloaded on Lina's position, forcing her to duck behind the boulders in a shower of limestone splinters.

Crouching beside Mary at Lina's ten o'clock, Sofia had yet to enter the fray. "Cover me. I'm going down there," she said. "We need to find Estrella."

Lina pivoted on her heel, wheeling into the open to scatter fire along the front row of saddle horses, hoping to start a panic. As Sofia scampered away, Mary chimed in with a series of quick rifle blasts.

For a few seconds, the two women had Donovan's men reeling.

Lina hazarded a quick glance toward the far cave. Bloody Dixie lay sprawled across the footpath. There was no sign of Frank.

Where was Estrella?

"Here, dogs!"

"Oh, my Lord," said Mary.

Sofia was half-way down the slope, squatting in the grass.

"You like to see death and destruction?" Estrella had appeared from inside the center wagon carrying two sparkling packages, one is each hand, and both trailing a curl of windborne soot — Dynamite.

"You want to see carnage?"

Lina expected the men to open fire on her friend. Instead, the men on foot back-peddled and ran for their horses. The soldiers in the saddle turned and spurred their animals toward the open range. With their brief appearance, the smoking brown paper bundles had delivered a powerful message.

Rayburn and Booth hustled for the row of mesquite trees and Lina's clothesline as Estrella pitched one of the explosive parcels at the main body of retreating men.

Lina threw her arm in front of her face.

The head-pounding concussion tossed a column of fire, dirt, and smoke into the air more than a hundred feet. Sharp-edged debris fell across the camp like sleet.

Booth and Rayburn were knocked off their feet and Mary took advantage of it, pummeling their position with rifle fire. The earth erupted around the sheriff, forcing him backwards up the side of the canyon landscape.

Lina concentrated on Booth, hoping to get a clear shot between the mesquite trees, but her aim was always slightly off.

While they hammered at the two men, Sofia had descended into the camp. In Lina's peripheral visions, she was perched on a wagon tongue between two of Ma's vans. At a break in the retreating gunfire, she leapt into the main camp, dodging .45 caliber lead.

Estrella had caught the edge of the dynamite blast and Sofia knelt by her side.

The second package of dynamite had fallen only a turkey's flight away and it still smoldered and popped even as a row of the mounted uniforms swept back around.

Sofia saw it, acknowledged the army advancing upon her with an obscene gesture, and charged ahead. She scooped up the dynamite and hurled it toward the oncoming brigade with one, smooth underhanded motion.

Unlike the first detonation, the second blast was airborne.

Horses reeled and screamed in the clap of thunder and flame and men were pitched, wailing, from their saddles. A cloud of black smoke hung over the camp for several minutes and the silence was cut only by the continuous ringing in Catalina's ears. She wondered if Ma's caravan held any more munitions.

She hoped not, but was thankful for the explosive packages.

Thanks to Estrella and Sofia, Donovan's army was in complete disarray. In the blowup's immediate after effects, bays galloped away absent their riders in a stampede of hooves. Haggard uniformed figures limped away from the canyon. Men desperately called to their comrades with no response.

At the center of the camp, Lina watched as Sofia

approached Estrella and slipped her arms under her, bringing the smaller woman to her feet. Together, the two found shelter behind the front van as a few of the horsemen swung back around.

With one easy shot, then a second, Mary plunked two of them from their saddles.

"Just like a carnival game," she said, "Quack, quack, little duckies."

Catalina turned her attention back to Booth and Rayburn. The two men had climbed to the level of the cave and stood just inside the mouth with a clear shot at her and Mary. If they'd been armed with rifles, the danger would be imminent. As it was, only the visible puffs and audible pops from their guns showed their intent.

"They're out of range," said Lina.

"Not for me," said Mary. She put her cheek on the rifle butt and took aim...Click.

In frustration, she shoved the gun away. "I'm spent," she said.

Lina tossed her rifle across the space between them. "Take mine. Cover me."

"Where are you going?"

"An injustice has been done this day, Mary." Catalina opened her tin of ebony paint and dragged a dark streak down her forehead and onto the bridge of her nose.

She said, "I'm going to talk to the sheriff."

Donovan's brigade might not be broken, but the main body was in retreat.

Lina peered across the gap at Booth and Rayburn. The job now was to cut off the head.

CHAPTER TWENTY

The cave was five feet high at its apex and less than twenty feet deep into the hillside. Not so much a cave, as a hollow. But it featured an interesting formation — a second entrance behind a bosky of brush in the hillside.

The Black Rose entered with complete silence. Glued to the back rock wall, she merged with the shadows like a bat, watching Booth and Rayburn's outline against the onrushing twilight, waiting for the precise instant to strike.

Booth stood just inside the mouth of the cave, partially concealed from the campy, his bent arm holding his .45 at a ninety-degree angle. Across the opening and tucked farther inside, Rayburn reclined on a crumbling outcrop of dark volcanic rock, his left leg casually draped over his right knee. He held the makings in his hand and sprinkled a trail of leaves along a creased rolling paper. Catching the thong of his tobacco sack with his teeth, he cinched it tight.

"You got a light?" said Rayburn.

"Uhmm...no," said Booth without shifting his attention from the camp.

Rayburn spun the paper into his mouth and patted his shirt. "Down to my last lucifer. That's what my dad used to call a sulfur match. You ever heered 'em called lucifers, Booth?"

"Uh-uh."

"Old way of talkin'"

Rayburn found his match and brought it to life on the heel of his boot. He lit the cigarette and aromas of apple butter and oak filled the cave. "Guess I'm pretty much for the old ways of doing everything," he said.

"Yeah?"

Booth still hadn't moved from the door and Lina didn't think he was paying any attention to the sheriff's meanderings.

"Take the law as an example," said Rayburn. "What happened here today?"

Booth grunted. "What about it?"

"Looking back at it, there's quite a bit of ground that will need to be covered." Rayburn took a deep drag from his smoke and the bright cherry red end blazed in the dark. "I'll need to type up a report."

"Shouldn't take you too long," said Booth. "Seems real straight forward to me."

"See now, there's the hell of it," said Rayburn. "It ain't straight forward to me at all. Seems a little sideways to my way of thinking."

For the first time, Booth turned to glance over his shoulder at the lawman. "Is that so?"

"That's so."

Rayburn smoked a while, then dropped the short end of his butt and squashed it under his boot.

"You aim on staying up here all night?" he said.

"One of 'em's still over there with a rifle. Been watching her."

Rayburn shook his head. "We walk out of here peaceable like, I don't think she'll bother us."

"You're insane," said Booth. "Besides, we have a job to do."

"And killing civilians sure as hell ain't the way to do it."

Booth's laugh was wet and came from deep inside his chest. "You dumbshit locals are all alike. No battlefield experience and think you've got all the answers."

"And you do?"

"In 1902, I was in the Philippines."

"Had an uncle fought over there," said Rayburn.

"Then I was fighting against your uncle," said Booth.

Rayburn didn't say anything.

For the first time, the Black Rose realized he didn't have a gun.

"What happened here today was wrong," said the sheriff. "We both know you had no call to shoot the woman."

"All wars have casualties. It can't be helped."

"This casualty had a name. It was Martha Grell. Her friends called her 'Ma.'" Rayburn stood up and hitched up his belt. "I was one of her friends."

Booth put the muzzle of his gun under Rayburn's nose. "I'm sorry for your loss," he said.

The two men stared at one another for a full minute.

When Booth turned back toward the camp, the Black Rose struck.

The man outweighed her by more than a hundred pounds, but she had the element of surprise on her side. And she had momentum. Springing from the back of the cave, and with a running charge, planted the heel of her boot in the back of his left leg, buckling it out from under him.

Felled like an oak tree, Booth came down on the knee with a crash and the Black Rose whirled into a roundhouse kick, connecting with the right side of his jaw, snapping his head sideways. He toppled against the wall of the cave, then rolled forward and tripped over the ledge, his gunhand leading the way down.

The Black Rose recoiled into a fighting position to face Rayburn.

"You dressed up for a costume party, purty lady?"

"I heard what you said about Ma Grell."

Rayburn chewed his lip, took his time answering. "She wasn't a bad woman. She sure as hell didn't deserve what she got."

"You're a party to it."

"I suspect I am."

"You lose your gun?"

The sheriff said he did. "During the altercation with your friend over there."

Across the divide, somewhere in the black background of a score of green-tailed lightning bugs, Mary would still be on guard.

The Black Rose made her demands. "I want Booth

charged with Ma Grell's murder."

When Rayburn stood up to stretch, careful not to bump his head, the Black Rose took a wary step back. He waved away her caution. "Hell, I agree with you, girl. But I wasn't about to get my head blowed off telling him."

"The other men? They should be charged also."

Rayburn shrugged. "Can't help you much there. You folks were, in fact, shooting at them."

"We don't have the sword."

"Yours is a hard face to forget. I guess I saw you at Old Central on Sunday afternoon."

"I stole nothing."

"The big round window in Mr. Donovan's office didn't break itself."

"I don't deny the trespass. But somebody else got the sword before us. You need to tell Donovan."

"Somebody else? Who?"

"Ever heard of the Sainted Brotherhood of Monterrey?"

"Matter of fact, I have," said Rayburn. "That's you, ain't it?"

The Black Rose shook her head. "I assure you, sir, it's not me. It's definitely not us."

"Then who?"

They were quiet and the outside desert night air still smelled faintly of dynamite and gun smoke. In the distance, an owl trilled and the first stars winked on above them.

Rayburn rubbed the back of his neck. "What do I even call you? You got a name?"

"Not one you need to know."

"Catalina…Rivera, wasn't it?" Rayburn raised his eyebrows at her surprise. "Like I said, I wouldn't forget your face. Or your voice."

The Black Rose couldn't deny her first impressions of Rayburn from Sunday morning. She liked him. More so she trusted him.

She turned to go. "Tell Donovan what I said."

"Wait," said Rayburn. "Will I see you again?"

"I think—"

The clatter of falling gravel alerted her before the gunfire.

The Black Rose lunged to the floor of the cave and rolled backwards in the dark, springing up from her shoulder into a ready crouch even as the echo of percussion started to fade.

Clutching his ribs, Rayburn collapsed with a groan.

On the lip of the cave, Booth was climbing to his feet, waving his gun. He fired into the cave once and the slug ricocheted off a sidewall, thudding into earth. The gun's slide made a ratcheting sound. Out of ammunition.

Before the Black Rose could attack, Booth turned his back and scurried away with a clumsy gait, letting his prodigious weight pull him down the hillside toward his waiting horse.

Rayburn groaned and the Black Rose hurried to him.

"You need a doctor," she said.

"Heh," he coughed, and grimaced in pain. "You got one handy, do you?"

"Sofia has had medical training."

"Who's Sofia? One of your pals?"

"Sister Sofia is a nun of the convent of Senora Maria in Santo Tomas."

Rayburn whistled. "So you really are a covey of nuns."

"No," said the Black Rose, positioning her shoulder under Rayburn's outstretched arm to lift him. "Only one of us is a true bride of Christ."

"What a...damned shame, because...I got a feeling I'm gonna need all the prayers I can get."

Before she got Rayburn out of the cave, he was out cold.

CHAPTER TWENTY-ONE

Long after dark, Cassidy led Diablo into Candelaria from the north, opposite the College of St. Vincent's campus. From what Hodges had told him back in the jail cell, there was every chance he'd end up on the college grounds before everything was said and done. Sullivan was involved with some big-wig who worked there. Apparently this Shanahan fella was the leader of the Sainted Brotherhood and planned to nick the same sword Catalina had come down to get.

How the stolen girls from Santo Tomas fit in wasn't clear, but Hodges said Sullivan had carried them along to Candelaria. It wasn't exactly a garden resort. So far the village looked like a run down pile of drunken frame hovels and sagging jacallas no better than Santo Tomas, and in many ways worse.

Maybe it would look better in daylight, but Cassidy doubted it.

He found himself walking alone beside a row of sad, gray buildings asleep under the stars, wondering where he'd find the hotel Hodges mentioned. Lantern light fell onto the boardwalk from a place at the end of the street. At least somebody was awake. They'd direct him to the hotel.

The long billboard over the door and windows read *The Snorty Horse* in faded script.

Cassidy tied Diablo to a hitching rail and mounted the boardwalk in front of a rotted door jamb with rusty screws. The saloon may have lost its batwing hinges during the last century, but inside the mahogany bar was polished to a fine luster. Cassidy didn't let it fool him. He knew from the first faint whiff of puke-soaked sawdust and open rotgut what kind of place it was.

Most of his years as a United States Deputy Marshal had been spent drunk and doubled over in rooms like this one, tinkling piano music hammering at his eardrums, kerosene lamps like the one on the bar filling his nose with black smoke.

He knew the kind of people who would still be lingering here at midnight. The toothless old raisin slumped over his drink at a table near the door. The farmers playing a tired game of cards far in the back. Even though he'd never met them, he recognized them.

Cassidy had never before laid eyes on the blonde with dark roots who was perched on a cloth upholstered stool at the end of the counter, but he maybe knew her best of all. Her lips parted when he crossed the threshold. All her attention was on him. Stirring her shallow drink with a finger and sticking it into her mouth was an obvious invitation.

Cassidy made his way to the bar, steeling himself against the temptations of emerald green jugs and sparkling amber bottles on display behind the bar. A rainbow of labels listed the names of past infatuations — Warner's Rye, Mestigo Rum, Jamie's Scotch Whiskey. How many nights he'd gone to bed caressing their smooth curves with his hands, feeling their warmth in his belly.

Cheap rotgut.

But even cheap lovers have a certain allure.

The polished glass tumblers made his mouth water.

He caught the attention of the willowy barkeep. Thinning hair told a story of long years behind the counter pouring drinks to whoever could afford them. The smudged apron tied around the waist said it had been a long day.

"What can I get you, mister?"

Cassidy swallowed hard. "Water," he said again.

"Water all you want? You sound like a man's not too sure?"

"I'm sure. Name's Cassidy."

"I'm Max." The bartender filled a glass from a tin pitcher and put it down on the bar. "Water's free."

"What about information?"

If anybody in town knew about an old man with two lovely virgins in tow, it would be Max.

Cassidy put two gold dollars on the counter and the blonde slid off her stool and crept toward him.

Max sniffed the coins like a dog regarding a head of lettuce. "I guess it depends on what kind of information you need? I can tell you the weather tomorrow — sunny. I can tell you the lady on your left is named Edna, and she's always real thirsty."

"Lookin' for the hotel."

"I can tell you the hotel is two doors down and charges three dollars a night." Max put his hands on his hips and leaned back with a satisfied smile. "All that's free of charge."

"Just like the water," said Cassidy.

"Just like the water," he said with a nod.

"Ever heard of an old man named Sullivan?"

Max didn't even pretend to think about it.

"That's the information that'll cost you."

"Mick Shanahan?"

This time the look of recognition crossing his face was obvious. Fleeting, as Max clamped down on his jaw and wrinkled his brow, but obvious. He nodded at the coins on the counter.

"Like I said."

Cassidy tossed down two more coins.

While Max pondered the offer, the blonde approached with casual ease. Edna wore a white button shirt with a ruffled bosom and no top buttons. Her hair was twisted and piled into a fancy stack with a few choice ringlets dropping to her shoulders. She wore tight jodhpur pants and no shoes. The toenails at the end of her calloused feet were painted red.

All her virtues were on display, but a lot of it was window dressing.

"Max has what you call a selective memory, stranger." She breathed on him and her breath smelled like turpentine. "Me, I've got a good memory. Why not try me out?"

When Cassidy turned back to Max, the four coins were gone.

"Can't stand the competition?"

Max shrugged his shoulders, but shot Edna a dirty look, nonetheless.

"Shanahan...yes, he works up at the college," said Max.

"He ever come in here?"

"Sometimes."

"He ever come in with an old man named Sullivan?"

"Sure he did," said Edna, jumping into the conversation. "Just today as a matter of fact." The two of them were here this afternoon and sat at the table in the corner. They ordered Irish whisky — good stuff — but wouldn't buy me a glass.

Cassidy grinned at the scowl on Max's face and turned his attention to the blonde.

"What do you know about a couple new girls in town? Maybe at the hotel? Maybe with Mr. Sullivan?"

Edna's answer was an exaggerated pout. "Mister, if you're looking for a girl...?" She ran her hands down each side of her waist until they rested on her hips.

"I'm not—" Cassidy bent his elbow and leaned against the bar. "Maybe I am."

"Buy me a drink?"

Cassidy tossed Max another eagle. "Whatever the lady wants."

"Tomato beer," said Edna.

Cassidy pursed his lips. "Nutritious," he said.

"I gotta keep my figure." Once Max had the drink made, Edna plucked it from the counter and drank.

"What kind of girl did you have in mind?" she said.

Max leaned over the bar as if he were still part of the conversation. Cassidy picked up his glass of water and put his other hand on Edna's elbow. "Shall we?" he said, leading her to a table near the stoic card players.

"I'm flattered, sir."

One of the farmers worked up a wad of tobacco from his lower lip and launched it into a sloppy brass cuspidor where it landed with a splash.

"How long have you lived in Candelaria?" said Cassidy, pulling out Edna's chair.

She sat down, and polished off the remains of her drink before answering. "Too long."

"I find it easy to believe."

Edna put her elbow on the table and set her chin into the cup of her hand. "You got a name?"

He told her.

"Bounty hunter or jilted lover?"

"Neither?"

"You're a tease," said Edna, touching the end of his nose with her fingertip. "There's only two kinds of men come in here asking about traveling men with women in tow — bounty hunters want the man, jilted lovers want the women."

"There might be other possibilities," said Cassidy.

Edna had just enough hooch running through her to be brazen. She leaned over and pushed her attributes up against his arm. "What about me, Cassidy? Do I have something you want?"

Cassidy put his arm around Edna's shoulders. "What if I told you the two girls I'm looking for are nuns?"

Edna pushed away hard enough to make the legs of her chair screech on the hardwood.

"You're a law man," she said. Like taking a bite of rotten fruit.

"You know something about nuns?"

"I know there's three of 'em been tearing holy hell out of the college."

Cassidy's eyes fluttered briefly closed. "That has a familiar ring to it," he said.

Dammit, Catalina.

"Tell me what happened?" said Cassidy.

"Buy me another drink, law man?"

He did and she told him all about the whore named Estrella and the Sunday morning murder of Miguel with some sort of outlandish contraption you've ever heard about, like a bear trap on a stick. Then she told him how Ellis Donovan — the famous historian — had his office destroyed. "And a good man, a security guard named Nolan, was lost in the commotion."

Edna ran her fingers along Cassidy's sleeve. "How about I tell you a little more about it at my place?"

"Where's your place?" said Cassidy.

"Right here. I live in the back room."

"Could you tell me some more about the nuns?" He waved at Max, motioning for another round of drinks.

"Like what?"

"Where are they now?"

Edna took her red beer from Max and half of it disappeared in the time it took to fill Cassidy's water cup.

Edna ran the back of her arm along her lips, leaving a red smear on the white fabric.

"I heard they was with Ma Grell."

"Who's Ma Grell?"

Edna fell back in her chair. Her laughter was quick and ironic.

"You said you're looking for girls. Well, if you're looking for a girl, you need to find Ma Grell," said Edna.

"Is that right?"

"Runs a nice little wagon train business hereabouts. Got a couple girls on the string. Couple boys too, if you're so inclined." She lowered her eyelashes and looked up with exaggerated discretion. "Naturally, they'll ask for a fee. Me? Since you bought me a couple of drinks, any fun you'd like to have tonight is on the house."

"Where do I find this wagon train?"

Edna rubbed up close and whispered in his ear. "They've been out of town a few days, but they always camp out at Stark Canyon. There's a nice little clearing up there. How about you and me go together?"

"I'm not against the idea." Edna finished her drink and swayed to the left and then to the right. Her eyes nearly crossed and Cassidy put his hand on Edna's cheek. "How about you draw me a map just in case you want to take a nap on the way?"

"Thash...thash...a good idea." Her teeth were bright in the lantern light. "For one more drink, I'll draw you a map," said Edna.

Cassidy dug into his pocket for one more coin.

At least the water was free.

CHAPTER TWENTY-TWO

Catalina tossed a few stray pieces of mesquite into the fire and stared into the flickering orange flame. The wood smoke smelled good and warm, but after what had happened Stark Canyon didn't feel safe. As soon as Rayburn was fit to move, they needed to climb into the wagons and move.

"You think the men on horseback will come back?" said Estrella.

Lina clenched a piece of jerky between her teeth and pulled. Was it only a few short hours ago Estrella had said Ma would want to prepare a meal before they left?

Now Ma and her boys were dead and the sheriff wavered at the threshold, unsure which way he was going.

One thing was still the same. They would leave tonight.

"They'll be back," said Lina. Thinking about Booth, she washed her supper down with a swig of spring water. "They may wait until morning, but they'll be back."

They each sat alone together with their thoughts.

On the other side of the fire, Sofia and Mary tended to the sheriff. Rayburn was stretched out perpendicular to Lina's line of sight, his head propped up with two pillows from Ma's van, a colorful hand-pieced quilt covering all but his face. Sofia cradled a canteen of spring water in her lap and occasionally spilled a portion onto his lips.

The bullet had gone straight through. Rayburn didn't appear to be bleeding inside, at least he wasn't losing a lot of blood on the outside.

Sofia had bandaged the wound. Mary made him comfortable.

They had done all they could.

Farther from the fire, Ma, Dixie, and Frank were wrapped in blankets, waiting for the grave.

"I have no words," said Estrella.

Lina rose from the fire and walked to the lead wagon. She came back with a long-handled shovel.

"No words are necessary," she said. "Especially when we've got work to do."

It was past midnight when they finished their task. Ma Grell, Frank, and Dixie were peacefully at rest under New Mexico stars, enjoying eternal slumber in the canyon they had considered more of a home than anyplace else. It was small comfort.

The women's grief was palpable. There would be no sleep.

"How soon can we move him?" said Lina, keeping her voice soft and low.

Sofia brushed the hair away from Rayburn's

sweaty forehead. "He was restless, but now he's sleeping quite sound. I'd like to let him rest for at least another hour."

"There is a doctor in town, not far from the hotel," said Estrella. "We can take him there."

"In the meantime, how about some coffee?" said Mary. "Ma had a good store of it in the first wagon."

"I'll get it," said Estrella.

Lina watched her walk to the wagon in a kind of drunken stroll.

"She's torn out of the frame, ain't she?" said Mary.

"Estrella has lost three of her closest friends in one horrific night. How would any of us feel?" said Lina.

Sofia's voice was firm. "While we have a few moments alone, I'd like to suggest we leave here. Tonight."

"I concur," said Lina. "Estrella knows a place on the other side of town. We can be there before dawn."

"No. I want the three of us to leave, to travel back to Santa Tomas."

"Without the sword?" said Lina. "This is not possible."

"Of course it is! Who gives a hang about the sword? We have no idea where it is, and we've got people shooting at us." said Mary.

"For once, I will agree with you," said Sofia.

Lina studied her friends' expressions in the dim firelight. They looked as exhausted as she felt. Her feet, ankles and calves were sore from clamoring around on the rocks all evening like some kind of goat and since digging the graves, her shoulders and back muscles screamed with every movement.

The problem of the sword made her head hurt and trying to imagine another assault on the college was beyond imagination.

She knew exactly how Mary and Sofia felt.

But she had decided to stay.

If it was simply a question of the retrieving the Sword of St. Agnes, Lina might have given in to strain she felt. But this business about the secret society...

Demetrius feared the Sainted Brotherhood of Monterrey.

Lina wanted to find out why.

"You two may do as you please," she told them.

"I think I—"

Mary put her fingers on Sofia's lips. "Hush." Her eyes cut to the left, then right. "Did you hear that?"

"What?"

"A single rider, alone," said Estrella, rejoining them with a paper sack in her hand. She handed the coffee to Sofia. "Somebody approaches the camp."

Mary rolled onto her side and came back up with one of the Spenser carbines. She tossed it across the fire to Catalina. "Reloaded," she assured Lina with a wink.

Rayburn murmured something in his sleep and Sofia dabbed his face with her cloth.

Lina rose up to her full height and passed the rifle back to Mary.

"You need this worse than I do. You three stay here."

"Be careful, Black Rose," said Sofia. "Even one such as you is not invincible."

Something the screaming muscles of her lower back and hips were happy to remind her.

Lina snuck behind the caravan, then edged forward, keeping the wagons between her and the campfire. Once there, she followed the corral fence, careful not to stir the horses. D'oro nickered at her smell and the shuffling of hooves from the others covered the sound of the rider coming toward the camp on the hilly branch trail. The same trail used by Rayburn and Booth during afternoon when they assailed the camp.

Moving fast, Lina cleared the horse pen and crept along the road beside a quarry of heavy rock and gravel strewn ground. She stayed low.

The intruder stopped short of riding into camp.

For several precious moments Lina couldn't pick out his shadow from the array of tall vegetation and outcroppings of rock. Then he coughed and lit a cigarette with a match and the flare lit his face and the brim of his Stetson hat.

Booth! Less than thirty feet away.

And even as she recognized him, two additional men came near to the horse. One of them wore the outline of a cap similar to the ones worn by the soldiers. The men whispered between themselves, but Lina couldn't hear them for the rush of blood in her ears.

Sinking to earth, she steadied her breathing and pulled a band of leather from her waistline.

Practiced fingers traced the ground beneath them, seeking out just the right stone…

******

Cassidy rubbed the sore nub at the back of his head and reached for Diablo, but the donkey wasn't at hand.

A rough slap sent him staggering back a step. "Get'cher hands off my horse," said the raspy thick voice in the saddle above him. A second pair of hands held his shoulders, pulling him sideways and off the flat rock where he stood into a patch of scrub and buffalo grass.

The man in the saddle coughed, then struck a match to light a cigarette, illuminating his features. He was a brawny man with ruddy skin and pouches under his eyes. His jowls hung low, anchored to his face with a thick hairbrush mustache, and he wore a tall Stetson hat and a soldier's uniform with brass buttons.

The other man was equally tough-looking, with the same blue garment and polished accoutrements.

Cassidy shook his head.

Who were these two jaspers? How had he arrived here?

Again he worried the bump on his head. The last thing he remembered was setting out with Diablo from the cantina with Edna's hand-drawn map in hand. He'd followed the wavering trail out of town until it ended at a trickling muddy creek bed beside an old juniper tree growing sideways out of a split rock. From there, the map directed him eastwards to the rim of Stark Canyon.

After another mile or so, he'd stumbled across the man at the cold camp.

He remembered it now, though the picture was still a little fuzzy. The man he'd seen reclining on the ground was the same one on the horse above him, the one with the hat.

The fellow had greeted him friendly enough, but when Cassidy had mentioned the nuns, something heavy hit him from behind.

Yes, that's when it was, directly after asking about the nuns.

Now the three of them waited on a trail at the edge of the canyon. Cassidy could smell woodsmoke from a nearby fire.

"Where are we?" he said.

"Shut-up," said the soldier who pinned his arms. "Or I'll give you another knot on the skull."

"Ease up, Morgan," said the man on the horse. Then he turned his attention back to Cassidy. "I think your holy Catholic women-friends are just over this next rise. I'd like you to walk in to their camp ahead of me and Mr. Morgan." He pulled back the action on a big iron .45 automatic and chambered a round into place. "Slow and easy, now," he said.

Cassidy stayed his ground. "Holy Catholic women friends?"

"The way you asked me about those nuns made it sound like they were more friend than foe."

"I told you, I'm a town constable—"

"Looking for the three nuns involved in the incident at the college on Sunday," said Booth. "I know what you said."

"I didn't say I was a friend."

"It's not so much *what* you said as *how* you said it."

"You just do as Mr. Booth says to do," said Morgan, prodding him in the back with bare knuckles.

If only he had his hickory stick.

Or his rifle. For rattlesnakes, he'd told Mercy.

Well, these two were starting to look pretty venomous.

Unfortunately both weapons were back at the cold camp with Diablo.

Booth put heels to his horse and the heavy bay took a step forward. "Get on with you now, Mr. Town Constable."

Morgan shoved him again and Cassidy shifted his balance, stalling, deliberately swaying off to one side rather than taking the lead. "Guess I'm more dizzy than I thought," he said, bending slightly at the knees, letting his hand fall to keep himself upright.

"You think you're dizzy now…," said Morgan.

Cassidy raked a handful of gravel into his palm and pitched it into the soldier's face.

The distraction worked better than he could have hoped. The debris had caught Morgan with his mouth wide open and he reeled backwards toward Booth's horse, gagging and sputtering. "Mmph—son of a—brff."

Cassidy followed up fast with a sweep of his right leg, catching Morgan off-balance, tilting him sideways like a hatchet-chopped cottonwood. "Tim-mmberrrr," he thought to himself, but when he spun back toward Booth, he didn't feel so amused.

The muzzle of the automatic was an inch away from his nose.

"I guess I've had about enough outta you," said Booth, but then there was a whistle of air and he was reeling from his saddle as the bay cried out in defiance. Before Cassidy could react another pelting of rocks—two of them this time—slapped into the horse, sending him into a braying restlessness. Hopping up and down on front legs and back, he thrashed his rider up and down by the stirrups before dragging him, bellowing, off into the canyon.

With his boss out of commission, Morgan was back up and forging ahead. Cassidy repositioned himself to face the man head on when a third barrage of rocks hit home, one of them plonking the soldier in the forehead, knocking him out cold and another slapping him square in the back.

Cassidy turned on his boot heel and complained loud, with a curse. "Ya cowardly goldang polecat, stop throwing rocks and get out here where a man can see you."

"Cassidy?"

The voice of an angel. Or devil. Who else could it be to exhibit such unerring accuracy?

"Catalina?"

Crouching down beside the road, she rose up in a hurry, then propelled herself toward him with arms held open wide. He caught her and her embrace was sturdy and true.

He pulled back to gaze into her face, her eyes. He brushed gleaming blue-black hair from her forehead.

No war paint.

Flooded with relief, he kept a gentle hand on her arm and kissed her lips.

"Mercy didn't hear from you," he said.

"There's much to tell," she admitted.

"But you're all right? You're not hurt?"

"I'm not hurt," said Lina. "But what about you? These men, Booth, and his partner? How did you come to be with them?"

"Entirely by accident. I was looking for you." He tripped over the toe of his boot and she and she reached out to steady him. "I have news for you. From Hodges."

"Come with me to camp. You can tell me there. You can tell all of us."

Grateful for her support, he leaned into her as they walked. "Did you get the sword?" he said.

Lina didn't answer him until the fire was in sight. As they came into camp, she whispered the answer more to herself than to Cassidy.

"Not yet," she said. "But we will."

CHAPTER TWENTY-THREE

Ellis Donovan reached for his whiskey glass, but it had tipped over and rolled across the desk, out of reach, spilling a squalid little river along the edge of his blotter.

The dark room was lit by a single electric bulb mounted in a lamp encircled with a spider's web of dangling crystal shards. Shadows filled the room and produced menacing shapes on the covered remnant of the huge rose window. A cool evening draft carried in scents of lilac and the wood smoke from a far off fire.

He had fallen asleep behind the desk and a knock at the door had awakened him.

It came again and he straightened himself up in his chair. "Yes? Come in?" he said.

The door opened a crack, pulling through the cross breeze and there was Honey's lovely visage poking out from behind the door.

Even as the night air whistled through the broken pane, Donovan felt a great weight off his chest. His anxious thoughts and worried feelings were picked up and cast aside by the sight of his true beloved. A great blanket of warmth grew within, spreading from his heart, sending tingles through his extremities, forcing him to rise.

"Am I disturbing you, Sugarplum?"

"No, no, of course not," said Donovan. He stood beside his desk, waiting for her to enter, righting the fallen whiskey glass at the last instant.

She came in with a flourish.

Her dress was tight across her breasts and hips, slim and cut short above the knees. It was the coming fashion, daring and urbane. Not the lush Victorian era dress he was more used to seeing wrapped around his most prized possession.

Because, in the end and he wasn't ashamed to admit it, he considered her his.

She was as much a part of his collection as the Book of Ragnarök, the vase from ancient Babylon, or the parchment fragments from the Gospel of Thomas. Their summer wedding would make it official. By then too, the sword would be recovered.

Donovan would then be complete and Honey would never again wear such brazen attire. He eagerly anticipated how he would bring to her heel once she was his wife.

Tonight, he was torn between taking her in his arms and scolding her.

She took the decision away from him by wrapping her arms around his shoulders. "I know you don't like the dress, Ellis," she said. "But it's so scrumptious outside, I couldn't resist." She put her lips close to her ear. "Nobody will see except you and Mr. Shanahan."

"Shanahan?"

"Here I be, boyo."

Donovan disentangled himself from Honey's embrace and straightened his rumpled white shirt. "I...uh, didn't know you were there, my friend."

"'At's okay, boyo. I kinda like watching you and the lassie."

Not sure how to respond, Donovan turned back to Honey. "We had supper plans?" he said.

"I was just coming to see you when...ah...Mr. Shanahan intercepted me."

"Intercoursed her is what I did all right, Donny." Shanahan came full into the shadowy office and closed the door. Between the stink of his breath and the slur of his tongue it was easy to tell he'd been drinking heavily. "*Intercepted*, I mean." When he smiled, all his teeth glistened in the lamp light and his gums were a bright red. "What she said."

"You need to go home and sleep it off, Mick. Before you say something you'll regret in the morning."

"Oh, yes?" Shanahan continued to speak even as he raised his attention to a row of books on one of Donvan's massive shelves. "Go home? I hope this isn't your way of saying I'm not welcome. Tell me the truth, Donny? Am I not welcome?"

With the last two words, he clutched the book spines in front of his and dragged them away from the shelf, letting them fall to the floor. Again Shanahan turned and bared his fangs. "Not welcome, eh?" The veins in his head pulsed in rapid time with his heart.

"Good Lord, Mick."

Honey kissed Donovan on the cheek. "Babykin's been drinking," she said.

Babykins?

Donovan staggered back as if Honey had slapped him. Now he could smell the liquor on her breath as well. A trembling unease rippled through him and he felt his stomach latch on to his spine.

He watched in horror as Shanahan strolled in and wrapped his arm around Honey's waist.

"What's this all about?" said Donovan.

"Shall we show him, Dumpling?"

Honey squinted her eyes. "Let's show him, Babykins."

Shanahan cleared his throat and brought himself to full, military-style attention. "Colonel Sullivan," he called. "If you'll please, come in."

In spite of his trepidation, Donovan couldn't help but be fascinated by the performance playing out in his office. Shanahan stood erect like the Captain of the Guard and Honey lounged seductively against the pillaged bookcase, a cat licking at her lips with gleeful anticipation.

But the next shock was greater still.

When the old man with the long gray whiskers marched into his office with the Sword of St. Agnes, he knew the universe was rewarding him.

The strange antics of his dear Honey and drunken Shanahan were forgotten.

Donovan could hardly breathe. "The sword," he said.

In the old man's parchment hands, the relic almost seemed to glow with an eerie gold light all on its own.

"Colonel…Sullivan, is it?" said Donovan and the elder nodded his assent. He gripped the boney spindle of a hilt with one hand while the other rested on the chipped blade. Sullivan was dressed in a musty green uniform of some kind and against such a backdrop the blade seemed formidable indeed. No frail scrap of archeological detritus, this was the find of the century.

Maybe the millennia. For Donovan, who saw the culmination of his life's work returned by lamplight, the Sword of St. Agnes gleamed with the intensity of a million suns.

"Thank heavens, you've found it," said Donovan. "Oh, thank the Lord." He bounded forward, but Sullivan was stoic and unmoved.

"Hut, hut, hut," said Shanahan, quickly inserting himself between Donovan and the oldster. "Afraid it's not quite what you think, Donny."

Oblivious to Shanahan's words, Donovan strained his neck around the younger man's slender form to gaze on the recovered treasure.

Shanahan put a hand on Donovan's shoulder and shoved him back.

"I said, it's not what you think."

"It's not?" Donovan's thoughts went into a whirl. A score of questions darted around inside his head like bees at a church picnic and he hoped blinking several times in succession would push at least one of them into focus.

Finally, he said. "Where did you find it?"

Shanahan laughed. "I didn't have to find it," he said. "Honey gave it to me."

"Honey?" Donovan's eyes cut from Mick to Honey to Sullivan and back.

"I canna tell a lie," said Honey. "I took it from your office."

"But...but, why?"

Shanahan seemed weary of the conversation. "Because, for one thing, you have no idea what you have here. You don't deserve to wield the power enchanting."

"Power enchanting?"

"The eldritch energy courses through the blade," said Shanahan.

"Honestly, Mick," said Donovan. "It's the liquor talking. How much whiskey have you had tonight?"

Shanahan shouted loud enough to make even Sullivan flinch. "It's not the liquor talking, you bumbling idiot. It's the voice of destiny. My destiny! Mine and the Sainted Brothers of Monterrey."

Shanahan swung around to the Colonel. "Give me the damn thing," he said.

Sullivan handed him the sword.

Donovan took a step back, tripped on the rug and fell against his desk, spreading his arms wide to hold himself upright.

Shanahan held the sword up into the light above him and wrapped his drunken mouth around a series of garbled phonetics. "Thoir spiorad Agnes. Fuil na beatha. Coisrig stailinn dhomh."

Honey giggled. "Amen," she said.

Shanahan's eyes were glazed and bereft of sanity. He moved from light into shadow. Two steps and he hovered over Donovan with malicious glee.

"I told you, Donny. The day you asked me to go to the board and plead for funding. I told you."

"What did you tell me, Mick?" said Donovan.

"I told you that you owed me."

And then he did the unexpected. He wheeled around in a perfect about face and put the sword against Honey's collar, drawing a line of blood so rivulets of blood seeped onto the blade. Astonished, Donovan watched the droplets soak into the thirsty blade or was it a trick of the light?

Honey scream was pain mixed with astonishment and Shanahan followed the cry with a hard right hand rocking her jaw. She slid to the floor, senseless.

Shanahan addressed Sullivan. "Put her with the others," he said.

"Others?" said Donavan.

"Blood of a virgin," said Shanahan. "Just like I promised you, beloved."

He was talking to the sword.

Shanahan plunged the blade straight into Donovan's chest.

The hilt was awash in blood and the room seemed to glow with a new amber energy pulsing in time with Shanahan's temple and Donovan's scholarly chamber seemed to echo with pagan Celtic chants.

If it was all just his imagination or truly a manifestation of ancient sorceries, Ellis Donovan, the famed professor of history and metaphysics, would never know.

Because in less than a minute, he was stone cold dead.

CHAPTER TWENTY-FOUR

Traipsing along the boardwalk of Candelaria, Cassidy and Lina were dressed like any wealthy American couple of the Edwardian era.

Catalina wore a two-pieced ivory dress. It was tight through the hips and flared at the hem, so much so she looked and felt like a walking trumpet. "Whoever thought a dress should be this tight should be strung up and garroted." She carried a parasol against the sun, its emerald green matching Cassidy's tie.

At her side, Cassidy wore a sack coat in neat navy with light gray pinstripes and matching vest and pants. The silk tie gave the costume a pop of color. A pocket watch chain dangled across the center of his chest and atop it all, a Panama straw boater.

They were stunning in their obvious extravagance.

And miserably hot.

"There seems to be no end to Estrella's wardrobe," said Cassidy. "I don't think I've seen so many clothes in one place in my life."

"She has suffered much from helping us." Lina pulled at the edges of her cramped dress. "Would that we have to ask no more favors."

"When this is over, we should invite her to go home with us," said Cassidy. "Maybe we can repay her. There's certainly nothing for her here in Candelaria but sad memories."

From across the road came the sound of somebody chopping wood. Lina looked to see the small shanty where she had first met Estrella Perez. There was the weed patch where Sofia had no choice but to kill Miguel. There was the lemon tree worth dying for.

A small man with a hatchet was busy hacking away at it, cutting it down in a flurry of bark wood chips.

"This town is a treasury of contradiction," said Lina. "On one side, a place of scholarly retreat, on the other hand a breeding ground of vile ambition. A bastion of progress and a haven for primitive beliefs, like two sides of a coin."

Abruptly, she realized she could have been describing the mission in Santo Tomas. Monsignor Andronicus had plenty of vile ambitions and she had seen for herself there was no shortage of primitive beliefs.

"It's one of those places the railroad passed by. Despite the college, I have a feeling Candelaria won't be here in twenty years," said Cassidy.

"I won't disagree," said Lina.

"Will you disagree if I ask you one more time to turn back and wait for me in Estrella's wagon?"

Lina felt the constable's hand squeeze her own and she withdrew from his touch, placing both glove hands together on the shaft of her parasol. "I'm offended you even asked."

"I figured as much." His knowing smile was playful and he scratched the back of his neck. "I had to ask."

"To satisfy your sense of chivalry?"

He held her gaze as long as he could without blinking. Which is to say, not long at all. Having grown up the only sister among brothers, Lina had learned early on to out stare any of them. Finally he said, "Consider my chivalry satisfied."

"Good," said Lina, "because Colonel Sullivan is as much my responsibility as yours. I should have cleaned out the entire nest of hornets when I had the chance at Sullivan's Way."

"I should've helped you. Had we taken Sullivan along with Hodges, the girls from your convent would be safe at home right now." Cassidy chewed his lip. "We had no way to realize the Colonel was a part of it."

"Under normal circumstances, I would have sensed it."

"Normal circumstances?" Cassidy cocked his head with the question. "What wasn't normal about that night?"

"Don't you think one soul is enough for tonight?"

"We can't all afford to be as docile as you, Cassidy."

"Don't mind me," said Catalina, pushing away the memories. "My head is...somewhere else." She breathed in deep and exhaled slow.

A teamster with a load of hay on his wagon nearly broke his neck cranking his face around to watch them walk. Cassidy offered him a friendly wave.

Four children followed in his wake, two of them with pitchforks, scooping up the clumps of hay he lost.

Across the street, Lina saw the square house with the doctor's shingle out front. Inside, Sheriff Rayburn was fighting for his life. Another victim of Mercy's quest for the sword.

But no, Lina corrected herself. It wasn't about the sword any more.

Cassidy had explained about Savannah Diaz and Emilia Martinique. Now it was about finding them.

They stood in front of a white-washed two story frame building. A porch hung off the facade at both levels and tall brick chimneys braced each side. All the windows were open and white curtains stretched out, beckoning them inside. They crossed the threshold of the open door and a short man with a heavy gray wool suit welcomed them to the Candelaria Arms. He leaned on his counter with a crooked arm and doffed an invisible cap.

"I'm Jacobs," he said, wispy blonde hair sticking to his forehead.

Cassidy introduced the two of them as Mr. and Mrs. Jones.

The lobby was a narrow space with walls on either side cut by open doorways which led to a dining hall on the right and a common area with a player piano on the left. Behind Jacobs, a carpeted stairway led to the second story. A heavy oak telephone with dual bells hung on the wall at the foot of the steps.

"Welcome to Candelaria — a friendly community, ready to serve." Jacobs wiped the sweat away from his puckered red face with a damp hanky. "Are we looking for a room, then?"

"Upstairs, if you please."

Jacobs asked for payment up front and while Cassidy handed him the money, Lina signed the guest registry. Colonel Perry Sullivan's signature floated on the line directly above.

Jacobs offered a key from under the counter. "Room 5," he said.

"Excuse me," said Lina. "I couldn't help but notice Colonel Sullivan's name in your book."

"Yes, indeed."

"Is he a guest here?"

"As a matter of fact he is. We don't often have such an influx of travelers. It's been a busy week."

"Who else besides Sullivan?" said Cassidy.

Jacobs continued to mop his face and neck. "Oh, I was only referring to yourselves and Colonel Sullivan's family."

"The Colonel and I are old acquaintances," said Lina. "I wasn't aware he was traveling with...family?"

"His daughters," said Jacobs.

Lina exaggerated her smile and fluttered her eyelashes. "Are they here? I'd so like to say hello."

Jacobs face filled with mock sympathy. "I'm sorry, no. The Colonel's party are early risers. I believe they're on a bit of an outing."

"I see," said Lina.

"Would you like me to take a message?"

"I'd rather surprise him," said Lina.

"Of course." Jacobs dabbed at the back of his neck.

"Will you be going up to your room now?"

Cassidy bent backwards and slapped his chest. "Truth is, the wife and I are famished. Where can a man get a good plate of steak and eggs in this 'burg?'"

Jacobs seemed eager enough to please, especially after Cassidy laid a gold eagle on the counter in front of him. "As it turns out, the Snorty Horse has a real nice steak and eggs lunch special. You'll find it at the end of the street."

"End of the street?"

"You can't miss it."

Lina walked to the door and opened her parasol. "It's been a pleasure, Mr. Jacobs." She stepped into the sunshine with Cassidy on her heels.

"Just a friendly community, ready to serve, Mr. Jones," Jacobs said as they walked out the door.

Once they were outside, Cassidy stopped to glance back through the open window. "Here's your friendly community for you," he said, motioning for Lina to look as well. She poked her head down past the curtain just in time to see Jacobs speaking, ending a telephone call.

A few minutes later, they stood outside the Snorty Horse and listened to the clink of glasses and soft conversation. It was just after noon.

"Would you care to join me for an aperitif before we dine, ma'am?"

"I'd be delighted."

Lina closed her parasol and hooked an arm around Cassidy's elbow.

She was oddly satisfied with the morning's plan.

While they tracked down Sullivan, Sofia and Mary had taken Rayburn to the doctor. Meanwhile, Estrella nosed around the college administration buildings to locate Honey.

Together, Lina and Cassidy walked into the saloon and moved quickly back to the far table where Lina slid the parasol under her chair. Cassidy pulled at his collar and looked around the room with a nervous tic in his jaw.

"Anxious?" said Lina.

"Saw a couple hombres playing cards at this table last night," said Cassidy. "I'm surprised they're not still here."

"You're not looking for old men," said Catalina.

Cassidy leaned over and whispered. "These clothes might hide our identities from some people around town, but they won't fool Edna, the woman who directed me to the canyon last night, or my bartender friend, Max."

"It doesn't appear Edna is here. And if Max is a slender beanpole on legs, he went out the back door the moment we came in."

"Well and good, but—" Cassidy stopped talking. "Did you say he went out at the same time we came in?"

"Yes."

"Did he see us?"

"Yes, he was talking on the telephone."

There was a change in the air and Lina immediately understood their predicament.

She looked around the saloon. The conversations they heard from outside had faded. The clink of glass had settled and gone.

They were absolutely alone in the room.

Lina carried her parasol to the edge of the bar and dropped it when she saw a furtive shadow brush past an open back door.

She whirled around at the sound of a heavy tread on the boardwalk. Figures passed by the frontage window glass.

"It's a trap," said Catalina.

They both recognized the big man in the doorway as Booth. Heavily bruised with a swollen eye and bandaged ear, he was still as dangerous as ever.

"Fancy duds you're wearing," he told them and stepped aside to allow in two men with matching uniforms. "You ought to present well in your coffins."

All three of the men had their automatics out of the holster.

Booth kept his attention on Lina and waved his piece back toward Cassidy's table. "Go sit down," he said.

She did as she was told, sliding her chair close to Cassidy.

Booth and his men approached the table, guns level and pointed straight ahead. Before anybody spoke, Perry Sullivan limped in from the back door with Max close behind. His big rubber overshoes seemed two sizes too big and they clomped down loud and hollow as he walked. He held a brown bottle in his hand.

Max carried a short barrel coach scatter gun.

Sullivan took a long pull from the neck before setting his bottle down on the bar next to Lina's parasol.

His eyes sparkled with recognition. "I didn't expect to see you here…Sister," he said.

Lina nodded.

"And the constable as well."

"Why the costumes?" said Sullivan.

"We were attempting to be…discreet," said Lina.

Sullivan chuckled. "I understand," he said. "Believe me, I do."

"What do you want us to do with 'em, Colonel?"

Sullivan scratched his chin, then picked up his bottle for a second drink. "I don't know," he admitted. "On the one hand…," he let the words trail off and ticked off unheard options on his pickled fingertips. "But then, on the other hand…"

Lina said, "I think it would be a good idea for you and your men to turn around and leave peaceably."

Impatient with Sullivan, Booth ignored the comment. "What's the problem Colonel? Give us an order."

"I've a wee bit of a problem, sir. I'm not exactly sure why these two are here in Candelaria and perhaps I should ask Mr. Shanahan about it."

"Shanahan will agree with whatever you decide," said Booth. "I'll back you up, too."

Sullivan accepted the endorsement, but then turned to Lina. "And why is it you're here, lassie?"

"Savannah Diaz and Emilia Martinique."

Sullivan's mouth opened in a perfect oh without sound. He understood.

"Why don't you kill them?" said Max.

Sullivan's eyes popped open wide and his cheeks pulled back with the realization: "I could, couldn't I?

We don't have to worry about the law anymore." He moved his attention from Max to Booth and back again. "Do we? Or...or do we?"

"We are the law," said Booth. "Right here. Right now."

Sullivan agreed. "Let's kill 'em then."

Max lowered the shotgun. "But outside," he said. "It takes me forever to get blood off the wood floors."

"Outside it shall be," agreed Sullivan. With a looping roundhouse swing, he made a grab for his bottle, sweeping it from the bar straight into his mouth. After he swallowed, he told Max to lead the way. "After you, my good man."

They left the building, Max in the lead, with Sullivan dragging his heavy boots behind.

Once more, Booth waved his pistol. "Out the back," he said. "Follow the Colonel."

Lina stood up and a note of defiance crept into her voice. She held up a single index finger.

"Mr. Booth...isn't it? I did want to tell you something," she said.

Annoyed but curious, Booth leaned forward with pursed lips. "And what's that, dearie?"

Slowly she sauntered forward, leading him with a bent finger.

After several steps, near the edge of the bar, she turned and leaned into him, whispering in his ear.

"When this is done and you're on the ground dying, remember this was the choice you made and we gave you the opportunity to leave peaceably."

CHAPTER TWENTY-FIVE

The midday sun cast severe shadows on the wood floor of the Snorty Horse saloon and pictures formed in the sawdust. Shape of a dog. A bird. A death's head.

Lina moved her eyes from the floor and back up to Booth's thick mustache, his violet nose a roadmap of broken veins. "You had your chance," she said, brushing at the clutching waistline of her dress sending a tuft of glowing motes between her and the security guard.

Booth pulled his enormous weight back and cut loose with a guffaw. "Did you hear what I heard, boys? The little hen here says we can leave peaceably."

The men didn't answer.

"Boys?" said Booth.

Lina's brother, Carlos, had taught her much about the martial arts. Swordplay, gun craft, and how to wield a blade. But he'd taught her about science too. About orders of magnitude and how to measure time. In 1909, a prominent physicist had coined the term millisecond — meaning one one-thousandth of a second.

In the millisecond Booth took to avert his eyes from Catalina in search of his silent comrades, she moved. A shuffle on soft sawdust, a sideways grab. The parasol secure in her hand, it's tapered ferrule a spear traveling upwards into the soft underside of Booth's chin.

With both arms, Lina drove the steel spike through Booth's fleshy jaw and up, into the roof of his mouth and beyond. The sound was like pulling tendons from a chicken or slicing round steak from the rump of a cow.

Except for the screaming and still hot gushing of blood.

Booth fell against the wall, clawing at his neck, conveniently making way for Lina to confront the two standing guards.

Their expressions were both blank and unseeing. As Lina watched, the guns toppled from their hands and Mary stepped out from behind them, a bloody shiv in each hand. Casually, she blew on each of them in turn and they dropped to the floor.

Mary was about to speak when a double-barreled concussion ripped through the air behind the cantina.

"That would be Max," said Cassidy.

"Sullivan—" said Cassidy, rushing to the bar.

"Sofia," said Mary.

Catalina held her breath. If Sullivan were hurt, or worse — they'd never find Savannah and Emilia.

At Lina's feet, his jaw broke and impaled, Booth had stopped squirming and lay gasping in a growing puddle of blood. His crazed eyes darted one way, then another, finally straining up to land on his attacker. Lina stepped over him and crouched down. "I told you so."

"I think this is the fellow you're looking for, constable."

Lina, Cassidy, and Mary all turned at the voice as Sofia marched Colonel Sullivan into the room ahead of her. His arms were raised and bent with his fingers laced behind his head. Behind him, Sofia had the man-catcher turned at an angle and pressed against the nape of his neck. When he got to the bar, she gave him one last shove and he stumbled ahead, bumping into the mahogany frame with a thud.

Lina offered Sofia a nod of thanks. "Max?" she said.

Sofia's negative move was barely discernable. But clear enough. "He fell on his weapon," she finally said.

Sullivan's countenance was madly animated. "You'll pay for this. Enemies of the Battalion always pay! Erin go Bragh!" he cried.

"Shut up," said Cassidy.

"No, constable," said Catalina. "Let him talk."

She walked up to one of the barstools and sat down, facing the old man across the polished mahogany surface. Then, without breaking her gaze, spoke to Mary and Cassidy. "Please keep watch? Make sure we're not disturbed?"

Lina's arm shot out and she gathered a fistful of his emerald shirt. Pulling him halfway across the bar, she let her voice grow husky and seductive. "You need to tell me where those girls are, Colonel. You need to tell me right now."

"Erin go Bragh," he said.

Sofia cracked him across the back of the neck.

"Again," said Lina. "Savannah and Emilia."

"You can't have 'em. Can't have 'em. Can't have 'em." Sullivan gibbered with sheepish abandon and drool ran from the corner of his mouth.

"You don't seem to understand your dilemma," said Lina.

Sullivan cackled. "I understand fine," he said. "Oh boy, do I understand."

"Where are the girls? I won't ask again."

"It don't matter if you ask again or not, lass. The simple fact o' the matter is that you can't have them because they're dead."

The words hit Catalina like a thunderclap.

All the air went out of the room and the walls of the Snorty Horse wrapped around her so she was staring down a long dark tube with Sullivan's face at the end, lit by the sun.

She let go of his shirt.

"I can see it's hittin' ya hard, girl," The Colonel nodded. "Aye, and I can see it."

"You're lying," said Sofia.

Sullivan had both hands in the air beside his ears and spoke over his shoulder. "I'm not at all. I'm telling you the truth, and it doesn't matter how hard you poke me with that thing or e'n if you kill me. It won't bring y'r little nuns back."

"But it would bring me some satisfaction," said Sofia.

"Where is Honey Shaw?" said Lina.

Sullivan cocked his head from one side to the other. "I believe I'm getting a wee bit parched," he said. "If I could but have—"

Lina's voice cut through his chatter like a sledge-hammer. "Where's Honey Shaw? Where's the sword?"

Sullivan winced at the volume of her query. "I gotta tell ya, that's some kind of wind you've got there. If only you were in the Brotherhood, the songs we could sing. But, oh," he grinned. "the Sainted Battalion is only for the menfolk, doncha know?"

He winked at Lina, then delivered the final blow.

"As it turns out, Miss Shaw is gone, flown the coop, absconded with the sword across the meridians. It was an incredible disappointment to me and Mr. Shanahan, as well. The loss is…well, it's a tragedy." Sullivan spread his fingers on the cool wood. "A tragedy — but there you have it."

"I don't believe it," said Lina.

From the open doorway, Estrella spoke. "You may have to," she said.

Lina met her halfway across the floor, grasping both of her arms. "Honey's gone?"

Estrella said she was. "It's not the only thing I found out."

"Come, sit," said Lina.

"I'm eager to hear all about it," said Colonel Sullivan.

Lina gave the old man one last look of contempt. "Take him to the wagon," she told Sofia. "We'll be along presently."

"Wagon? What wagon?" said Sullivan. "Where are you taking me?"

Sofia directed Sullivan toward the back door. "You're going back to Santo Tomas, where the truth of those girls' deaths will come out," she said. "If you're lucky, you'll hang."

"Lucky? You mean if I'm lucky, I won't hang."

"If the judge doesn't sentence you, the Black Rose will."

Lina acknowledged Sofia's backwards glance. "If fortune is with us, maybe we can still retrieve the sword."

Sofia shook her head. "It isn't worth any more lives, Lina."

The two disappeared out the back door, leaving Lina alone with Estrella at the table she'd first shared with Cassidy. "I can't believe those girls are dead," said Lina. "I think he was lying."

"He wasn't lying about Honey," said Estrella. "She's gone."

"You're sure?"

"On the college campus, I ran into an old professor I know. He took me to Old Central. I spoke with Mr. Shanahan in his office."

"And?"

"Ellis Donovan is dead."

Lina sat back in her chair. Here was something unexpected. "How?"

"Killed with a sword. Probably the blade you're looking for."

"Honey?"

"That's what Shanahan says."

"She would kill her fiancé?"

Estrella's reaction was whimsical and reflected

years of experience in affairs of the heart. "The course of true love…"

"Never did run smooth," said Lina, finishing the quote. "A Midsummer Night's Dream. I'm surprised you know it." The sentence slipped out before Lina could stop it.

Estrella didn't seem to take offense. "You've heard of the whore with a heart of gold? I'm the whore with a library of books."

Fair enough, thought Lina. But she hadn't seen any books in the wagons except an old Bible beside Ma Grell's mattress.

Estrella continued. "Shanahan is literally in tears, Lina. His heart is broken."

"I don't understand."

"He also loved Honey. And to see her life ruined, a fugitive from justice. His best friend slain."

"There's too much death surrounding this entire affair," said Lina. "From the very beginning."

Estrella's face was pained. She wanted to say something, but she kept quiet.

After a while, she said, "Why don't you just go home, Catalina? You've got Sullivan. Go back to Santo Tomas to your Mother Superior and forget you ever heard of Candelaria."

"Sullivan says the girls we are looking for are also dead."

Estrella winced. "They are," she said.

"How do you know this?"

Estrella pulled a folded piece of parchment from her pocket and smoothed it out on the table in front of Lina.

"I took this from Shanahan's desk when he wasn't looking," she said.

The note was written in a hasty script with black ink. Some of the lines had been smudged, but most of it was legible. Based on the flourishes and curves, Lina assumed the hand who penned the missive to be feminine.

I've done something so utterly horrible, so heinous and cruel, I can never be forgiven. The life of Mr. Donovan is now forfeit at mine own hand and may God save my soul.

I'm taking the sword and going away forever. The memory of what I've done, and the death of those poor girls be forever on my conscience.

--Honey Shaw

"You knew Honey when she worked for Ma Grell," said Lina. "Is this her handwriting?"

"It is."

"The flowery language she uses here doesn't seem like the woman we met."

Estrella understood Lina's meaning and explained. "Honey was always putting on airs. It was her goal in life to be part of the wealthy, learned society." Estrella pulled the letter back across the table. "With Donovan, she almost made it."

Catalina stood up and contemplated the bodies of Booth and his two soldiers.

The sheriff was at the doctor's office, but there were other people in town. Men who wouldn't appreciate dead bodies stacked like hay bales in the saloon. The sooner Lina and her friends were away from Candelaria with Sullivan in tow, the better.

"Will you come with us?" she asked Estrella.

"I wish I could, but no. I grew up here. I came to love the canyon. It's where Ma is — where Frank and Dixie are." She blinked back the tears. "Maybe I'll build a cabin there."

"You have a fresh-water spring there."

"It will do. Remember when you once told me — it will do." Estrella held Catalina's eyes with gentle sorrow. "I guess it will have to."

Lina kissed Estrella on the forehead and turned away.

There was nothing to do now but to go home.

CHAPTER TWENTY-SIX

No matter how deserving they were of their fate, four dead men littered the Snorty Horse property in Candelaria and without Rayburn to lead them, the citizenry would seek justice the old fashioned way. With rope first, and questions later.

There was no time to waste.

After a fast supper of beans and canned peaches in Stark Canyon, Catalina offered Estrella a sorrow-filled goodbye.

Setting out for Santo Tomas under cover of night, Catalina insisted Cassidy ride Diablo parallel with Colonel Sullivan's mangy nag. The swayback suffered under the old man's weight and the going was slow. But given Sullivan's age and his squishy big boots, forcing him to walk on foot would take even more time.

Sofia and Mary followed behind on their Andalusians with Catalina trailing on D'oro.

The healthy mare resented being held back and complained by shaking her head with pinned back ears, then chomping the bit and pulling the reins from Lina's hand. "Easy, niña," she said, but D'oro hardly listened.

They rode for two hours, away from the mountains, south across the open range on a tranquil road through fields of moonlit Mexican poppies. The lustrous blossoms along with the sway of D'oro's gentle saddle threatened to lull Lina to sleep.

The physical toll of the day weighed her down. It had been a taxing afternoon.

And though Cassidy had retrieved the Colonel, they left town without securing the sword worse yet, Lina's urumi was gone. She felt naked without its weight at her waist. And in the most crushing defeat of all, they'd left whatever earthly remains were left of Savannah and Emilia.

Failure was a painful burden.

Mary drifted back on her mud brown mare, its black mane contrasting sharply with D'oro's cremella radiance. "You're awful somber," she said.

There was a time Lina would have rebuffed Mary's concern, firing back a harsh denial, venting her anger unfairly. She liked to think she was learning.

"As a child, I was immensely competitive," she said. "In a house filled with men, I had to be."

"Woman, I don't know how you survived."

Lina's jaw twitched with the memories and she watched as the road made a long looping curve to the east. "I survived by being better. By becoming, better."

"I liked to run," said Mary. "When I was nine years old, I ran faster than anybody I knew."

"You would not have been faster than me."

"I would've run you and your pretty horse both to ground."

"Do you suppose that's still true?"

"One day we'll have to find out, won't we?"

Lina appreciated Mary's candor. Of all the women in the convent, Mary was the only one who understood Lina on her deepest levels. The banter lifted her spirits, if only for a few minutes.

"We left those girls behind."

"They're dead," said Mary. "And the bastard riding ahead of us will hang for it."

Lina shook her head. "Not without proof. We should've tried to find them."

"Aw, hell. Cassidy won't let him and Hodges get away with it. And there's always Lucia. She was attacked too, and she'll say so at the trial." They rode down through a draw and up a sandy hillside. "At the very least, those two are gonna spend time behind bars."

"Do you remember the first time you saw them? Savannah and Emilia?"

"I do," said Mary. "The Rosary Maker introduced us."

"Lately, the Rosary Maker seems to introduce all the new candidates for the order."

As mysterious a personage as Catalina had ever known, the odd resident of Santo Tomas was an apparition wearing the white cotton clothes and the toeless shoes of a peasant. He appeared seemingly out of the ether, stepping up to offer his wares, hand carved rosaries of oak or stone, mahogany and glass, each one different, but each one the same in their polished jet black manifestation. Freshly birthed from the Maker's hand, without odor or corrosion, they were nonetheless scorched, as if in invisible, eternal flame.

Reminiscing, Catalina said, "We met him near the train station."

"I never will know how he gets around town, blind as he is."

Lina agreed, "It's a mystery."

The Maker appeared on a late winter's day when the sky was low and the clouds were like a child's finger painting of colorless swirls and flat-bottom mud pies in the sky. Catalina and Mary had accompanied two elderly women from the convent, Sisters Theresa and Elizabeth, to the train.

The nuns were old, each approaching their 80th birthday, and both of them had expressed a calling to go back east, back to their homes in Ohio and Maine.

The younger women walked through a cold rain, not just to shield their dependents from the rain with umbrellas, but to offer spiritual support for the long journey ahead.

The irony of course being neither Lina nor Mary had taken any vows.

"The Seven Sisters became five on that day," said Mary.

It was true, because at the mission of Santo Tomas there are orders within orders and just as the Order of the Black Rose exists independent of the other Sisters of Senora Maria, so too the Seven Sisters of Sorrow have their own agenda.

Almost as mysterious as the Rosary Maker, the Sorrow Sisters share the common bonds of rape and family tragedy, appearing in public only when dire events are soon to transpire. At first doubting their gloomy prophesies, Lina had seen evidence of the Sisters' gifts. They took special care to get Theresa and Elizabeth securely on board the train out of town.

Once the task was finished, they turned into the gale and the old man stepped in front of them.

Startled, Lina had instinctively reached for the steel belt at her waist, but Mary touched her arm. "The Rosary Maker," she said.

The man's bald head was dark and wind burnt, his eyes, flat and unseeing.

"This is for Savannah Diaz," he said, holding out an ebony length of beads. "This is for Emilia Martinique."

Catalina had accepted the two rosaries without knowing the names.

With a warning tone, the Maker said, "Sorrow will have its seven."

"Can the cryptic mumbles, Baldy," said Mary.

The old man had ignored the juvenile comment, turned, and walked into a crowd of travelers recently disembarked from the train.

Lina and Mary met the two girls on their way home from the station.

Savannah was her Georgia home's namesake personified in manners and voice, but with a Spanish temper thin as moss hanging from the magnolias. Her skin was the color of an old wheat penny, but her hair was a stunning blonde.

Emilia was the opposite of her cousin in every way. With blue-black hair, pearl white skin and buxom curves, she was brash and cynical, but her anger was slow to burn. They had both suffered under an abusive uncle.

They had escaped to the West with their lives.

As they traversed the New Mexico plains toward Texas, Mary said, "It seems awful unfair to come half-way across the country, only to get caught up in this senseless Fenian nonsense."

"Is it?" said Lina. "Senseless, I mean. You're right about it being unfair for the girls, but is the cause of the Sainted Brotherhood truly senseless?"

"I sure as hell don't call it anything productive."

"My point is we don't really know their goals," said Lina. "Sullivan rants about his ancestors and apparently Shanahan and Honey are active in the group. But beyond a desire to possess the sword, we don't know their aim. We've traveled hundreds of miles, nearly a dozen people are dead and we don't know much more than we did when we left."

"Under John Riley, the original St. Patrick's Battalion was unhappy with the treatment of Irish immigrants in the United States Army. They were forced to attend Protestant church services and fight against Mexican Catholics they considered to be their close spiritual kin."

Mary obviously relished the opportunity to parade knowledge Lina didn't have. As they rode, her voice was more strident, catching Sofia's attention. The quiet nun fell back and rode her horse at Lina's left hand.

"A lot of Irish settlers in San Patricio, Texas sided with the Mexicans in the revolution. Some of their decedents live around Candelaria and Shanahan is in contact with them."

"And you know all this...how?" said Lina.

"Estrella told me, when we were riding in the van and you were recuperating from your initial run at the sword. She grew up in Candelaria, you know."

"None of what you're saying helps explain what they want now," said Lina.

Sofia interrupted the conversation. "Isn't it clear? They want what any gathering of evil people wants. They want power."

"Power over who?" said Mary.

"Anyone who happens to be at hand?" said Sofia.

The three rode behind Cassidy and Sullivan in silence for another hour until they came upon a flat acreage with a fence to tie the horses to and an abandoned wood shed filled with dry grass, bark and wood shavings. While Lina gathered the tinder and set it ablaze, Mary boiled water for coffee and Sofia helped Cassidy secure his prisoner.

Before long, everybody was asleep.

*****

In the dream, Lina crawled through the tunnel and the floor was made of bones, crackling under her knees and bare palms. Splintering and sticking to the wet of her palms. On three sides, hungry darkness smothered her like a funeral shroud, but the bones gave off a faint amber glow and piled up in front of her.

They were human bones.

Ribs and collars. Femurs and a humorous. A jawbone. A skull. Gravel sized bits like masticated chewing gum with scientific names she couldn't remember. And the assault on her nose was the rotting flesh of a man Catalina stumbled over outside their Hacienda when she was 14.

The man had been a local drunk, a ne'er-well the Rivera family had tried to help. Over the years they had given him food, shelter and employment working horses and cattle. But nothing worked with the poor sodden fellow. Nothing ever stuck, except a self-inflicted bullet to the brain.

And Lina found him many days later, rotting in the weeds, great pieces of his meat gone to feed coyotes.

The tunnel smelled the same way, an odor carved into her mind forever.

Worrisome were the dreams Catalina knew weren't of the waking world, but seemed real enough to believe. She knew she was asleep under the stars of New Mexico on a chilly blanket surrounded by friends. But crawling through the tunnel, she couldn't make herself wake up.

The grisly surface beneath her gave way to a muddy clay sticking like glue to her every move. Catalina held her breath against the overpouring sour smell of it as it mixed with the decay already clinging to her nose, mouth and tongue. When a cool breeze tossed back her hair, she lifted her chin. Deep underground, there was no access to the outside world, nothing in any direction but the earthen floors and ceilings thick with layers of squirming maggots.

The breeze was the breath of another person crawling toward her. If the emaciated, rotting thing could truly be called a person. It had jerking arms and legs that spasmed forward and back. It had torn rags and wet tendrils of dripping hair clinging to its skeletal form. The figure was human, but its hand and feet were claws and its grinning countenance was from the very pits of hell.

She recognized the face. Savannah Diaz, the missing novice from Santo Tomas.

Catalina sucked in a quick breath and tried to stop her own forward momentum, but her limbs wouldn't obey. She was on a collision course with the macabre vision.

"Catalinnnnaaaa."

The hollow call, bypassing her ears and ringing only inside her head, came from behind. Another demon. Another lost soul. Because wasn't this what Mercy's church taught? Wasn't a demon simply another lost soul? Somebody like Savannah or Emilia... or Catalina Rivera?

Now it was Emilia who snapped at her heels, crawling with the speed of a recluse spider, flinging her unholy screech at Lina's retreat.

Ahead, Savannah advanced with gnashing teeth. Behind, Emilia reached for her.

The dimensions of the tunnel shrunk with abrupt speed, closing in behind each of them.

The three of them were trapped together.

In a fetid, worm infested grave.

She opened her eyes in the real world of whip-poorwills and cactus, fresh scents of juniper and pinon trees. Above her, a vast panorama of soft indigo and deep blue, ebony swaths of night lit by endless, flickering stars. The breeze moving across her face was fresh and warm and washed away the remains of the horrific dream like a tonic cleans the throat and clears the lungs. She flexed her muscles against D'oro's blanket and willed them to relax. She calmed the rolling waves inside her stomach and drank deep of the rural sage brushed atmosphere.

To her right, Sofia and Mary breathed easy on their bedrolls. Across the still smoldering campfire, Cassidy sat upright against a broken log, his hickory pole not far out of reach. Staked to the ground and tied between the lawman and the nuns, Colonel Perry Sullivan snored with fitful starts and stops.

Lina's right hand involuntarily reached for the rosary she'd wrapped around her waist before bedding down — a practice she'd kept for the past month or so. She squeezed the black crucifix tight enough for the stations of the cross pricked her skin.

The burnt wood, passed down from her birth mother, Mercy's sister, gave her immediate comfort. More than a simple keepsake, it had become a symbol of the special Order inside the Sisters of Senora Maria and it brought her back from the abyss. She was awake and ready for what must surly come next.

She knew what she had to do.

The camp was wrapped in slumber.

Catalina was going back to find the girls.

CHAPTER TWENTY-SEVEN

In the predawn light the village of Candelaria looked like a bleached skeleton splayed out on the scrubby plains. The mountain range behind it served as the marker of its vast grave and the air ahead was rife with balls of swarming gnats.

Hoping to avoid even the most casual traveler on the roads leading into town, Catalina steered D'oro around the sorrow-filled town in a wide, lonely circle. Earlier in the morning, having successfully led the mare away from the other horses, she had returned across the country they had so eagerly, if too slowly for D'oro's blood, crossed the night before.

Had she stayed with her friends and returned to Santo Tomas, the entire incident could have been put behind them. Naturally, Mercy would be upset — at first. But as time went on, the inevitable truth about the sword would be clear.

It wasn't worth any more lives was the truth Sofia spouted.

"It's not worth the lives already lost," Lina said to herself.

But if there was even the slightest chance Savannah and Emilia were alive…

As long as you don't intervene, sorrow will have its seven.

Theresa and Elizabeth had resigned from the convent, leaving five Sisters of Sorrow.

At first it had seemed clear the Rosary Maker intended for the new girls to join the melancholy order, as long as she and Mary didn't intervene. But how was she supposed to divine the proper interpretation?

The Sisters of Sorrow didn't carry the burnt rosaries. The blackened beaded prayer chains were intended only for Mercy's order of the Black Rose.

If the Maker wanted the young women under Mercy's direction, maybe there was a different meaning to his caveat. Maybe the seven he spoke about, maybe the sorrow, had nothing to do with the gray ladies of the convent.

Maybe the Maker *wanted* Catalina to intervene — so sorrow could be avoided.

The morning's terrible dream had jogged a memory that had been nudging the edge her conscious mind for a long time. The ghastly wraiths in the earthen pit reminded Lina of the tunnels under the college campus. Tunnels where she had seen recent footprints, handprints and more importantly, a lock of blonde hair.

She spurred D'oro along the road, the same road she had used to first escape Donovan's army. The same road where they had encountered Ma Grell's broken wagon and become reacquainted with Estrella.

The outskirts of Candelaria were quiet, most of its citizens asleep. Estrella had described a once vibrant Western town, filled with enthusiastic settlers. There had been restaurants and beauty parlors, three churches and an opera house where traveling theater companies from all over the country stopped to perform. In those halcyon days, the College had been founded with a rich endowment from a slate of well-known industrial magnates.

And then the railroad decided to bypass the town. A contract not only for service, but for a hub of railway access, went to a smaller city more than forty miles north.

Candeleria suffered horribly, losing half its population and nearly all of its economy.

Catalina bypassed the main street, cutting across the back yard of a blown-apart hut, pulling up to the back of the doctor's house where Rayburn would still be recuperating.

She meant to pay the sheriff a visit.

Touching ground beside a grove of pinon trees, she had a clear view of Old Central in the distance.

Though she'd had precious little sleep during the past 24 hours, Lina felt energized by the first rays of sunlight glittering on the crimson shards of Donovan's broken window, visible behind a tall repair scaffolding. Even shattered the round aperture made for a dazzling focal point and the intricate lattice work of lumber now reaching up to the third story level was a sign of hope.

She had done her best to take away Ellis Donovan's prized possession, but it had never been personal. Pompous and self-important as he might have been, Donavon was somehow as much a victim in all of this as Ma Grell or Rayburn. She felt a passing sadness for his loss and hoped his lost sword might someday be avenged.

At the very least, his window would be repaired.

At the back door of the doctor's square built home office, she knocked surreptitiously. A dumpling of a woman with barely five strands of gray hair to cover her liver-spotted head answered. The cotton dress she wore once had a fancy pattern, but eons of hard water and sun-dried afternoons had turned it into a threadbare pinkish-gray blur. "Yes?"

"Is the doctor in?" said Lina. "Is the sheriff still here?"

"My husband is out, but he should return shortly. Mr. Rayburn is doing well, having his breakfast," said the lady. "Who are you?"

"Would you tell Sheriff Rayburn it's Catalina Rivera to see him?"

"Wait here, dear."

The space behind the house was piled high with crates and tin bushel baskets, buckets and assortments of rusting tools and wire. Yet, among the discard piles were well-tended plots of wildflowers. Indian paintbrush and orange groupings of devil's trumpet grew up through rusty perforations. White jewel flowers with purple details grew from a pail full of dirt. When the woman returned to open the door, Lina said, "Your flowers are beautiful. You must work hard to keep such a wonderful garden during the summer."

"My dear, the flowers would grow anyway. I just encourage them." She smiled. "It's what my Dr. Leonard says too. He encourages healing the body does anyway."

"Either way, Mrs. Leonard, your garden is lovely."

"You said your name is Catalina?"

Lina nodded and the lady indicated one of the paintbrush blossoms. With its yellow green petals and blazing red bracts, it had a distinctive star shape which made it stand out from the rest. "This variety is called Santa Catalina."

"It's quite beautiful."

"It is indeed. It's also quite resistant to my wishes as to where it blooms." She opened the door for Lina, inviting her in. "Perhaps it is a bit like you in more ways than one?"

"Perhaps."

Mrs. Leonard led Lina through a narrow hall past a cuckoo clock ticking a steady beat in time with their steps. They emerged in a cramped room with a cedar wood floor grown crooked and bowed over the years. Rayburn sat upright in bed wearing a tan nightshirt, holding a campfire mug full of coffee. Beside him, a tin plate with the yellow remnants of scrambled eggs and crusts of toast waited on an old spindle-legged chair.

Lina picked up the plate and passed it to Mrs. Leonard before sitting down.

"I'll leave you too alone," said the old lady. "Before you go, Catalina, I want you to stay on and eat lunch. It doesn't take a doctor to see you've been pushing yourself. You look to me like you could use some a good meal and some rest."

Lina agreed to stay.

"Much obliged, Marta," said Rayburn.

The door closed behind her but didn't latch, swinging back open a few inches.

Rayburn ignored the door and when Lina turned to look at him, his good-natured expression was full of curiosity.

"What the hell are you doing here?" he said.

"Checking on you." Lina motioned toward the door. "She says you're recovering well."

"I been better." Rayburn sipped his coffee and grimaced for effect. "But, yeah — all in all, it's better than being six-feet under."

"Ellis Donovan is dead."

"So I have heard. You know anything about that?"

"You might find this interesting." Lina withdrew the wrinkled letter Estrella had taken from Shanahan's desk. "It seems his fiancé did it."

Rayburn read Honey's note twice, flipped over the paper, then folded it and let it rest on the bed beside him. "How did you get this?"

"I assure you, it's authentic. Honey Shaw's handwriting has been vouched for."

"Vouched for, by who?"

"Estrella Gomez."

Rayburn pursed his lips. "Those two were close

friends, real close. Once upon a time you wouldn't see Honey without Estrella by her side. They roomed together." Rayburn snorted in amusement. "Worked together." He gauged Lina's reaction from the corner of his eye.

If he was disappointed by her stoicism, he didn't let on. Then he gestured with the letter.

"You came here to give me this?"

Lina nodded. "And to see how you were doing with my own eyes."

Rayburn's study of her face was backed by years of experience. "You ain't responsible for what happened to me." He let his head fall back on his pillow. "Looking back on it now, I do believe I was led into a bad situation by bad people."

"How so?"

"The way things worked out, I think Booth had it all planned out ahead of time. I think he knew he was going to kill Ma and the boys before we even got there." The sheriff shook his head. "The way it happened was too perfect. I think we both got played, Catalina."

"By who?"

Rayburn played with the corner of his blanket. "Donovan? Shanahan, maybe."

"The Sainted Brotherhood of Monterrey?"

"Ay-yuh. Them too."

"What reason would they have to kill Ma?"

"I wish I knew."

They sat awhile and Rayburn finished his coffee. Then he reached for her hand. "Thank you. For the campfire, for bringing me here. I owe you and yours a debt." His voice was firm and sincere. "If it wasn't for you, I wouldn't be here anymore."

"We did what we had to do," said Lina.

Still holding his hand, she stood up and pushed the chair aside.

"I should go now."

"Marta makes a mean pan of eggs and sausage. Make sure you eat your fill."

"I will."

"Then what?" said Rayburn.

"Then, I have errands to run before I leave Candelaria."

He nodded. "Would you be willing to do me a favor?"

"If I can."

"Don't kill any more people in my town."

Lina squeezed his hand. "I believe that will be up to the people in question."

******

After Mrs. Leonard's lunch, Catalina took the opportunity to rest on a straw-filled daybed. She fell asleep immediately and when she awoke, she felt refreshed, even if most of the day was gone. After offering her thanks and making her goodbyes, she stopped in the Leonard's outside privy to change clothes. She donned her tunic, gauntlets and cloak. She applied the Apache paint and the lace-up boots.

The missing urumi at her waist was like a wound.

But there was nothing to be done about that. She could find a replacement of some kind after she got home to the mission.

No, not a replacement.

A new weapon, but there would never be a replacement for the urumi she'd carried for most of her life. Her brothers had presented it to her. Carlos had taught her in its arts. She'd rigorously trained for years. It was every bit as much a part of her as her right arm.

Nothing would replace it.

Soon after, leaving D'oro behind, the Black Rose adjusted the leather satchel she carried on her shoulder and traversed a discreet path along a narrow creek to the campus of the College of St. Vincent of Maccabees. On foot, she mounted Windsor street beside an old wooden bridge full of holes in its deck. Approaching the campus through a veil of trees, she saw two uniformed guards on horseback patrolling along the wide open egg-shaped acreage on the campus.

The Black Rose couldn't afford to draw attention to herself. If only she could slip past them.

She was in luck. Almost as soon as she decided to chance an encounter, the two rode together and dismounted beside a garden bench to share a smoke.

The Black Rose moved quickly across the opposite end of the egg, taking note of the soft, warm grass under her feet. In the late afternoon sunlight, a cadre of gardeners pulled a steel-wheeled tank wagon full of water along the far sidewalk in front of Old Central. One of the men wrestled a measure of thick rubber hose from a turning roll while two more stood over a see-saw hand pump.

Watering the grass must be a full time job to keep it so lush in the arid environment.

Even as she slipped along the side of the grand old building underneath the scaffold in her black tunic, gaucho pants and cloak, a sleepy carpenter carrying a tray of tools met her coming around the corner. Yawning with eyes closed, he offered a noncommittal wave and shuffled past.

If the tradesman noticed her crimson forehead or the garish black cross scarring her face, he doubtless chocked it up to the regular shenanigans of an adolescent student body. He'd probably seen all manner of peculiar things working on campus.

At any rate, the Black Rose had vanished swiftly behind the building before he might take a second look. Within minutes she stood at the iron lid of the concrete cistern leading into the tunnels.

Grabbing the cold steel handle, claustrophobia like an iron mesh wrapped itself around her. For what seemed like an eternity, she couldn't move, the gruesome phantoms of her nightmare plaguing her.

It was all she could do to lift the lid and drop down to the rungs of the crawlway ladder. Holding her breath and gathering her cloak and satchel close with one hand, she closed the entrance above with the other, cutting off all light and sound, melting into an early night.

CHAPTER TWENTY-EIGHT

Inside the tunnel, the smells were familiar the same stale air, the same odor of decay. Just like the Black Rose remembered it. Bending at the waist, she flung her satchel to the floor and quickly unbuckled its hasp, digging through its contents until she wrapped her fingers around the welcome tube of her electric torch. She slid the switch forward, illuminating the corridor.

She let go of her cloak and breathed out a sigh of relief.

This wasn't the nightmare scenario from her dreams. The walls here were brick and mortar, not clay. Poured cement, not flaking layers of worms.

The floor was hardpacked clay with a thick layer of dust.

The light picked up signs of recent activity.

Footprints. And not just from one person. Several impressions stood out.

Two people, maybe three. She studied the prints carefully.

One of the shapes was clearly made by the military style of boot worn by Booth and the men in Donovan's guard. Another imprint was small and rounded, the shoe of a woman or child and if she hadn't been looking carefully, the Black Rose would have missed it.

The third print was impossible to overlook, the sloppy mark from a heavy clodhopper overshoe. Those were the shoes worn by Colonel Sullivan.

Unable to stand fully upright, the Black Rose bent her knees. Crouching low, she crept forward through the tunnel as she had once before, ever more vigilant this time for signs of occupancy — past or present. The earthen floor became less dusty as she went, so there were fewer prints and she didn't find any additional locks of hair or fragments of cloth.

She was unable to tell which direction the tunnel's earlier occupants had taken, impossible to know where they had gone, so the Black Rose chose to take them all — one by one.

When she came to a small crawlspace veering to the left off the main way, she moved into it. Eventually it narrowed to less than three feet square and served as a resting place for a stack of long lead pipes six and seven inches in diameter. Sewage pipes, maybe.

This storage nook wasn't on the map she had memorized and she wondered why.

She wondered if there might be a few more forgotten corridors.

Carefully she backed out of the tight quarters into the main channel and proceeded along the main path to the open elevator shaft under Old Central.

The passage opened up here and the Black Rose could stand in a confined cubicle roughly ten feet square by six feet high which opened into the elevator's vault.

It was just as she'd left it on her initial run for the sword.

All senses alert and making sure she was alone, the Black Rose poked her head into the shaft and ran the beam of her torch up and around. All was still. The heavy Otis car hung suspended at the top of its climb, locked in place three stories above by a series of safety levers.

She examined the steel beam structure of the tower and its deep concrete moorings, traced fat woven fiber electric cables, big around as a silver dollar, running down from the mechanism to where they branched off and ended in a heavy iron box.

From there, they ran along a stone wall at the building's deep foundation, up and over a thin groove in the cement, then back down where they dove straight into the ground.

Which seemed odd. Why would they be embedded in the ground?

And why the odd hitch up and over at the wall?

Her fingers found the horizontal groove underneath the wire's course and followed its path across, then down to an iron ring, like the one on the lid leading into the tunnel.

The Black Rose had discovered a heavy, hidden door.

Given the architecture of Old Central, she figured the egress opened onto the building's flight of stairs.

Tucking the information away, she continued to play her light over the walls, again following the electric wiring until it disappeared under the floor where she stood.

She was almost ready to turn back, when she saw a flat rectangular void in the corner of the chamber near the floor. Approaching the low horizontal access way with caution, she fell to her hands and knees and shined the light inside.

Made of poured concrete like everything else down here, it was crawlspace of some sort, an air vent maybe? Or coal chute?

It was just high and wide enough to crawl through and dust on the surface inside had recently been disturbed.

Less than six inches inside the crawlspace was a handprint. A handprint decidedly smaller than any man's hand.

The Black Rose squeezed into the narrow cut.

Immediately, a squall rose in front of her, and she jerked back, nearly bumping her head on the low concrete ceiling. The foul smell overwhelming her could only have one source.

Rats.

In the light of her beam, brown tufts of fur soared through the air in orbit around a spiraling mass of shrieking motion.

Rat wars to choose a king.

Each of the animated combatants were at least eight inches long and their hair, except where mussed and bloody, was sleek with a greenish tinge.

They were so engrossed in their battle they ignored the light and the Black Rose didn't have anything to throw at them.

She hissed and told them to get away. "Rapido," she ordered. "Rapido." But she didn't want to call out loud and risk the chance of discovery by other vermin — all too human.

The hissing seemed to do the trick and the rats finally noticed the light and scurried away along the path ahead, their naked pink tails fading into the edge of the dark.

Not for the first time, she missed her urumi. Deep in the campus' concrete arteries, there was no way to utilize its full length, but if nothing else, she could have shoved the coil ahead of her to clear away encounters with such hazards.

Eventually the passage ended at an abrupt ledge leading into another open chamber, this one slightly larger than the room beside the elevator shaft. The Black Rose jumped down to a full cement floor covered in several inches of dust and a collection of sloping black pyramids. There were dozens of the strange floor ornaments around the perimeter of the vault, mounds of molding black granular slime. At first she thought they were piles of explosive black powder, then she figured them for debris from the wooden joists above.

She was under the first floor of Old Central.

Shining the light up and across the ceiling, she instinctively recoiled at the scores of restless, fluttering bats hung directly overhead.

The pyramids were piles of guano.

Careful not to disturb the animals any more than she already had, and assuming she'd come once more to a dead end, she prepared to turn back.

Then she saw the electric cables again, coming out of the cement floor at the far edge of the room and proceeding up the wall to a terminus at the ceiling where they continued on through the wood sub floor of Old Central itself.

So why did the wiring travel under the floor she stood on? Why not just string the wire along the way she had crawled? Wasn't this what a crawlspace was designed for?

Unless…? Was there another area below her?

Maybe a dungeon of some kind with electric light?

Doing her best to ignore the piercing high pitch complaints of the skittering vermin above her, the Black Rose examined the confines of the room with her light. When she moved her light away from the far west corner, she saw a dimly lit square outline in the dark floor.

Exploring further, she found square grooves and an iron ring to serve as a handle.

A trap door.

Dim pinpricks of light trickled along the edges of the jamb.

"Once more into the breach," she said.

She pulled at the door. It was stubborn and heavy and didn't budge. She repositioned her feet and grabbed the handle and pulled, slowly and steadily, using her legs and back for leverage. Finally, the hinges squawking like a bird of prey, it cracked open.

Suddenly, a man bulled his way up and through. He slammed back the door and it crashed over to the floor, the noise driving the bats into a frenzy of flight.

The Black Rose stumbled at the sudden appearance, fell onto her back, but directed the light on the intruder. She didn't know him, but he wore the same blue uniform and black leather belt Booth had worn. His automatic was till sheathed in its holster and she didn't intend to give him a chance to draw.

With lightning speed she was up and swinging, catching the guard in the short ribs with a kick she knew could shatter cordwood.

Unlike Nolan or Booth before him, this one wasn't made for fighting and he sagged immediately, slumping down to the floor with a whimper, one hand holding his side, the other desperately raking at his gun.

Again the Black Rose struck, stomping hard on the soldier's hand, leaving him to jerk it away with a high-pitched scream. Then with a move born of countless drills in agility and finesse, she swooped in and took his gun, pivoting into a fighting stance. She pointed the automatic at a spot just below his belly button. "Who else is in the basement?"

"N-n-nobody," he stuttered.

The Black Rose dropped her stance by two inches and fired, sending down a fountain of orange and slapping a bullet into the concrete where it pinged away. The ruckus stirred up a squadron of bats and the soldier quickly threw his arms in front of his face. "For the love of God, stop," he said. "I'll tell you, I'll tell you."

The Black Rose blew smoke from the muzzle. "I know you will," she said.

Staying firmly planted on his backside, the guard said, "Seven girls, it's—"

"It's me," said Honey Shaw, standing hallway out of the floor, her hair disheveled and her bodice ripped. Her right breast was nearly exposed and her sleeves hung from her arms in tatters.

Keeping her light shining in the guard's face, the Black Rose helped Honey up and out of the pit.

"Thank God," said Honey. "You…you…" Startled by the dimly lit war paint and shadows cast by the electric torch and cloak, Honey seemed unsure what to say. "What are you?"

The Black Rose ignored the query to deal with the guard.

She waved the automatic with savage menace. "Back up against the wall over there." The man picked himself up and was positioned to bolt. "You do, and I'll blow the back of your skull off," said the Black Rose.

Then she spoke to Honey, "Six more were down there with you?"

Honey nodded. "Yes, oh…yes," she said. "There are six more of us."

Hope was a surging wave of joyous energy, but the Black Rose kept her voice calm. "Tell them to climb up."

From where she stood, the Black Rose could see the lower room was lit by a single incandescent bulb and in the midst of the stink of bat droppings and mold, she could smell the vile, burning death of singed moth wings.

"Quickly, girls, come quick," said Honey into the hole.

A hand appeared on the visible top rung of the ladder, then a blonde crown of hair. With more elegance and grace than should've been possible, young Savannah Diaz pulled herself free.

The Black Rose felt the burning sting of tears in her eyes.

No, she had no time to cry. No quarter for sentiment.

Not while she kept the gun trained on the man at the far wall.

Savannah slid her blue eyes sideways to her rescuer, then back to the opening in the floor. She bent down as another hand appeared. Gripping her friend's arm, Savannah hauled the second girl up with a single jerk.

Emilia cleared the lip of the opening and stood beside her friend.

The girls weren't dead after all. They were very much alive

And Honey was here, imprisoned with them.

The implications were clear. The letter Estrella had discovered in Shanahan's office had been a forgery or a letter written under duress.

Unlike Honey, the girls' wardrobe was undamaged and though they appeared malnourished and tired, they didn't seem to be hurt. The Black Rose greeted them by name and held the electric torch under her chin.

"Do we know you?" said Emilia.

"I think you do."

Savannah crept in close and cocked her head. "Sister Catalina?"

Emilia plunged forward with a happy squeal. "Catalina, thank the Good Lord above for sending one such as you to rescue us."

The Black Rose held the girls at arms' length with her words. "We must be on our way. Quickly, we need to get out of here."

They didn't need to be told twice.

Lina watched as Honey and the two girls helped four more young women up the dungeon's ladder. Two of the girls were blonde, one had dark hair like Emilia. The last girl's hair was short and rusty orange, her face covered with freckles.

Who were they? How did they come to be here?

Questions to be answered at a later time.

Honey brushed past the guard and led the way to the horizontal exit half-way up the wall. "This way, girls. Hurry."

At the wall, Emilia put her foot in Honey's clasped hands and let herself be boosted up and over the sill and the other girls fell into a line.

"Now you, sweetie," said Honey.

While Savannah climbed out, the Black Rose dealt with the guard. The sneer on his face was pronounced and made macabre shadows in the torch light. His face was a contorted mask of fleshy mountain peaks and deep abnormal fissures. Twirling the barrel of the gun, the Black Rose sent him a message: *Follow them.*

When the guard turned his back on her, the Black

Rose clubbed him on the back of the neck with the pistol. Rocked senseless, he fell into a heap.

Tucking the gun into her waist band where the big iron butt rubbed her hip bone, she made for the exit. The six girls were already scurrying through the underpass on their hands and knees, but Honey had stayed behind.

As the Black Rose approached, Honey held out her hand.

"There's one more thing," she said.

Quickly she ran back to the trap door and vanished beneath the floor.

Wary, the Black Rose pulled the automatic and kept it trained on the opening.

She didn't trust Honey. If this was some kind of trick, the blonde temptress Estrella had called "Ma's number one whore" would rue her actions.

It wasn't a trick. Instead, Honey popped back out of the dungeon with a round steel coil in her hand.

In the dying glow of the electric torch, a razor line of yellow-orange ran like wildfire along its rim.

"Donovan had this," said Honey. "I believe it belongs to you."

Handing Honey the light, the Black Rose kept one hand on the gun and quickly wrapped the steel spring around her waist like a belt and latched the hilt.

"I am in your debt, Honey Shaw."

"We aren't out of here yet," said Honey. "But if and when we are, drinks at the cantina are on you."

"Agreed."

But as the two prepared to follow the girls back through the tunnels, Honey hit a patch of guano and her feet slid out from under her. She hit the floor with an agonized cry and a bone-crunching thud.

The Black Rose quickly spun and ducked down beside Honey. "Are you alright?"

Stretched out prone on the floor, she managed to roll to her side and balance on her hip. Holding her torso up with one elbow, Honey stretched her right leg out from her upraised skirt. She tried to stand, but immediately cried out. Sinking back to her elbow, she said. "I…I don't think I can walk."

She looked toward the exit. "You'll need to go on without me."

The Black Rose resisted the suggestion and reached for out. "I'll carry you."

"You can't carry me through this passage."

"I'll pull you."

"Towing me will take an hour." Honey pushed aside the offer. "No. You need to help those girls. They're waiting for you. Get them away from here. Get them safe, then come back for me."

Lina looked at the unconscious guard sprawled nearby.

"I'll be fine," said Honey.

Sizing up the situation, the Black Rose knew the woman was right. But she wouldn't leave Honey defenseless in the dark. She pressed the .45 automatic into her hand. "Keep this. Don't be afraid to use it."

In the light of the electric torch, the two shared a look of comradery.

"You took the sword from Donovan's office," said the Black Rose. It wasn't a question.

"I did," said Honey. "I was in love...am in love." Her expression was confused defiance. The battle she fought wasn't with the Black Rose. It was with herself.

"I was blind. I got caught up in Mick's vision." Her voiced pleaded for compassion. "You understand, don't you?"

"I didn't ask for excuses," said the Black Rose. "Where's the sword?"

"Shanahan's got it."

"What's he going to do with it? Why is he keeping you here?"

Honey's answer was filled with anger and self-recrimination. "Just get the hell out of here, okay? The girls are waiting."

Honey was right.

The Black Rose stood up. "As soon as the girls are with Rayburn, I'll be back for you." She waited a beat and Honey spoke up.

"It's not the first time I've been alone in the dark with a man and a gun," she said.

"That's what I assumed," said the Black Rose.

"Go," said Honey. "Hurry."

The Black Rose scurried into the crawlspace and the torch light shot ahead toward the next chamber.

CHAPTER TWENTY-NINE

Once reunited with the girls, the Black Rose took the lead with Savannah and Emilia close behind. She led them past the open elevator shaft to the long tunnel leading out. "Who brought you down here to begin with?" she asked.

"Two men," said Savannah, "the guard, the one you saw and another one, an old man with a beard."

"He's called Colonel Sullivan," said Emilia. "He's the one who brought us from Santo Tomas."

"But it was Henry Hodges who grabbed you first?" said the Black Rose. "At Sullivan's Way back home?"

"Yes, it was Hodges. He stopped me in town," said Savannah. "He wanted to show me a prize winning horse. He led me to a barn in the woods behind Sullivan's house. Then he put some kind of awful smelling cloth over my face."

"Is that what happened to you too, Emilia?"

She said it was.

"But he didn't hurt you otherwise? Didn't...touch

you?"

Savannah's sneer was apparent in the tone of her voice. "He wanted to. Kept telling me how he wanted to. But, no. Something held him back."

"He was the same way with me," said Emilia. "I think Colonel Sullivan paid him to leave us alone."

When the Black Rose got to the entrance to the tunnel, she let Savannah hold the torch while she climbed the ladder, cracked the iron lid, and peered outside. "All clear," she whispered. At a rapid pace she stepped out onto solid ground and helped the six girls escape.

Once they were free of the tunnel, the Black Rose led the string of girls to the back wall of the blonde brick chapel building. "From here we will circumnavigate the campus oval," she said.

Suddenly several shots rang out and the Black Rose felt her heart push through her rib cage.

Not shots, she realized.

Hammers on nails. The workmen at Old Central.

Fourteen wide and expectant eyes landed on her for guidance and the Black Rose reassured her charges. "They are constructing a scaffold to repair the window damage in the tower of Old Central. They don't know we are here." Her words were as much to reassure herself as the girls.

"Where can we go?" said Savannah. "How can we get away?"

"We ought to go to the sheriff," said the freckled girl with orange hair. "His name is Rayburn. I met him once and he's a good man." She moved down the length of the building. "His office is this way," she said.

The Black Rose put a firm hand on her arm and reeled her back. "Rayburn isn't in his office," she said. "A lot happened while you were being held prisoner downstairs. The sheriff is at the doctor's house, so we need to go there."

"Doc Leonard is a good man too."

"I'm glad you agree with me. Now, here's how we get to Doc Leonard's house."

The girls huddled around the Black Rose as she drew a crude map in the dirt. "This is the grassy oval with Old Central at the forefront." Then she drew the chapel and a few additional buildings. "We're here," she said, marking the place with a big X. "You'll sneak along this line of trees and cross the street here, near the bridge over the creek."

"Where will you be, Catalina?" said Emilia.

"I'll be behind," said the Black Rose. "Dealing with the men who are stationed here and here." She showed them two points on the far side of the campus oval. "They are on horseback. I saw them when I came and managed to slip past them undetected. I don't think seven of us will be so lucky."

"Don't worry, she has the guard's gun," said Savannah. She turned to the Black Rose. "Don't you?"

"I left it with Honey."

"But, then…how will you…?"

"Dealing with the guards is my concern, not yours." She took up the instruction again. "Once you've crossed the street, run for all you are worth down Windsor road. After three blocks, you'll see the back of the doctor's house. It's a square, white-washed building with a junk pile behind. There too, you'll see my horse." She looked at Savannah and Emilia. "It is a white Andalusian named D'oro."

Both of the girls nodded.

"Now, say it back to me," said the Black Rose. "Each of you in turn, so if you are separated for any reason I can be sure you all know what to do."

When each girl had repeated the instructions, she put Savannah in charge. "Lead the way. And once you start, don't stop. Don't look back until you are safe with the doctor and Sheriff Rayburn."

"We understand," said Savannah, crossing herself and folding her hands in a quick prayer.

With that, the Black Rose sent them on ahead of her.

******

The two horsemen had separated since the Black Rose arrived earlier in the day. One of them loitered a long distance away at the opposite end of campus standing next to his horse beside a tall flagpole. The second man was closer, patrolling the road on the near rim of the grassy oval. Hiding behind a two-story brick dormitory with ivy crawling up the north face, the Black Rose waited for the rider to disappear behind a neighboring structure. Once he did, she looked over her shoulder and gave Savannah a wave.

All six girls bolted cross the grass as the Black Rose purposefully strode into the egg between them and the re-emerging guard. When he saw them, he blew a whistle and spurred his horse into a charge.

As the fugitives made their way toward the street, the far-away sentry had his back turned and didn't hear his partner's signal.

All the more tragic for him.

The guard reached for his holstered weapon and shouted. "Hold on there, you! Stop, or I'll be forced to shoot ye down." The powerful bay stallion charging down on her was a beauty and the Black Rose vowed to take the villain without injuring his steed. A magnificent animal should never pay for the mistakes of its rider.

She unsnapped the steel whip-sword coiled around her waist.

The guard pulled his gun.

With a flick of her wrist, the Black Rose sent the urumi arcing out six, ten, twelve feet, timing the recoil to perfectly coincide with her attacker's first pass. The tip of the blade flayed the knuckles on the guard's left hand and he jerked the reins before dropping them.

The bay pounded into a sideways gait even as the guard tried to swivel his gun arm around to the left. The weapon went off with a crashing boom. Already off balance in the saddle, the heavy recoil put the rider into a panic, desperately holding on to his horse.

Hazarding a look back, a grateful Black Rose noted three of the girls had reached Winsor near the bridge.

But then, having heard the percussion, the second soldier took note of the action.

There was enough space between the lead girls and those trailing behind for him to get between them. The Black Rose would have to move fast if she were to intervene.

Before she could act, she had a problem of her own to deal with. With his horse under control faster than she anticipated, the first guard resumed his attack with a withering four shots of sizzling lead. Spinning into evasive action, the Black Rose whirled the urumi into a broad arc that when unleashed would take off the man's head.

But this time he was wise to the weapon and drew his mount up short, dodging the deadly swipe. Another two shots nearly ended the Black Rose — one pierced her cloak near her left hip, another grazed the leather on her arm. At this range a .45 slug would play hell with anything it hit, splintering flesh and bone, knocking her down flat.

The bay's thundering hooves came straight for her and she launched herself to the side.

At least she was buying the girls some time.

But, rolling to her feet, her hopes were shattered.

The second guard had managed to intercept three of the girls, herding them like lost calves. Meanwhile, Savannah and Emilia with the orange-headed girl had stopped at the bridge to wait for their friends.

"No, dammit," said the Black Rose. "Keep going."

But instead, Savannah was deliberately turning back.

The voice over her shoulder was like gravel on a washboard. "Drop the whippy-dippy, Indian girl."

The Black Rose turned to feel the breath of the bay steam across her face. She stared into the muzzle of the automatic. She heard the rider's command once more. "Drop it," and she could smell his rancid breath even above the equestrian smell of his horse.

"What's your name, solider?" said the Black Rose.

"Corporal Thomas Johns."

"Well, I'll tell you what, Tom. You drop yours and I'll put away mine."

"You seem to think you've got some sort of say in this here—"

The urumi bit deep, slicing across the corporal's wrist with the speed of thought itself, taking tendons and bone, catching the corner of the gun in its recoil and carrying the weapon to earth. Thomas Johns screamed and raked the air with a geyser of blood before plummeting into the ground.

The bay sidestepped away with a nervous stride.

"Be seeing you," said the Black Rose, but she scooped up the gun before catching the horse's reins.

In a flash she was up and into the saddle, riding toward the girls.

But in the time it had taken the Black Rose to deal with Corporal Thomas, the other guard had the girls corralled near a flower garden beside the street and was holding them at gunpoint. If only she could draw him away, the girls would have time to escape.

She leaned into the withers of the bay, coaxing the anxious beast to do her bidding, careful not to spook him any more than he already was. When she got close enough to call out, she did and the girls and their captor turned toward her as one.

"Let those girls go you bastard son of a wormy possum!"

The horseman's answer was less creative, but just as insulting. He fired two slugs in her direction. Not for the first time, the Black Rose realized she owed her life to the lack of professional training these men evidenced. As she closed, the urumi whirled above her head in a widening gyre.

And then she saw their salvation.

Not forty feet away, coming down the street with an easy cadence, a familiar blue van with four horses marching in front rocked across the street's brick lined pavement. Estrella sat in the wagon seat, dressed in a light blouse and butternut trousers, the reins easy in her hand. A cockeyed bowler hat sat on her head and a rifle rode on her lap.

The Black Rose waved with frantic abandon and Estrella acknowledged the sign. She snapped leather and the horses raced into a turn, pulling the van over the curb and onto the lawn. Surprised at the intrusion, the guard's horse rose up on its hind legs and swung around in a circle.

The Black Rose shouted at the girls. "Go to the van! To the van!"

Savannah was the first to comprehend the words and she pulled in Emilia and two others, crouching low, taking advantage of the guard's confusion to run toward the wagon.

By this time, Estrella had the rifle in one hand and the door open on the van with the other. Quickly she shepherded the girls inside.

Two, three, four.

With her urumi at the ready, the Black Rose

closed in on the uniformed guard and his bay.

Five.

Only the orange-haired girl remained and the Black Rose drove her mount directly into the other bay, toppling both horses and sending the uniformed guard sprawling across the grass in a hard tumble.

Leaving her saddle to land catlike on all fours, the Black Rose saw the last girl disappear into Estrella's van. Quickly she joined her friend at the wheel of her wagon.

"What's going on?" said Estrella. "I thought you had gone?"

"I couldn't leave," said the Black Rose, working to catch her breath. "I had a hunch. Couldn't leave. Without the girls."

Estrella seemed to understand.

The Black Rose wrapped the urumi back around her waist and snapped the clasp on the hilt closed, latching it in place.

"Let's get you into the back," said Estrella, "and we'll be away from here." She swapped hands with the rifle and the Black Rose let Estrella guide her arm toward the van's side door. She unhooked the latch. When the door swung open, a hand reached out to help the Black Rose crawl inside.

Mick Shanahan's hand.

Behind him, the six girls cowered in fear as he sat on his haunches wearing a green uniform not unlike Colonel Sullivan's.

Shanahan's lunatic smile was all teeth and bright red gums. "Hello, dear. Fancy meeting you here."

The Black Rose recoiled in horror, tried to spin out of Estrella's grasp, but then the rifle butt was coming down on her forehead.

There was a sharp, agonizing thud and a thick dark wave carried her out to sea on a boat of two resounding words echoing over and over inside her aching head.

"Stupid bitch," said Estrella.

CHAPTER THIRTY

The heat woke her up before she even opened her eyes. Her skin felt scorched and tight, like she'd been outside in the sun far too long. The smell of smoke mixed with kerosene made it hard to breathe.

The sound of flames crackled through her ears before the clamor of the mob.

When they roared it was a ponderous throbbing thing growing louder and more insistent.

"Erin go Bragh."

"Erin go Bragh!"

They demanded to be heard by the whole town. By the entire state.

Ever more demanding.

To be heard by the entire world.

The Black Rose opened her eyes to the blinding light of the fire before focusing on a scene of flickering madness.

What had happened?

She had rescued Savannah and Emilia, along

with four other girls from an almost certain death or worse. She remembered how she had disarmed their guard, led them from the tunnel to the street, and devised a plan of escape.

The seven of them should have been ensconced safe with Sheriff Rayburn.

But in her haste the Black Rose had blundered with the two mounted security guards. She'd taken a risk she and the girls wouldn't be seen, or her own fighting prowess could protect the girls over the distance of Old Central's lawn.

Instead, the girls had been ushered into Estrella's blue wagon.

And Estrella…

Estrella was the one who had betrayed them.

How long had the whore's deception been in play? The Black Rose couldn't believe it was a spur of the moment weakness.

She remembered her conversation with Rayburn.

"The way it happened was too perfect. I think we both got played, Catalina."

"By who?"

"Donovan? Shanahan, maybe."

Estrella.

Now the Black Rose knew the truth and damned herself for not seeing the connection with Shanahan sooner. The clues had been there.

The easy way Booth had led Rayburn to Stark Canyon. Almost as if he had known exactly where they would be camped. Because he had.

Estrella's casual acceptance of Ma's death, because she had planned on putting an end to Ma and the boys from the moment they took off.

Her knowledge of scholarly works with no evidence of a library at hand. Because how would a garden-variety prostitute in a small town in the middle of nowhere know the scholarly works Estrella seemed familiar with.

It all added up.

From her high vantage point, the Black Rose looked down on a sea of bodies in forest green uniforms wearing polished black leather belts and holsters, their voices thundering up at her in unison. There were four rows of them and though it was hard to focus, she sensed more than a score of soldiers in each row. Their mania was mesmerizing, their voices unstoppable.

"Erin go Bragh."

"Erin go Bragh!"

As a single body they pumped their fists into the air in time with the call. Behind the assembled mass, a brush pile of tree limbs and lumber, old carpet and stacks of newspaper were being fed by dozens of young men and women — students from the college.

The bonfire burned with fat flames and a hypnotic flickering.

Dizzy, the Black Rose struggled to make sense of the scene. The air was a chaos of swirling red embers and trails of blue-green fireflies. Her eyes watered and her nose burned from the acrid smoke. Her ribs struggled to give support to her meager struggles for breath and her lungs ached at the effort.

Each breath was a painful struggle, but she willed herself to remain calm, even as her shoulders felt like knives were plunging into the meat at her neck.

Her shoulders and wrists were pulled from their moorings.

She clenched her teeth and jerked her head around in a spasm of panic. Savanah hung limp on her left, Emilia on her right.

Along with the girls, she'd been crucified on the scaffold in front of Old Central.

Strung up with taut hemp like a carcass in a slaughterhouse, she hung twenty feet off the ground, her wrists bound to a pair of vertical wood beams, her middle section lashed to a horizontal brace. She kicked empty air and gravity pulled her weight down hard against the bindings holding her fast.

Below her flailing feet, the other four girls were equally trussed — thankfully still asleep to the horror around them. A scent of pungent rotting wine lingered on the Black Rose's lips.

They had been drugged, likely with chloroform.

Sorrow will have its seven.

In front of the girls, a makeshift wooden platform had been constructed, and a tall T-shaped lectern held center stage.

Somebody in the assemblage had noticed the Black Rose was awake, and now the chant changed its course. From below and to the right came a snarling lead voice and the mob followed along: "Sacrifice," was their demand.

"Sacrifice!"

"Sacrifice."

The Black Rose strained against the ropes to no avail.

Again, she turned her head, this time in hopes of waking her friends. "Wake up, girl. Savannah!" But the blonde's chin lolled against her collar bone and her only response was a sad whimper of pain. "Savannah, please."

Likewise, the Black Rose tried to rouse Emilia with equally dismal results.

Again, she pulled against the bindings, but each effort seemed only to strengthen the bonds against her. The spiny hemp dug into her skin, cutting off circulation and her fingers and thumbs felt heavy and numb.

If only she knew what was happening, or why, she might be able to buy some time.

To do what, she thought?

Escape hardly seemed possible.

Even if she did get loose, the wild-eyed pack of slavering soldiers arrayed against her would rend the flesh from her bones in seconds as surely as if they were wolves who had gone too long since eating.

The Black Rose could feel the lunacy as a palpable wall of force, crushing her into the tower of wooden beams, smashing her to a bloody pulp. She tried to breathe, but even the shortest intake of breath caused a stabbing pain to shoot through her torso.

The cries of "Sacrifice, sacrifice" reached a crescendo.

If only Rayburn could appear with a posse of men.

If only Cassidy wasn't more than a day's ride away with Mary and Sofia.

At least the urumi was still wrapped around her waist.

With mind-numbing abruptness, the chanting stopped, its final echo rebounding off the edifice of Old Central. The din careened over the chapel and dorms only to fade through the Candelaria night.

The malevolent voice returned, carried over the egg to the chapel and dorms.

"Erin go Bragh," said the voice. "Welcome, ye Sainted Brothers of Monterrey. Welcome ye knights of the new Holy Crusade."

The Black Rose recognized the powerful, robust voice. The Irish brogue was exaggerated but familiar. As quickly recognizable as the man's lanky, overbearing stride when he had walked around the building to meet them on the previous Sunday.

Mick Shanahan raised his arms in the air, accepting their accolades as he walked across the boards to take his place behind the lectern.

A bully pulpit.

Mick Shanahan, dressed in a flowing emerald robe with a black stole over his shoulders and a cowl resting loose behind his neck, addressed the crowd.

"This journey began almost a century ago, when in Clifden, County Galway, our beloved Seán Ó Raghailligh was born of a virgin to a world lost in a fog of confusion. I believe even as a boy, John Riley had a vision of our struggles today and a prophetic understanding of the solution we offer. His vision led him to service, first in his own land, then across the immense Atlantic where awaited his disciples —

our passionate ancestors. Our devoted mothers and fathers. In truth, it is *we* who waited for him in spirit. It's we who will see him come again bodily on this very night to lead us to victory over the current age."

"Erin go Bragh," the crowd cheered with reckless glee and the inferno behind them raged to ever greater heights. Shanahan delivered his oratory with the inflection and drama worthy of a Shakespearian actor, but without the Bard's material to work with.

If the Black Rose was going to escape, now was the time to do it, while Shanahan held his audience in rapt attention.

But how?

Trial and error proved there was no chance to break the ropes around her wrists, and the pine wood she was tied to was newly pieced together with square-headed iron nails. If she could get some leverage, to brace herself, she might eventually force her way loose.

But hanging like she was, between Savannah and Emilia, there was no chance.

Breathing alone took every ounce of effort she could muster.

Perhaps the three of them together could sway the edifice? Again, she tried to rouse her friends. "Savannah, wake up."

The blonde girl's head wagged in bothered confusion.

"Wake up," said the Black Rose.

Again, the blonde complained, shaking her head vigorously before she opened her eyes. "What? No, leave me be." With consciousness came an immediate shock of fear, and anguish played over her features.

Savannah's voice was demanding and teetered on the edge of panic. "Where am I? Where are we?" Her face flushed red with terror.

"We've been taken by a madman," said the Black Rose. "If we want to escape with our lives, we must do all we can to get loose and away from here."

Savannah looked out over the animated crowd. "What do they mean to do to us?"

"I don't know," said the Black Rose, "but for now, their attention is diverted by their fanatical leader. The longer he speaks, the more time we'll have."

With a wild series of gestures, Shanahan continued. "At the peak our grandfathers' power, we were more than 700 strong. From our core here tonight and with arcane magic we now possess, we will surpass . Our membership tonight will grow by thousands. We will seize our destiny, the destiny our forefathers only dreamed of."

The Black Rose ignored the enthusiastic cheers and tried without success to wake Emilia.

"At San Luis Potosi, our precious silk flag was embroidered," said Shanahan. "Our grandfathers marched 'neath the angel's harp. Tonight we will find our eldritch energy there, once again."

Shanahan held aloft a bronze staff with a green flag suspended from it. Eagerly, he marched across the stage, swinging the staff, unfurling the banner in the hot bonfire's wind. The angel and harp design from the tokens Catalina had seen was emblazoned on the flag along with the Brotherhood's slogan of *Ireland Forever.*

The crowd was ecstatic.

Taking the waving flag as a signal, four students ran to the bonfire and lit torches made of fabric-wrapped sticks. Then each carried his fire in one of four directions to perimeter points on the egg. Once there, they touched the grass. Trails of flame coursed over the lawn, drawing out the shape of the harp and the angel in lines of fire.

The Black Rose had seen men soaking down the egg earlier in the day with hoses. She had assumed they were watering the grass. As the fire burned into sooty black tendrils of smoke, she realized the truth. The workman had been drawing the Brotherhood's symbolic icon in kerosene. They too, like Donovan's army, were loyal only to Shanahan.

"Does the man have this entire town in his thrall?" said the Black Rose under her breath.

Filled with despair, she bucked against the rope at her midsection and her eye took note of something odd. Something else seemed...familiar.

Shanahan posted the flag into a socket on the boardwalk, then crossed to the edge of the stage. A woman, previously unseen, appeared from behind two soldiers. She extended an arm, and Shanahan helped her to the stage.

It was Estrella.

Like her lover, she wore a long, shimmering green robe with a Satanic black stole and her head was uncovered. Her eyes reflected the orange and red chaos of the inferno.

Back behind his lectern, Shanahan preached his

unholy gospel. "What our grandfathers lacked, we have achieved. Wealth, prestige, power. It's ours for the taking. What our fathers only dreamed of, we will achieve in the future." Shanahan wrapped his arm around Estrella's lithe form and pulled her close. They came together in a lustful kiss and she handed him the Sword of St. Agnes.

"Tonight we call on powers beyond the earthly plane," said Shanahan. "You have seen these powers at work in Europe. In Mexico. In the orient. In our own greedy, vile nation. There's a restless energy of conquest on the horizon. It's there, lurking, waiting for any of us to pick it up." He held the sword high and the fire gleamed along its cracked iron blade. "Tonight I choose to pick it up. Tonight I seek to use it for the newly reborn Batallón de San Patricio."

"What's he talking about, Catalina?" said Savannah. "What's he going to do?"

The Black Rose shuddered involuntarily. "I've got a grim idea," she said. Again, she twisted against the rope lashed around her middle. A pair of loose ends dangled from the tie and again she felt a niggling familiarity. If only the smoke would clear from her eyes and nose.

If only Shanahan would shut up.

The professor was ecstatic. "Tonight the thousand year wait is over. Tonight the St. Agnes sword will drink again of virgin blood."

The sword flashed through the night.

Savanah's voice as ragged and shrill. "Good God, Sister. He means to kills us! What are we going to do?"

"We're going to stop him," said the Black Rose.

CHAPTER THIRTY-ONE

Shanahan's eyes were saucers and flecks of foam formed at the corners of his mouth.

"Just as Agnes of Rome was chosen by providence to die for our cause more than a millennia past, these seven will help forge a new engine of martial destruction. The sacrifice of these seven will call the spirit of John Riley from the land of shades."

The crowd responded, "Sacrifice! Sacrifice."

"Tonight we quench the sword's thirst for virgin blood. Tonight Riley will come to reside in me. And I will speak with Riley's voice. My hand will be Riley's hand as it holds our flag high in battle."

"Riley! Riley."

Then, at the back of the crowd, having ridden in along the student-lined ring of fire, Sheriff Jeff Rayburn appeared on a roan horse. A small group of four men in tall hats rode behind. The amber light of the fires played reflective tricks in their horses oiled leather tack and cast weird shadows across their forms.

They carried rifles on their laps as they approached and the students let them in.

The crowd parted, some moving to the right, some moving to the left.

Like the Red Sea for Moses.

The Black Rose felt her heart swell in her chest. Rayburn would save them from this mad folly.

Shanahan held his tongue and his followers fell silent while the fire popped and squealed around the horsemen.

Into the relative silence, Rayburn pitched an authoritative tone. "What's this all about, Mick?"

Arrogantly planted at his perch, Shanahan called out. "It's my pleasure to welcome you to the fold, Mr. Rayburn. If you'll kindly lay your weapons on the stage, we'll do our best to enlighten you."

With more effort than should've been necessary, Rayburn lifted his rifle and rested the butt on his thigh, pointing the barrel at the stars. "I'll keep my rifle, thanks." The Black Rose knew the sheriff was still weary, could see his weakness even as he tried to hide it. She felt a hint of trepidation skitter down her spine.

Rayburn lifted his chin, saw the Black Rose and her friends tied to the scaffolding. Immediately he directed his men, "Thompson, Schulz, cut those women free."

His order was rapidly countermanded. "Don't you move an inch," said Shanahan, brandishing the sword. His voice carried the amused tone of a child. "I think you forget the precarious position you're in, Mr. Rayburn."

Rayburn leveled his gun in Shanahan's direction. "Likewise, sir."

The stand-off lasted exactly five seconds.

Shanahan called out, "Take them, my brothers. Show them the spirit of the San Patricios!" Without hesitation, the crowd flowed in over the five horses and their men, none of whom managed to get off a single shot.

Rayburn tried to keep his balance, but the combined weight of ten soldiers grabbing at his arms and legs pulled him out of the saddle. His four comrades were likewise consumed under the shrieking swarm.

When Catalina was young, she'd seen a colony of red ants devour a grasshopper in less than a minute. This was like that times four and the curses of the sheriff and his men were cut abruptly short. It was like watching swimmers drown in the midst of rough waters.

There would be no help from the law. There would be no help from anyone.

The Black Rose pushed against the rope at her waist and it drew tight. She relaxed and the loose ties pulled back into the knot.

"They never shoot when they have the chance." Shanahan's laugh was short and guttural. "They always wait, and talk, and talk, and talk — and then you call their bluff." Once more Estrella was in his arms, at his mouth. Always the good whore.

And not just a whore. A trickster. A deceiver. Hadn't she lured Catalina in with soothing words and shared interests. How like Lina's relationship to Mercy was Estrella's love for Ma. How, like the Black Rose cared for Cassidy, Estrella cared for Rayburn. How they both enjoyed the outdoors, reading, tying knots.

All lies.

But not all untrue.

Not *all*…

In a flash of insight, the Black Rose saw what had been at the back of her mind. She knew what had seemed familiar about the ropes.

It was the knot. A perfect widow's grip.

The kind of knot Estrella tied back in Stark Canyon and Catalina had found wanting.

The Black Rose cocked her head to the side and craned her neck back. Her wrists were each fixed with a widow's grip and at her right hand the knot was within reach of her bent thumb.

A sense of expectant urgency fueled her fingers.

It was clear Estrella had helped Shanahan secure the Black Rose to the scaffolding. The widow's grip was too peculiar, too unique to be used by anybody else. Thankfully, it was equally clear to the Black Rose where the knot was weakest.

Just as she had immediately seen back at Ma's camp, the grip was fine for securing a heavy load because the more resistance it encountered, the stronger it became. But at the same time, the loose remnants dangling from each end were prominently displayed in the design. And one of them was the binding's Achilles' heel. One good yank of the loose end would unravel the entire structure.

The Black Rose struggled to get the short piece of loose rope between her thumb and forefinger. If she could only get one wrist free...

Below, onstage, Shanahan had prepared for the final scene. His cowl now enveloped his skull and he stroked his followers' bloodlust with a song of Gaelic gibberish. "Thoir spiorad Agnes. Fuil na beatha. Coisrig stailinn dhomh" He balanced the sword upright in two hands, his fingers on the pommel, his thumbs at either side of the hilt.

Slowly he turned toward the scaffold and the first of his sacrificial virgins.

The girl with the orange hair opened her eyes, saw Shanahan coming toward her, and screamed.

The Black Rose frantically clawed at the loose end of the knot at her wrist.

She had rope. Then lost it.

"Sisters, help meeeeeee!"

Shanahan raised the sword high and the crowd held its breath in anticipation. "I call upon the spirit of John Riley to lead us, to join with me, so we might seek vengeance for those who died."

The Black Rose grasped the loose end of the widow's grip, bent her wrist down with a hard pull and the knot dissolved. The rope fell away free, and her right hand was free.

Within milliseconds, she had her left hand free as well and a gasp went up from the crowd. With both hands, she pulled away the bonds beneath her breasts and lunged from the scaffold to land on the wood stage behind Shanahan.

"You were right all along, Shanahan. You should have stopped talking and acted while you had the chance."

At the sound of her voice and the impact of her landing, the madman spun around to face her, sword still held in position above his shoulder for a high, stabbing, attack.

The Black Rose dropped into a defensive crouch, her urumi free and swirling around her like a living steel tentacle. "You like to play with swords?" she said. "So do I."

"Your fate was sealed the day you walked onto campus, girl." Shanahan threw back his hood and brought the sword into a ready position. "The sword of St. Agnes thirsts for your virgin blood."

"You'll find my sword isn't so particular whose blood it drinks. And I'm not so cowardly as to attack school girls."

"Cowardly?" Shanahan spread his arms wide. "You call all of this…cowardly?"

The fool had left himself wide open.

With a fast sweep of her arm, the Black Rose hurled the urumi straight for her opponent's chest.

With a lightning reflex Shanahan knocked the blade aside with his sword. "I have all the powers of the faithful on my side, Black Rose. That is what they call you back home, isn't it?" His smug face beamed with amusement. "The Black Rose. How very theatrical. And how juvenile. Estrella told me all about you, dear. About your strengths and about your weakness."

Shanahan skipped forward, driving the Sword of St. Agnes ahead in a reckless attack sending the Black Rose to her knee. Trained reflexes halted the blade's progress on the hilt of the urumi. The Black Rose shoved Shanahan away, then ducked low, swung up and around and fell directly into Estrella.

The jezebel made a clumsy grasp for the urumi and the Black Rose leveled a side kick into her sternum. Sucking wind, Estrella collapsed to the stage floor and curled into a ball of pain, gasping for air.

The Black Rose spun, pivoting from one defensive position into the next.

Once more, Shanahan was on top of her, but his attack went wild. The St. Agnes sword whizzed above her hairline as he tried to lop her head from her shoulders. With a flick of her wrist, the Black Rose sent the whip-sword out where it slammed into the ancient Roman blade with an ear-piercing clang.

Shanahan fell back and now the Black Rose pressed the attack.

Her flexible urumi was a flurry of razored steel soaring in three-dimensions, shredding Shanahan's robe, slicing into his shoulder, sawing through skin and muscle straight to the bone. Howling in protest, but not dropping his sword, the lunatic went into a perfect pirouette and came back around, hacking, stabbing and screaming a dozen vile oaths.

The Black Rose tried for his legs, whipping her blade across Shanahan's knees, but again he parried the force of the blow and came on. The shoulder wound alone would have stopped a sane man dead in his tracks, but by now Shanahan was far from sane, and from the smell of him, far from sober. Driven to bestial fury by his incoherent dreams and foolhardy expectations, he reverted to gibbering nonsense.

"Lestinu fraggish. Melinnium acu," he chanted as he closed the gap between them. His voice was a horrible snarl. Once more the Black Rose heaved the urumi and steel clashed against steel.

At the same time, gunfire erupted from the crowd.

CHAPTER THIRTY-TWO

Three blasts of a high-powered carbine rifle is enough to get anybody's attention.

Even the most obsessed zealot.

When the gunfire comes from an unidentified location, the end-result is chaos.

Even for the most organized battalion.

Which the newly christened Battalon de San Patricio was not.

From the comparatively high point of the wooden stage, the Black Rose immediately identified the three horses riding in across the smoldering egg, scattering the back two rows of troops.

Mary Rosetta bore down on one arm of the legion, batting at their skulls with abandon while Sofia came for the other side, man catcher at the ready. In between the women, Cassidy rode with the Spenser carbine, shooting into the air.

They had followed her back to Candelaria. Her friends had come back for her.

But what about Sullivan? Where was he?

No time to think about him now.

The diversion was enough to give two of Rayburn's men room to climb back on their feet. One of them still carried his rifle and he fired three more rounds into nighttime air, carving a clearing from the nearest block of green uniforms.

Momentarily unsure how to respond, the soldiers hesitated in going for their guns.

Taking advantage of their indecision Rayburn himself limped into the open space. "I told you to cut those girls down," he shouted. "I mean now!"

One of the soldiers stepped in his path and Rayburn punched him in the face, then jerked the .45 automatic from his hand.

"Who do I need to shoot to get those girls off the scaffold?" He pointed the gun at the next uniform he saw. "How about you?"

The guard drew his weapon and without missing a beat, Rayburn shot him through the center of his chest.

As the man fell to the ground in a crumpled heap, it was clear now all four of the posse were back in control — with hands firmly on their rifles.

But the frenzied mob, stoked to a mad rage by Shanahan's rhetoric wasn't about to back down. Caught off guard, they regrouped in splinters of four or five and ducked around the bonfire, shooting toward the sheriff's posse, drawing a bead on Cassidy.

Sofia employed the man-catcher, hoisting one of the soldiers from his feet. They rode a good forty feet with her holding him aloft through the air before she deposited his squirming corpse groundside.

The battle was furious, but the Black Rose didn't have time to follow the action. She had problems of her own.

Shanahan had taken advantage of the distraction to slide in close and rock her head back with a fast blow to the chin. Staggered, she took two steps sideway and nearly fell from the boardwalk stage. "You can't win against eldritch magic," said Shanahan, closing the gap between them.

"Then it's a good thing there isn't any such thing, you stupid little man," said the Black Rose.

Righting herself, she carried the hilt of urumi around in a wide arc.

But to no avail.

With his left hand, Shanahan snatched her wrist from midair and held her sword arm pinned, preparing to run her through with the St. Agnes sword.

He reared back for a killing thrust, but she surprised him by rolling in close, snapping a hard knee between his legs. The impact was just enough to make Shanahan gasp and loosen his grip. The Black Rose let go of the urumi with her right hand, plucked it from mid-air with her left and whipped it around Shanahan's back where it tore a hole in his robe, skimming his hide underneath.

The aggression hadn't hurt him much, but it was enough to get him to back away.

"You can't win," he said.

"You keep saying so," said the Black Rose. "Talk, talk, talk. It's all you ever do."

The urumi uncoiled in a spiral of death.

Like the honed claw of some great bird of prey, the ancient weapon soared down and tore skin away from Shanahan's forehead, leaving blood to pour over his brow.

But the man was powered by a hysteria bordering on the supernatural. He shrugged off the attack and pounded across the boards.

Again and again, the ancient Roman iron clashed with the forged steel of the urumi.

Shanahan's face was a swollen mass of rage, his teeth clenched together as he hacked and chopped, keeping the Black Rose on a constant defense. Behind him, two of Rayburn's posse mounted the stage, one with a folding knife in hand — presumably to free the girls and a second to cover him with his carbine.

When he saw them, Shanahan wheeled around, slashing through the air, and curving the sword toward the first man's neck.

But it never arrived.

Instead, the tip of the urumi shot through the air, peeling a chunk of flesh from Shanahan's hand knocking the weapon from his grasp.

Covered in blood, the sword clattered across the boards.

"It's over," said the Black Rose.

Shanahan didn't think so. Without pause, he continued the attack, jerking a gun from beneath his robe. Unable to see clearly with blood flooding his vision, he waved the automatic like wild man, finally settling on the man frantically at work cutting Savannah free.

But even as Shanahan brought the gun to bear on his target, the Black Rose snapped the whip-sword up and back, catching Shanahan just under the jaw.

The cold hard steel of the urumi sliced through the skin of his neck and drenching his chest in a torrent of hot, gushing blood.

With one last gurgle of mindless chatter, Mick Shanahan fell dead to the stage.

The crack of another .45 went off behind her and the Black Rose spiraled away from a new barrage of slugs intent on taking her down. At the edge of the stage, one of the Battalion uniforms crouched with a smoking gun. With a quick explosion from his carbine, the posse man on the stage behind her took off the top of the soldier's head.

"Thank you," said the Black Rose, and the man touched the brim of his hat.

"De nada," he said.

The fires burned down across the expanse of the egg and Rayburn together with her friends were forcing the St. Patrick's Battalion into ever smaller clusters of weak resistance.

The Black Rose turned back to the scaffold just in time to see the last of the girls cut free from her bonds.

And there was Estrella picking up the sword of St. Agnes only to disappear in a cowardly sprint behind Old Central.

✱✱✱✱✱

Estrella's blue van waited with its horses on the brick street in the silver light of a rising moon. The din of the skirmish was lessened by the grove of lemon trees around the back of Old Central. The Black Rose screened out what noise remained, the groans of pain from the wounded, the shouts of Rayburn and the others as they rounded up the rouge soldiers.

Every sense was alert to the presence of her quarry. She soaked in the smells around her.

One of Estrella's horses snorted into the breeze and the wagon's familiar scent of lavender water and lye soap drifted in on the breeze.

The side door was partially open. Curious. A trap?

With her urumi firmly in hand, the Black Rose moved quietly, making her way to the wagon and pulling back the entrance. Climbing into the dark space, she was prepared for an ambush — but no attack came. She tried to clear her mind and listen. Was she all alone?

Everything inside the wagon was as she remembered it. Ma's Bible beside the quilt-wrapped mattress. Cabinets lined with sacks of cornmeal, candles and fruit preserves. A wooden bar curving under the weight of heavy dresses on wire hangers. There were plenty of shadows where Estrella might hide, but there was no fooling Catalina Rivera's senses.

The living space was empty.

But then came a bump, and the wagon shifted ever so slightly...

Carefully, so as not to give herself away, the Black Rose slowly and silently left the confines of the wagon. When her feet touched the ground, she waited, resting on the balls of her feet.

Outside, the Black Rose approached the back rail of the wagon with caution. Letting her hand rest on an iron-rimmed wheel, she crouched to peer between the wooden spokes. Estrella wasn't hiding under the wagon, nor was she retreating along the street behind.

At front, another of the horses recognized her and nickered a greeting. The Black Rose gave his nose a pat, then stood tall and backtracked into the street. There was hardly any noise coming from the area of the egg now and the fire which had only so recently been indistinguishable from a circle of hell itself had dimmed to little more than a campfire. The smell of cooked coal-oil filled the air.

Whether it was a creak of the wagon as Estrella shifted her weight or the singing breeze as the sword cut the air — something alerted the Black Rose to a sudden attack from out of the darkness. She dodged left just in time to avoid being skewered. A half-second slower or a faction of an inch less and she would have not lived to see morning's light.

As it was, the sword of St. Agnes nicked her right arm above the elbow, leaving a ragged furrow that immediately welled up with blood. Forced from her hand, the urumi rolled away into the middle of the street.

Behind the Black Rose, the sword slammed into the hard brick street.

And shattered into four pieces above the cross guard.

Which it wouldn't have done were it truly made of fourth-century Roman forged steel.

The sword was a fake.

From the roof of the van, Estrella's laughter echoed through the empty street.

She raised herself up to her full stature, the green silk robe parting in the breeze to reveal her pale bare legs to mid-thigh. She threw back her hood and shook loose her wild mane of dark hair. Her voice was mocking and tinged with insanity. "Pretty Catalina Rivera — still she moves with the reflexes of a cat. After all you've been through tonight, I should think you'd be spent."

"You will be surprised at my reserves, wench," said the Black Rose.

In the white-wash of moonlight, the mad whore's expression was pained. "Wench is it?" She pressed her fingers against the robe at her chest. "I can't help but be hurt, Catalina. I thought we were friends. I thought we were beginning to mean something to each other." She thrust out her lower lip as the Black Rose took a step toward the urumi.

"Pretty Catalina Rivera, all dressed up in her makeup and gown. Had you but asked, I could have loaned you something more fashionable. After all, you've borrowed my clothes before." Estrella pushed out her chin. "It's what *sisters* do, you know. They borrow each other's clothes."

"How ironic to hear you speak about family," said the Black Rose, "after you betrayed Ma, and Frank and Beauty."

"They didn't have much of a future here anymore," said Estrella. "Ma wasn't willing to take orders and Frank and Beauty weren't willing to wear the uniform. They weren't destined for the new order Mick and I brought into existence tonight."

"New order? There's no new order, Estrella. There's no magic. Your army has all but surrendered." The Black Rose motioned toward the broken fragments on the street. "Even your sword wasn't authentic."

"You're wrong. John Riley is here among us. With the power of the sword, we called him forth from the ether to walk again in Mick Shanahan's form."

"Mick Shanahan is dead."

Estrella's footing slipped if just a bit and she swayed ever so slightly in the wind. "You're lying."

"I killed him, Estrella."

"You killed Mick Shanahan. John Riley will rise up in his body. This will be the new Ireland."

Never had the Black Rose witnessed such naked insanity. What could have happened to Estrella to so twist her mind? To so distort reality?

Still on guard, the Black Rose tried to be gentle. "Come down from the wagon," she said. "We'll work it out together. Whatever kind of man he might have been, the John Riley of history would want you to stand down."

Estrella hissed like a wounded animal. "Blasphemer. Don't you dare whisper his name."

"I don't want to hurt you. You said yourself, we're like sisters."

"That reminds me of something Ma used to say," said Estrella. "Turn out the lights and all women are the same under their clothes. What do you think I've got under my clothes for you, Catalina?"

"Please come down," said the Black Rose.

Estrella slowly reached inside her robe. "Don't you want to see what I've got under my clothes?"

Prepared for anything, the Black Rose braced herself. The urumi was three quick steps away, but it might as well have been a mile when Estrella came up with a stick of dynamite, the fuse already sparkling from a hastily scratched lucifer match.

"Shrivel up and die, Black Rose," screamed Estrella.

The last of her voice was overwhelmed by a blast of rifle which sent her spiraling like a child's top. Twisting sideways she lost her footing on the roof of the van, her fingers still clutching the hissing explosive stick.

The Black Rose had just enough time to see Cassidy behind Old Central, standing beside Diablo, his smoking carbine still at the shoulder.

Then Estrella toppled over the opposite side of the van and the world went boom.

CHAPTER THIRTY-THREE

Once Doc Leonard sewed up Catalina's arm with a half-dozen stitches and checked to see if she didn't have a concussion (she didn't), he hastened across the street to the livery stable to provide aid for the twenty-some odd injured men in Shanahan's army. Rayburn, Cassidy, Mary and Sofia stayed on with Lina, convening at the kitchen table while Mrs. Leonard poured coffee and served sugar cookies with candy frosting. Catalina was across from the sheriff, between Mary and Sofia. Cassidy sat between Mary and Rayburn.

The broken pieces of the imposter sword were spread out on the table in front of them.

Seated by herself on a stool in a far corner of the kitchen, Honey Shaw stayed quiet, balancing a cup on her knee, her injured ankle bandaged and propped up on a walnut sideboard.

"Doc's gonna have got his hands full at the livery," said Rayburn.

"No, no liver for me, thanks," said Lina.

The conversation stopped abruptly and everybody looked at her with blank expressions.

"What are you all looking at me for?" she said.

Rayburn increased the volume of his voice. "Livery," he practically shouted. "I was talking about the battalion of men down at the livery stable."

"Oh," said Catalina, poking a finger into her ear and shaking it up and down. "I couldn't understand over the ringing in my ears. What about them?"

"Mrs. Leonard says the doc is taking good care of them," shouted Mary.

"They'll need it," said Cassidy. "Half of them worm-suckers were goofy in the head to begin with. What could make men gather together and behave in such a...such a..."

"Savage way?" said Sofia.

"Yes," said Cassidy. "Savage is exactly the word."

Rayburn shrugged. "I don't pretend to understand what went on here tonight. But I do know there's been an underlying sense of anger and discontent brewing ever since the railroad chose a different path and bypassed the town." Rayburn swallowed some coffee and sucked his teeth. "I suppose it was only a matter of time before some idiot like Shanahan would tap into the anger."

"What about the men, sheriff? Were most of those soldiers local to Candelaria?" said Sofia.

"A good many of them grew up right here in town." He shook his head. "I sure ain't proud to admit it."

For the first time since they sat down, Honey spoke — hesitantly at first, then with deliberate candor. "When Mick got the College of St. Vincent's board of directors to approve his funding request, he set Estrella up in the recruiting business." Honey spread her palms. "I thought that was the extent of her involvement. I guess I was wrong."

Honey's tears seemed to be genuine, but Catalina felt ambivalent. The woman may have been double-crossed, but hadn't she also double-crossed Donovan. Honey Shaw was hardly a candidate for sainthood and Lina wasn't sure how much sympathy she actually deserved.

Again, Lina's attention turned to the broken sword.

Mrs. Leonard shook her head. "If anybody would know which men to go to—"

"It would be Estrella," said Rayburn. In the silence that followed, his eyes went far away. "It's too bad too. I knew what she was, but I always held some admiration for her because she appeared to be so honest." Rayburn continued. "Makes a man wonder about the secrets people hide."

Ever since Estrella's wagon exploded, Catalina didn't hear well — but she was fairly certain the last sentence was aimed at her. She shared a meaningful glance with Cassidy who lifted one eyebrow in silent commentary.

She went back to the subject of the new Batallón de San Patricio, and asked. "What will you do with Shanahan's men, Sheriff?"

"Take care of the injured ones, bury the dead ones." Rayburn's eyebrows arched up and he drank the last of his coffee. "And I guess, we'll let the rest go home."

"Let them go?" said Mary. She glanced over her shoulder to look out the kitchen window to the back yard where Savannah, Emilia and the other girls were brushing D'oro, Diablo, and the horses. "Many of them were all too willing to be a menace to society and terrorize those young girls — if not kill them outright themselves. Are you sure it's a good idea just to let them go?"

"No," said Rayburn, "I'm not sure. But I can't hold all these men and most of them are related to one another. Like any other town, there's three or four big families running everything. I can't lock everybody up."

"They're accessories to attempted murder," said Cassidy. "Ought to be some kind of punishment."

"I might tend to agree, but if I do anything, I'll have the whole community up in arms. You want to stay here and figure it all out, you be my guest, Marshal."

"Marshal?" said Mrs. Leonard.

"Our friend here was a deputy United States marshal before he took up residence in Santo Tomas," said Rayburn. The two law men stared at each other. "My offer stands," said Rayburn. "I sure as hell don't have the manpower to deal with something like this. You want to stay, you're welcome. You want to take the lot of 'em home with you, you're welcome to 'em."

Cassidy turned away and dunked a cookie into his coffee cup. But he didn't answer.

"The truth is, the college may never recover," said Rayburn. "Oh, the students will clean things up and Old Central will be made good as new. But that was some special kind of evil we saw on display last night. If that's the kind of violence the new century has in store…" He shook his head in despair. "I mean, can you imagine if this kind of mania were to grip an entire nation of people?"

"It'll never happen," said Cassidy.

"I wouldn't be too sure, constable," said Sofia.

"I'm with you," said Mary.

Catalina agreed with the women.

In no way did she believe in eldritch energy or ancient magics. The sword of St. Agnes — even the real one — had no more mystical power than a carton of baking soda.

But like Rayburn, she had felt the evil as a physical presence cascading through the air last night.

Evil, that once released, might surely grow.

Catalina turned her chair to face Honey. "I want to know the whereabouts of the true sword of St. Agnes."

Surprised to be included in the conversation, Honey blinked her eyes, but sadly let her chin drop. "I don't rightly know," she whispered.

It was all Lina could do not to stand up and knock the porcelain coffee cup from her hand. For Mrs. Leonard's sake, she reigned in her temper and tried again. "I don't believe you. I don't think anybody sitting at this table believes you."

"You're in this up to your pretty rouge-covered cheeks, girl," said Mary. "Maybe you thought you were doing it out of love, maybe you're just as demented as the mob of idiots across the street. I know from personal experience what both ways are like.

Either way, you need to 'fess up, now, before you land in even more trouble."

Honey's sobbing started deep in her chest and broke out from her lips in a series of wet, wracking spasms. Mrs. Leonard hurried to take the cup off the girl's knee before it crashed to the wood floor below.

"I loved Ellis Donovan," said Honey. "At first. Years ago. He made me feel special and important. Not like a...well...you know. But as time dragged on, nothing changed. Each new discovery and every new book manuscript took priority over me. I knew I'd never be as important as his work. I'd never really fit in with the people at the college."

"You grew to despise him," said Mary.

"Yes, I did," said Honey. "Why couldn't I be enough for him? Why was he more interested in an old hunk of metal or rock than he was in me?"

"But then why not leave him, dear?" said Mrs. Leonard. "A pretty girl like you could find land a dozen potential suitors."

"A pretty girl like me already did," said Honey, "and ten times a dozen more."

Mrs. Leonard understood, but said, "What you did in the past — what you were, isn't as important as what you could become."

"What I was to become was *Somebody* — with a capital letter S. I was going to be Mrs. Ellis Donovan," said Honey. "Heir to a scholarly estate I figured would carry me over the oceans of the world and into the finest company of the age where I'd be respected and my opinions looked up to and revered."

"So you kept on with Donavan but fooled around behind his back with Shanahan," said Mary.

Sofia interrupted the sordid story to cut to the chase. "Tell us this, Honey Shaw. Was the true Sword of St. Agnes ever here? Did Donovan possess it?"

Honey slid from her tall stool and joined them at the table. "Yes," she said, wiping at her nose. "Yes, Ellis had the sword. But this wreck on the table isn't it."

"But put together, it looked enough like the original to fool you?" said Lina.

Honey seemed ashamed of her gullibility. "I was so caught up in the adventure, I guess I wasn't paying attention."

Gazing at the remnants of the sword there on the table, Lina reflected on Honey's words. The replica was a good forgery, but a close up inspection showed that its nicks and imperfections had been laid into the blade in too orderly a fashion and the hilt and pommel were insufficiently scuffed. Rather than showing the wear of a millennia, the entire piece was too pristine, the edges too true.

"Where do you suppose the forgery came from?" said Mary.

"It's likely Ellis had it made," said Honey. "He was a very secretive man. He was so convinced somebody would try to steal the sword. He was obsessed with wanting – no needing – all the security. My guess is he replaced the true sword in his display with this one."

"But why?" said Mary. "Why show us a forgery and make such a big deal out of it?"

"Maybe he suspected us after all," said Sofia. "Catalina told us early on Ellis Donovan was no fool."

"I'll verify that," said Rayburn. "Before we came out to the canyon, I visited with Ellis in his office." The sheriff reached into this shirt pocket and retrieved one of Sullivan's Irish tokens. "Your man was more than a little suspicious of just about everybody."

"Perhaps he even suspected you, Honey," said Sofia.

The idea was obviously one Honey hadn't considered and another round of tears fell from her eyes.

"None of this sword business matters too much anyway," said Rayburn. "I imagine the college trustees will find it in time when they go through Donovan's collection."

"I imagine…," said Honey.

"After all, it does belong to Mr. Donovan's estate." Rayburn's declaration was firm with the weight of his office. "I guess it's clear enough to everybody here?"

"You've said what you needed to say," said Catalina.

Rayburn stood up and walked around the table to stand beside Honey. "I'm afraid I'm going to have to ask you to accompany me over to the jail, ma'am. I've got a bushel basket more questions for you." Then he turned to Cassidy. "And seein' as I've only got one cell, I'm going to have to ask you to take Colonel Sullivan back into custody."

"Which means we need to get back on the trail for home," said Catalina.

"Tonight?" said Mary.

"You have a problem with leaving tonight?"

"I figured after all the girls have been through that

a good night's sleep at the hotel would do them good."

"Hotel's only got two rooms," said Rayburn.

"We'll make camp a few miles out," said Cassidy.

Mary poked out her lip.

"I'll pack you up some sandwiches and cookies," said Mrs. Leonard.

"The main thing is to pick up Sullivan and get underway," said Cassidy.

Lina joined Rayburn and Honey in the door to the kitchen. "May I have a minute with Honey?" she asked the sheriff.

"What is it?" he said.

Lina lowered her head, putting on her best bashful expression. "Girl talk," she said. "Something Estrella asked about. Please, sheriff?"

Rayburn chewed his lip and Lina wondered if he might deny her request. Instead, he offered a curt nod and said, "Two minutes. Then I'll see the lot of you out to the edge of town."

"Thank you," said Lina.

She put her arm around Honey's shoulders and walked her outside.

Two minutes was all she'd need to learn the whereabouts of the sword.

CHAPTER THIRTY-FOUR

Dressed in her riding clothes of jodhpur pants, ruffled shirt, boots and black, wide brimmed hat, Catalina wore one affectation of the Black Rose — the steel urumi around her waist. She wasn't about to lose her sword again.

And with the current venture, she hoped to gain a second one.

After pulling the iron cover shut behind her, she dropped down next to Cassidy into the pitch black tunnel with it cool embrace and familiar smells. Her hearing had begun to clear and she was able to make out softer tones.

"We're taking a chance doubling back here like this," he said. "Rayburn didn't act none too prepared to brook any nonsense."

"And I'm not prepared to face Mother Mercy without the Sword of St. Agnes in hand," said Lina. "Pass me the electric torch, will you?"

Cassidy flicked on the light and handed it over.

"What if Rayburn decides to ride out to Mary and Sofia's camp? He'll find them with the girls and Sullivan…and us absent. He'll know immediately what you're up to and where to look for us."

"Let him come," said Lina. "By the time he rides out there and gets back here, we won't still be here. Unless you intend to stand here and talk for another hour."

"I just don't think it's the best idea you've ever had."

His lack of confidence made her cranky.

"You're free to turn tail any time you want. Me? I'm going to get what I came for." She ducked her head and pushed forward into the dim beam of light.

Cassidy sighed, but nonetheless followed quietly behind.

They had been through a lot in the past week. Alone and together. Her emotions for him ran the gamut of seasons from summer heat to winter's icy cold.

She had no idea how he felt.

"Do you know how long it's been since I had any sleep?"

The man was infuriating.

"We'll be in and out before Sofia has a proper fire made," said Lina. "Once we've got the sword, we'll sleep a few hours and be on the road."

"The same damn road I traveled all day coming back after you."

"Are you deliberately trying to make me feel guilty? Because it won't work. I didn't ask you to follow me here."

"Just a statement of fact."

"You'd do well to keep your facts to yourself."

Lina continued down through the corridor the same way she had twice before. "Watch your head."

"I'm watching it, thanks. Wouldn't hurt if you'd keep the light steady."

The ground underfoot was soft and showed the marks of Lina's earlier escape with the girls. Whether they found the sword or not, she had saved six young virgins from Shanahan's insanity. At least she could content herself with that.

As if he were reading her mind, Cassidy said, "Did Rayburn tell you anything about those other girls who were with Savannah and Emilia?"

"Only what they, themselves, told us," said Lina. "They'd been taken from their homes by Shanahan's guards."

Cassidy reiterated his earlier opinion on the matter. "I think Rayburn is wrong to let those men go."

Lina secretly agreed with him, but she felt contentious, so she poked at Cassidy with her words. "He's only one man. He can only hold them so long."

"What about his posse? Those men who rode with him?"

"From what he said, it took the promise of many favors to convince those few men to ride with him tonight. According to Rayburn, it's the only real posse he's ever been able to mount."

"I certainly could teach him a thing or two about being a lawman," said Cassidy.

"Maybe you should."

"What do you mean to say? Do you think I should stay?"

Catalina's stomach did a complete somersault at the prospect.

No!

"If you'd like," she said.

"It makes no difference to you, eh?"

It does!

But pride held her tongue.

They moved out from the confines of the narrow tunnel into the elevator chamber, and Catalina focused on the job at hand.

"There's a door here, to the right. It's embedded in the wall." She offered the light to Cassidy, then ran her fingers along the thin seam in the almost unbroken surface of concrete. "I noticed it when I came down after the girls. The electric line travels around it at the top." As before, she took note of the iron ring bolted to the cement at waist level. "I think it opens onto the stairwell."

Lina clutched the ring in both hands and dropped back, letting her weight pull the heavy cement from its frame. With an ancient scraping sound, the door opened a fraction of an inch. Like opening an ancient tomb.

"Would you lend a hand?"

"*Please*, would I lend a hand?" said Cassidy.

"Please," said Catalina rolling her eyes in exasperation.

The constable wrapped the fingers of both hands around the rough edge of the door, and with Lina keeping tight to the iron handle, they forced the aperture to open.

"Wide enough to slip through," said Lina, and she did.

Without waiting for Cassidy, she bounded up the first flight of rickety wood. Since the installation of the elevator, the stairway had fallen into disrepair. Chunks of plaster were missing from the wall near the highest point near the ceiling and debris spackled the steps. "Careful where you step," she called over her shoulder. "These treads aren't too sturdy."

Cassidy's boots produced a series of groans from under the wood. "There's an understatement if I ever heard one," he said, carefully moving from one step to the next.

They arrived together at the third floor door and walked out into the hallway where Lina had fought for her life with Nolan and Donovan's office waited with its hidden prize.

Lina held the electric torch on the entrance to the office. "Donovan's door is open," she said.

Cassidy touched her shoulder and she turned to face him.

"What is it? We need to be quick if we're to find the sword," she complained.

"Just a question is all," he said. Then he offered her his damned disarming smile, and her heart raced in her chest. "You haven't told me where it is." His hand stayed on her shoulder, and she didn't pull away.

Then he kissed her and the weight of the day came crashing in.

She put her arms on his shoulders and let herself slip away, just for a moment.

When he stepped back, she caught her breath and gazed into his dark eyes.

"Honey doesn't know where Donovan hid the sword," she told him, "but she made a guess."

"Where is it?"

"More than anything else in his collection, Donovan was most proud of the books he wrote. Honey said they have a place of honor on the third shelf down, straight across from his desk at eye level. She said just about every time she was in his office, he would pull one down and flip through the pages. Once, she claims to have seen a hatchway behind them."

"Like a cubbyhole? Or a safe built into the wall?"

"That's what she believes."

Cassidy kissed Lina's forehead and, reaching down for her hand, said, "Then lead the way."

*****

The true sword of St. Agnes was a gleaming jewel compared to the replica Honey had stolen. Catalina held the polished iron up to the electric light and the blade was a mirror reflecting her sense of awe.

"Too hold such history in your hand," she said.

"I'm just glad we found the blasted thing," said Cassidy.

The bone handle felt solid in Lina's grip, as substantial as any sword she'd ever trained with, the crossguard firmly affixed.

Cassidy slapped the cover back over Donovan's wall safe and shoved a pile of fat books back in front of it. "*The Last Century's Statistical Soil Analysis of the*

Holy Land, Volume One," said Cassidy reading the titles from the spines of the books. "*A History of the Catholic Interpretations of Paul's Letters to the Corinthians in Gaelic Translation.* Not exactly light bedtime reading."

"Donovan was more famous for his collection of artifacts than his published scholarship," said Lina.

"I can see why."

"Look, here," said Catalina, holding the sword close to the light. "Do you see where the fuller meets the cross-guard?"

"What's a fuller?"

"The groove in the middle of the blade. Do you see how it runs down into the handle? There are stains there — beyond the mere rust of iron. The old blood of battle."

Cassidy nodded. "Or sacrifice."

Catalina pressed the sword to her bosom. "We'd better go."

"One more question," said Cassidy. "If Honey had seen the original sword in Donovan's collection, why didn't she recognize the fake?"

"I don't think she ever saw the original," said Lina. "Knowing Donovan, he most likely kept the true sword locked away from the beginning."

As one, they slipped from the office into the hall and back to the creaking stairwell. In less than five minutes, they made their way back through the tunnel door and up and out the round access way to where their horses waited.

"I've been thinking about what you said up there," said Cassidy. "About Donovan putting the fake sword up for show while the real one was hidden away. There's a pretty good chance an awful lot of his display might be phony."

"And much of his true collection hidden," said Catalina, "perhaps never to be found."

"That would indeed be a shame," said Cassidy.

"I'll tell you what's shame," said a voice in the dark night behind them, "that after all the hard work you done, I'm gonna have to kill the both and take the sword home for myself."

Lina spun and brought the light to bear on the grinning visage of Henry Hodges.

"It's gonna be a real shame for sure," he said.

CHAPTER THIRTY-FIVE

Before Catalina could act, Hodges jumped forward with his heavy Army Colt and slashed the barrel across Cassidy's forehead. The constable of Santo Tomas crumpled under the onslaught like an empty grocery sack and Hodges kicked him aside.

He turned his attention to Lina. "I finally got away from your rotten jail cell and them damned caterwauling brats in Santo Tomas, spent all day riding in here half-ways hoping I'd find Sullivan in time for the party, the other half hoping I'd find you and we'd have a party of our own. Either way, I get the final say. Now, gimme the treasure, you dumb little filly."

Lina brought the Sword of St. Agnes up into the space between them and flicked off the torch.

The night flooded in and Hodges launched two explosive shots from his Colt.

But Catalina was already gone.

"You can't hide, pretty girl," he said, and the moonlight made it true. Once her eyes adjusted to the silvery glow, Lina saw her attacker as a moving black shadow, thundering across the lawn. For him, she would be equally visible and his gun gave him the advantage over her sword.

Two more shots and the earth spit up geysers of clay sod.

Even if she could somehow find a way to turn the tables and keep him from reloading, Hodges packed a couple more hunks of lead. Catalina needed an advantage, and she needed it now.

She sprinted to the front of Old Central and the shadow maze of the looming wood scaffold.

Think, think, she told herself. What would the Black Rose do?

Without a moment's hesitation, she catapulted up and deftly caught a horizontal pine beam, hoisting herself to a platform more than dozen feet in the air. The lattice-work assemblage swayed gently, as it had when she and the others were bound to its façade earlier in the night.

Catalina looked out over the scene of Shanahan's crime, a horse-trampled smoldering ruin. Two figures walked on the sidewalk at the far side of the egg. Otherwise, the battleground was silent and haunted, like the Civil War fields she'd heard about from her brother as he described his travels.

Like her own Rancho Rivera, forever a place of Armageddon.

With the sword welded to her right hand, Lina scaled the structure with her left, soon reaching the third story patio outside Donovan's broken rose window. She searched the grounds below for Hodges, wondering exactly how he came to be here in the first place?

Cassidy told her he'd left the bastard to rot in jail at Santo Tomas. Anderson, the postmaster, had been appointed as acting deputy and scheduled to keep an eye on him.

Anderson wasn't much of a postmaster, and apparently he wasn't much of a lawman either.

Or Hodges was more slippery and smarter than anybody had given him credit for.

Probably both.

A sudden lurch in the construction caused Lina to look again and Hodge's voice confirmed her suspicions. "Comin' up to get you sweet thing. You can't run from old Henry. Not after all you've put me through. We're gonna have a real good time once I catch up to you."

Lina hopped off the edifice and found security on the third-floor patio. If not entirely clear of rubble and with no rail fence around its perimeter, at least it didn't tip in the breeze. She reached out and put all her weight into toppling the scaffold.

"Woo-hoo, you trying to give me a ride?" said Hodges. "Or maybe you think you can buck me off? I don't think you're filly enough to throw me."

Catalina ignored the taunts and kept shaking the scaffold with all her might.

Joints creaked and a couple nails popped free, but she finally had to admit Hodges was right. He'd be upon her in seconds and the structure was built too well to simply fall apart.

It was to be a showdown after all.

Catalina backpedaled across the patio until her back was at the shattered pane of the tremendous round window. Then she unhitched the clasp at her waist and unfurled her urumi.

With the whip-sword in one hand and the sword of St. Agnes in the other, she waited in the moonlight for Hodges' head to appear among the beams and poke over the patio lip.

Instead, the Colt revolver sailed up and over the edge, landing at her feet on the tar covered surface with a thud and followed by a plea for peace.

"I wanna call a truce, girlie," said Hodges from below.

"I don't," said Catalina.

"You've got the gun, now. Go ahead, pick it up."

Lina stared down at the nearby lump of steel. In order to pick up the gun, she'd need to put down the urumi or the sword. No. Rather than touch it, she walked forward and kicked it to the corner of the patio behind her. Then she lowered herself into an offensive crouch.

This high up, if Hodges joined her on the open landing, there was only one way it could end.

One of them would go over the side.

The Black Rose meant to be sure it wasn't her.

"Come on, then. Damn you," she said.

Anticipating her attack, Hodges came off the scaffold like a cat and the pitched blade of the urumi cracked into the pine wood and ricocheted back, narrowly missing him.

"What a fine way to say hello," he said. From behind his back Hodges pulled a spear-point Bowie blade, both sharpened edges catching the moonlight, his beefy fingers wrapped tight around the heavy black handle. "Got this from an old blind beggar in Santo Tomas."

The reference to the Rosary Maker threw her attention off-balance.

"Ain't that how it works for you sisters of the convent? The old derelict makes them black crosses for you, don't he?"

The rosary was a familiar warmth inside her right hip pocket.

"You're lying, Hodges. The Rosary Maker didn't craft your knife."

Hodges mouth fell open in mock astonishment and he licked his lips. "Aw, hell. I guess you're right."

He was playing with her. Teasing.

Reaching out for her, he failed to connect.

"I was just trying to make a little conversation," he said. "Most gals like a little pillow talk before we get down to business. You know what I mean?"

"I know exactly what you mean," she said.

The Black Rose feinted left, then swept the St. Agnes blade right, using its longer reach to score a shallow cut across Hodge's chest. The wound was superficial, but it tore the fabric of his shirt, drew blood and surely stung like a son of a gun.

In the moonlight she saw Hodges wince, but otherwise he barely acknowledged the strike, Hodges drove into the Black Rose with brute force catching her sword on his tough steel dagger, using sheer brawn to shove her backwards toward the window. She wheeled around into a full roundhouse kick and a stray piece of glass rolled under the heel of her supporting leg.

She came down hard, cracking her hip on the steel remains of the old guard rail, losing her grip on the urumi. Hodges was on top of her, filling her vision with his snaggletooth snarl, choking her with the stench of sweat and grime. One more, she threw the sword up between them and once more it tasted his blood.

This time her blade cut deep and he grabbed for his shoulder by reflex giving the Black Rose time to snap a kick into his groin.

She rolled away and reclaimed her feet just in time to catch his bull run into her chest. Hodges drove the Black Rose into the wood paneling over the open round window and the boards splintered and cracked as her lungs practically collapsed. Bright red fireflies exploded across her vision and she gasped for air.

Hodges' callused hand was like a vice around her neck, his slavering mouth at her cheek. He held her pinned against the window, his breath hot and stinking of onions and chewing tobacco. "There was a day when you stood over me like a queen and kicked me in the guts. Do you remember?"

The Black Rose struggled to breathe and Hodges shook her head like a child's rattle.

"I said do you remember?"

Her fingers continued to grip the sword, but her arm was held under Hodges' weight.

"You remember what you told me? You said you should've broke my neck." He laughed. "You remember saying that?"

The Black Rose shifted her feet, felt more broken glass under the soles of her boots.

Hodges leaned into her. "Well, guess what? You were right. You shoulda broke my neck, because I can guarantee ya..."

The glass rolled around, loose, like sand. All her weight was on the shifting surface.

All Hodges' weight was on her.

"I won't make the same mistake," he said, letting off her windpipe long enough for her to answer.

"No," said the Black Rose. "You'll make different ones." Letting all her weight fall on the shards of glass gave her the result she hoped for. She fell straight down onto her backside and Hodges came with her. But instead of landing on the soft cushions of Catalina's breasts, he fell on the upraised sword of St. Agnes. Unlike the replica, the true sword didn't shatter with impact but instead ripped through muscle and bone to rise up between Hodge's shoulder blades.

He had just enough energy to roll over and cough out a muffled cry of agony before he died.

Back on her feet, the Black Rose retrieved her urumi first, then waited for Hodges' last breath before she pulled the Roman blade from his rib cage. Once she was sure he'd breathed his last, she rolled him to the edge of the patio and pushed him over the edge. He landed with a grisly crack on the sidewalk below.

One of them had to go over the edge. Just as she'd predicted.

******

Catalina helped Cassidy tied Hodges' body to Diablo, then she and D'oro walked with him from the college campus along the line of trees before the bridge over the creek. They stopped to listen to the water roll over the bedrock and were rewarded with the trill of spring peepers.

"Are you sure you're not hurt?"

Lina let her fingers trail along the wood railing. "I could ask you the same question," she said. "Hodges gave you a pretty good wallop with his gun."

Cassidy pulled the Army Colt out of his waistband. "And a nice gun it is." He checked the cylinder. "No bullets," he said.

"I didn't expect Hodges to toss me a loaded weapon," said Lina. "Are you going to keep it?"

"As a souvenir? Why not?"

"This entire fandango started with him. It's good he ended it."

"I'd just as soon the judge had gotten the chance to sentence him."

"Hodges sentenced himself," said Lina. "A long time ago. Same for Shanahan and Donavan too."

"Nobody got out of this one unscathed, did they?"

"We'll take Colonel Sullivan back to Santo Tomas," said Lina. "Maybe the judge will be lenient."

"Not if you get your way."

"You're right."

Then he put his hand to her chin and tipped her face toward the moon. "You've got a few cuts and scrapes."

"The least of my worries," she said.

"Oh?" said Cassidy. "How about you tell me your worries, Black Rose?"

She held his eyes long enough to let a tear spill across her cheek. "How about I don't?"

Cassidy looked up the street toward the sleeping town. The moon was low in the sky, soon sinking down behind the doctor's house and the hotel. Behind Miquel's house and the long building housing the Snorty Horse.

"It'll be daylight soon," he said. "The others will want to make tracks back home."

"You're staying here, aren't you?"

He took her hand and carried it to his lips.

"There's a lot of clean-up to be done here. Rayburn can use the help. And I think a fresh start would be a good thing."

"Santo Tomas will need a constable."

"I'll put out the word from here. Santo Tomas is a growing village. With the railroad and the popularity of the springs, you'll have ten applicants for the position before you get home."

"What will I tell Mercy?"

"Have Savanah and Emilia tell her I was successful."

He seemed to have all the answers.

And Catalina Rivera had run out of questions.

Diablo delivered an impatient snorting bray and Cassidy touched the brim of his hat. "I'd best be on my way," he said. "Will you do me the honor of allowing me to escort you to the edge of town?"

The Black Rose stepped into the stirrup and swung a leg over D'oro's broad back.

"I will," she said.

And together they rode into the first golden orange streaks of dawn.

A LOOK AT: VENGEANCE OF
THE BLACK ROSE

The Black Rose discovers that a small mission on the border of Texas and Mexico has been raided by someone locals call "The Beast."

Many are dead but most of the women and children are missing. The trail of the kidnappers leads the Black Rose into Mexico, into a hidden valley where "The Beast" is raising an army to restore the Aztec Empire. "The Beast," known by his followers as "El Tigre," is human but something of a physical mutant whose face resembles that of a Jaguar.

The Black Rose will face an army with only a good sword arm and a fast gun between her and death for them all on a bloody altar.

AVAILABLE OCTOBER 2020

ABOUT THE AUTHOR

Richard Prosch's western crime fiction captures the fleeting history and lonely frontier stories of his youth, where characters aren't always what they seem and the windburned landscapes are filled with swift, deadly danger.

His work has appeared in True West, Roundup, and Saddlebag Dispatches magazines, and online at Boys' Life. He won the Spur Award from Western Writers of America for short fiction, and his Jo Harper stories have received nominations for the Peacemaker Award from Western Fictioneers. Richard lives in Missouri with his wife, Gina, son, Wyatt, assorted cats, and a Great Pyrenees named Moose.